Wreck

THE FUEL SERIES BOOK 2

by USA TODAY bestselling author

GINGER SCOTT

Yep.
This is still for you, Lesley.
All 3 of these suckers,
born from your race-lovin' heart.

W hen I was stuck in Camp Verde, I couldn't wait to get out. Now, I officially feel I don't belong. What I don't get, though, is how unbelievably sad I am about it.

I spent the morning driving around this place in my rental car, and as familiar as every twist and turn in the road is, the curves no longer feel like they're mine. I'm not sure what's changed over four years. The landscape? Or me?

Colt's gone.

That's a big change.

I have to keep reminding myself that my father—scratch that, *sperm donor*—is dead. He can't hurt me, and I think maybe that's partly what has me feeling off. My natural instinct in this place is to have a heightened awareness for danger, and I find my neck craning constantly in search of either Colt's truck or his friends.

Of all the things that could have taken that man out, pancreatic cancer did the trick. I guess he spent the last four years of his life being a puppet for the ATF and FBI, ratting out players in the drug trade, and his reward was he got to spend the last year of his life slowly dying in that shithole he called home.

I wouldn't have come back at all if it weren't for the weird legal crap that seems to require my signature and a lawyer present. Seems Colt left something behind. A safe deposit box. I guess he never put my mom's name on anything. Only mine.

Yay, me.

I inherited the shitty trailer too, and all the junk around it. Only thing I don't own is the tiny plot of land the trailer's parked on, which means I need to have it hauled out of there before the landowner starts charging me rent. The guy gave me a break this month on account of my dad dying. He only collects the checks and doesn't live in Camp Verde. If he did, he'd know better than to think I was torn up over Colt's passing.

Just like that asshole to croak on the cusp of summer in Arizona. It was ninety-six degrees when my plane landed. Camp Verde is north, but it isn't *that* north. It's still smothering as fuck out here. At least I don't have Oklahoma's wet blanket of humidity suffocating me on top of things. There's the silver lining for having to come back home for the summer. Well, that and the bronzed legs in tall red heels striding across the newly minted pavement toward a car I never thought I'd lay eyes on again. I suppose those are legs I never thought I'd get to see again either.

Hannah's home from college.

And she's *all woman.*

My knuckle finds its way between my teeth as I slink low in the driver's seat, trying to blend in with the crowd parked out on the Straights. It's been four years since I left this place; four years since I left a trail of burnt rubber next to that yellow dotted line. Of all the tracks I've been on, nothing compares to this two-mile stretch that splits the desert in half. I don't think I will ever love driving a strip of road as much as I loved this one. The there-and-back pulse-firing races are what forged me, and every time I snake by a driver in the truck race circuit, I thank this little bit of highway.

I also thank that girl.

Hannah has to know I'm here. This town is too small for word not to get around that Colt Bridges has business that needs tending to. I kept my promise to Hannah's best friend Bailey, though, and I didn't call Hannah. I didn't call Tommy, either. Unlike his sister, he kept his phone number the same. We've texted a few times over the last four years, but that's it. Our exchanges are always cold and short, like the Christmas cards you get from people you knew in another life.

I got the disconnected notice for Hannah's phone the first time I tried calling her while in a drunken stupor out in my uncle's barn. I was too wasted to understand what happened, or rather, too easily convinced of my own denial. I called her cell phone provider to file a complaint and lodge my concern. The customer service guy politely informed me that I was a stalker. After that, I quit calling Hannah's old line.

It was four years of radio silence, nothing but the rare scraps of social media news I was able to find through my Google search, and the one time Tommy mentioned Hannah in a text. He said he couldn't message with me at the time because he was with her. I knew what it meant— that Tommy hates me for hurting her and he was refusing to pile on the pain. It's okay. I hate me for that, too.

The only connection I had with Hannah Judge was the

one in my imagination, the times we met in my dreams. And then Bailey called.

She didn't have to. She must have known I would be contacted about Colt eventually. But Hannah was worried about me finding out. At least, that's what Bailey said. Through all the hate, the impossibly thick wall she rightfully built around her heart with the sole intent of keeping me out, she still was worried about me losing my dad. I knew it wasn't in the way most people show sympathy when a family member dies, either. Hannah understood that this death was different. Losing Colt was bound to fuck with my head, tear open scars.

She was right. It has. Only, I'm so distracted with hope and the possibility of seeing her again that I haven't been able to feel the toxic cocktail of emotions left in Colt's wake. I'll have to cope with them eventually, but for now . . . for now I stalk the girl of my dreams as she bends down and talks to someone in the passenger side of my old car.

"Goddamn." The word falls from my lips, raspy with forbidden guilt as I take in the lush curves of her ass cheeks as they peek out from the frayed bottoms of her incredibly short denim shorts.

Maybe I am a stalker.

Laughter consumes her and she tilts her head back, letting her long waves of hair spill down her spine. I get a glimpse of the inside of my old car and recognize Bailey's prim and proper smile. Still the best of friends. I'm glad Hannah has her. If it weren't for Bailey, I'm not sure I would be sitting here. I probably would have slipped into town last minute and avoided any and all contact with people beyond the lawyer I meet with in the morning.

I was content simply waiting, too. After Bailey's call, I was going to be patient with hope. My body was full of this strange kind of faith—*blind* faith. I believed Hannah would find me when she was ready. But when I was pulled back to Camp Verde to deal with Colt's belongings, I decided that was fate's sign telling me to get off my ass and not wait around any longer. It's time for me to do the work, to earn my heart back and put it where it belongs.

"You have to be shitting me." My heart ratchets up to a thousand beats per minute at the familiar voice coming through the passenger window. I didn't plan on being recognized, but I can't help the warmth growing in my chest when I meet Ava Cruz's gaze.

"Hey!" I roll the window down the rest of the way and lean across the console to embrace her arm as she reaches toward me.

"Unlock this door, *mijo*. Give me a real hug."

I do as she says and she climbs in and wraps her arms around me all at once. Her palms find my cheeks as we part and she twists to the side, leaning back to inspect me. The sharp points of her deep red nails scratch against my scruff. She pats the right side of my face a few times before letting go.

"You don't look skinny. Good."

I cough out a laugh. Ava was always trying to feed me when I was younger. I'm glad to see I'm fat enough for her this time. I spent so many hours at her dad Earl's garage growing up, and she knew my story. I think if it weren't for the Judges, Ava would have stepped in and mothered me.

"What's this piece of shit?" She glances around the bland inside of my rental sedan. Ava's probably the only person more car-elitist than I am. That's what goes along with growing up in a garage and being the reigning queen of the Straights.

"Only here for a few days. Didn't want to drive my car

all the way out here from—" I stop short out of habit. I haven't linked my past with my present location for anyone other than Hannah and Tommy's dad.

"Baby, I know you're with your uncle. You're a little more famous than you used to be. Lots of people around here been following Dustin Bridges on the circuit. You know, your uncle and I were a thing back in high school." A coy smirk crawls into one of her cheeks.

"No. I absolutely did *not* know that!" I swallow down my surprise at her news—*all of it.*

Truth is, as much as life at my uncle's has been easy, it hasn't been full of earth-shattering revelations. We barely talk. He's busy with his small trucking business and I'm busy hustling to prove myself to anyone worth a damn.

"Yeah, me and Jeff were homecoming king and queen. He was this stud wide-receiver—"

"And let me guess, you were the cheer captain." I roll my eyes, but she smacks my arm to correct me.

"Hell no! I was all about racing back then. No time for that *rah-rah* shit! Your uncle was the only damn reason I ever went to a high school football game at all!" Her laugh comes out with the rasp of a pack of cigarettes a day and she sinks back into the passenger seat while memories seem to drift through her mind. Her smirk inches into her cheeks before she covers her mouth with the back of her palm.

"God, time goes fast. You know?" She flits her gaze to me.

I blink and let her words soak in.

"Yeah." I draw in a deep breath before letting my eyes wander back to my left, to the Supra and the girl now climbing in the driver's seat.

"She drives that thing almost as good as you. Just so you know."

I smile to myself and keep my gaze fixed on Hannah's profile as she checks the mirrors, pausing as she sits up tall to look at her reflection and fix the lipstick on the corners of her mouth.

"You should stick around. She's racing some new kid in town. His daddy has money."

I turn back in time to catch Ava's wink as she opens the door. Our smiles match. Ava and I both have a history of taking trust-fund boys who want to play race car driver down a notch.

"Maybe I'll put a little money on our girl," I say. Ava laughs and waggles a well-manicured finger at me before shutting the door behind her. I feel at my back pocket while she heads toward the Supra and pull my wallet out. I've got a couple hundred bucks on me.

I get out of my rental and spot the new kid's car right away. It's a bright red Honda Civic, modified in all the right places. The kid is maybe sixteen, seventeen at the most. He's trying to look older by sporting some gnarly long sideburns that look patchy from several feet away. He's also rocking one of those hard parts, the shaven part of his head fresh. I bet he's got a girl around he's trying to impress.

I feel ya, kid. I've been there.

If Hannah's gotten as good as Ava says she is, this kid is way out of his league. I slip behind a few clusters of spectators, mostly people I don't know, and find the familiar jacket and pale green ball cap of the money man. Matty's been at this about as long as Ava has. He takes a cut of every bet, which is even more illegal than all this racing shit, but whatever. Man's gotta make a living. Matty slings beers all day at the Lodge, and I know those old codgers don't tip him very well. He's got a family to feed, too.

"Hey, can you give me two hunny on the Supra?"

The way his shoulders lift and freeze by his ears amuses me.

"No fuckin' way." Matty makes the slow turn, and when our wide eyes meet, it's hard not to feel that tinge of belonging. *Finally. Something here fits.*

"Bruh!" Matty pulls me into his arms, patting my back with fists clutching rolled-up bills. When we part, he leaves his fists against my biceps so he can eye me the same way Ava did. "You're really here!"

A few people nearby are looking our way, and I know it's a matter of seconds before the whispers about my presence make their way to Hannah's ears. I duck my head to shrink a little anyhow, not wanting to distract her. *Also, a little afraid of her.*

"Just for a few days. Family business," I say.

"Yeah, yeah. I heard about Colt. Real shame." He smiles through his words to be funny.

"Thanks, man," I respond. I glance toward Hannah and Bailey again, relieved to see their eyes are still trained straight ahead. The news hasn't traveled that far yet. "So what do you think? Got room for one more bet?"

"Shoot, for you? I'll even waive the commission." He winks and takes the two hundreds from my fingers, folding them in with the dozens of others in his right palm. I'd worry about him getting jumped with all this cash on him, but Matty's former military, and he's got a gun he knows damn well how to use tucked in the back of his jeans. It's always on him; always loaded.

"Thanks, brotha." I give him a nod and step back to let him get on with his business.

Doing my best to blend in with the crowd, I pull the brim of my hat down low on my brow and shove my hands in the pockets of my black jeans. I wish I had worn a less bold shirt, but behind a few bodies and in the dark, away from the headlights, the bright orange and yellow on my Tulsa Wings Racing T-shirt is a little less . . . *loud.*

Whistles from the crowd alert me that a race is coming up. It won't be Hannah yet; I would guess they hold hers third or fourth, given the novelty of a girl driver. Sexist, but lucrative. Matty and Ava work together on these races. It's an informal agreement that's lasted years and was passed down from relatives before them. Ava, or someone she decides to leave in charge, sets the lineup for the night, and Matty handles the money business.

The deep rumble of a classic Chevy gurgles forward through the crowd and I fall in step, careful to remain tucked behind someone at all times. I breathe in the sharp notes of gas and oil, and acknowledge to myself that everything smells better here. *At home.* Sure, I get the same scents for races in Florida or down in Texas, but the mixture is always missing something. Maybe it's the cottonwood trees or the red clay dirt that gets kicked up by the summer monsoon. The smell is never quite as sweet as a Friday night on the Straights.

The Chevy lines up next to a familiar Dodge and my mouth ticks up with a grin. *Good for you, Jimmy. Glad to know you're still racing.* I'm half-tempted to sneak up to his window and say something to encourage him, but then a whole different sight causes me to panic.

The Supra—it's empty.

"Shit," I mutter to myself.

Tucking my chin to my chest, I scoot back inches at a time, apologizing on my way for every elbow and shoulder

I bump into without looking. I think I'm finally clear of the crowd when I'm brought to a hard stop with a stiff arm against my spine.

"Leave."

That's all Hannah says. One word, and though probably not the coldest thing she could have said, it fills my chest with ice that cracks and shatters to pieces in a breath.

I wish I'd practiced this part more. I played conversations in my head, trying to predict how it would go, seeing her again. It always ended in a mess, like it's bound to now, so I quit pretending. I figure, *What's the use?*

Drawing a slow breath in through my nose, I keep my eyes on the ground and turn slowly, a quiet nervous laugh inching out my lips. I glance up from the shadow of my hat before lifting my chin completely. Her eyes are ice blue to match the single word that left her mouth. I can't be afraid, though. It's too important. *She's* too important to tuck my tail and go running when I just got here. She'll be mean. I'll deserve it. I'm going to have to endure it.

"No." I huff out a laugh after my response. In a millisecond, I decide to play this out by instinct. And that's what I come up with.

Her eyes dim and her mouth, already a hard line, somehow emits a growl despite her tight lips. Her nostrils flare. The urge to shift my feet is strong in my legs. I can feel my nerves firing from my quads, through my knees and calves, all the way into my toes. I don't give in, though. I stand rigid and tall, lifting my chin a little more. I'm being smug despite my racing pulse. Inside, I'm scared shitless.

"Fine." She shoves her hand back into the center of my chest and I stumble a step backward as she marches through the crowd, back toward the Supra. The *ooohs* sting a little and I feel heat hit my cheeks.

"Dustin, why did you come?" Bailey's voice lulls me to turn to my other side. I don't have to put the same guard up with her, and frankly, I'm embarrassed from the smack-down. I shrug as I square myself with her, my mouth a crooked and very guilty smile.

"In town to deal with Colt," I say.

That's not what she means.

"You didn't have to be here, though. This is hers." Bailey's hair is shorter now, almost a pixie cut. She's wearing silver crosses in her ears and I catch a glimpse of what I think might be a tattoo of a word on the inside of her wrist. Her parents must hate that she ever went away to college.

"This place used to be mine." My palms are sweating in my pockets, but I leave them there. I feel safer somehow.

"It did. And then you left."

Bailey's arms cross her chest and I note the accusatory tone in her voice. She's not wrong. I did. It's just, I can't understand why nobody seems to get all the nuances that came along with that decision. I know the details weren't public, but they had to see Colt around town when he got out. I read about the big arrests that came a year after he was out of prison, about the plea deal he took to take out some of the major cartel players. Simple math explains how dangerous it was for me to be around that. To expose Hannah to that.

"Nice tattoo." I nod toward her wrist, changing the subject. I'm being a bit self-righteous in my response. I've got Hannah's initials over my heart, buried under the vibrant T-shirt hugging my chest.

"Thanks. Hannah and I got them together, when she was at rock-fucking-bottom." She tightens her grip on herself, rolling her wrist inward to bury the word against her body. She's hiding it from me, which makes me wonder if it's all a bunch of bullshit and her tattoo is something frivolous and Hannah doesn't have one at all.

"Oh, yeah? What does it say? Nowhere but up from here?"

Fuck, Dustin. That was shitty to say.

Bailey's eyes harden and her body flexes with a deep breath before she unfurls her arm and holds her wrist out for me to read.

"Mine says TODAY, because I need to learn to live the moment." Her mouth twitches angrily, and I soften a little.

"That's . . . nice. I like it. Sorry." I scratch at my chest, where Hannah's initials burn my skin.

"You want to know what hers says?" Bailey pushes into me a step, cutting off my air and my sense of escape. I glance around, and thankfully everyone nearby seems to be minding their own business.

"It's okay. It's personal. If she wanted me to know, she'd—"

"Hers says TOMORROW. Because she needed to learn how to live until it came. Over . . . and over again."

My mouth goes dry and my throat closes. I shut my lips and briefly flit my gaze to Bailey's as I nod. Why didn't her dad tell her the truth? Why did he let her suffer so much, be so sad?

"I see," I utter.

"Yeah. You see. Your eyes are wide open now, aren't they? I never should have called you. It was wrong of me. You should have stayed gone. If you have any heart left at all, Dustin—"

"I understand. I'll take care of my business and be gone in a few days. I'm . . . I'm sorry. Tell Hannah . . . you know what? Don't tell Hannah anything. You're right. I shouldn't have come."

I pull one of my hands from my pocket and hold up a palm. My heart squeezes so hard I swear it's shrinking, shriveling into itself. Bailey put me in my place. This was so unfair of me. It was selfish. Because I'm ready to move forward with Hannah doesn't mean she is. I'm armed with the truth, and she still only sees the pieces. I'm not sure how to let her in, though. No matter what, at the end of the day, I left. I left without warning, and without a word. Warranted or not, she has every right to hate me for it.

The roar of engines fills the air as I sulk back to my rental car. Instead of slipping inside, though, I pull myself up on the hood and lean back to look at the stars. It's a special kind of dark out here. That's the one thing this place has in common with Uncle Jeff's land in Oklahoma. Wide open skies filled with diamonds.

I'll keep my promise. I'll leave. I'll be gone before Hannah sees me again. But I'll be damned if I'm not going to stick around and see my baby girl race. All the Colt Bridges in the world can't keep me from this.

2

I swear, if Bailey asks me if I'm all right one more time, I'm going to push her out of the car when I make the flip and revel as she tumbles down the road.

Wow, that was dark.

Ignoring her last words of concern, I turn my attention over to the feeling. Am I vexed a little? Sure. Dustin showed up after four years of complete and utter silence, and I'm about to rev his old car up to one-eighty in the dead of night with my best friend in tow. She may have a reason to be concerned. But I'm fine.

"I'm fine." My response is so delayed it causes a major brow scrunch on Bailey's forehead. I meet her stare. "I'm just anticipating you asking again. For last time, and for the time coming up—I'm fine."

My palms are sweating and it makes things feel *off.* My bare legs glisten with perspiration too because it's hotter than an engine block outside. I can't run the air because I need every ounce of power to compensate for my shifting.

I'm rusty. It happens every time I'm gone for a semester. One or two races, though, and my groove is back.

It wouldn't be a big deal if I didn't have a mountain of pride to defend tonight. I'm not worried about winning. Dustin's car could probably take this kid on its own, driven with nothing more than a garden shovel jammed in place to hold the gas pedal down. It's more than showing off what I can do in his car. This is about showing him what I can do *without* him. It's about proving I'm still whole, that he didn't break me.

Only, he did.

Dustin Bridges broke me into a thousand and one pieces. And rather than putting them back together, I merely swept them to the side and invented a whole different me. His presence ruins that. Seeing him is a reminder of who I was before he left. It stirs feelings, scratches at memories, and hollows out my insides. I can't afford that.

Tomorrow.

That's what it's been about for the last four years. Learning how to put one foot after the other, how to get through one task and on to the next. I've found a balance between excelling at school and living on the edge. If Dustin knew the kinds of things I've done while he's been away, he'd see that I'm not the same girl at all.

This Hannah Judge isn't afraid of swimming naked in front of frat boys. She thrives off of their attention, especially knowing that she'll never give in and say yes to any of them. She walks through fire, literally. Twice—because someone dared her to. And she's getting ready to leap from an airplane for the third time next fall, only one jump away from getting to do it solo. Roaring down the Straights in the middle of the night isn't about venturing to a wild side for me, not anymore. It's about keeping up my skills, scratching an itch, and reminding myself where center is. Racing is the only thread I've let remain that connects me to Dustin. And now that he's shown up and ruined it, I think it might be time to cut ties there too.

"You ready, lady?" Ava's lips pucker as she pats my window frame. I give her a confident smile.

I roll the window up as she walks around the front of the Supra and crosses the short distance to the new kid, Kyle. He's wearing gloves, which Bailey cannot stop laughing about. My best friend has been with me for every dangerous step of my journey. I've leaned on her, needed her. But I think this has been good for her in a way. She's blossomed. In the last year, she's stood up to her parents, resisting their demands that she study law and follow in her father's footsteps. She wants to go into psychology, and I think she's meant to. She has this deep understanding of what makes people tick, and her advice—and her welcoming ears—have made a world of difference for me these past four years.

I give a polite nod to Kyle. I'll give the kid this, at least he seems to treat me with respect. I've raced a few other teen drivers who have wandered out here over the summer, bored and looking for a thrill. They're quick to comment on me being a woman and somehow that makes a difference in my ability to shift and haul ass. Kyle's a local boy, though. New, but he's learned quick. Maybe I won't totally embarrass him.

Ava saunters through the dust lit up by our headlights, and she turns to face us when she's a few dozen feet out in the road. My body still doesn't feel right, but there's no time to dwell on it. I blow on my palm since everything else on me is soaked with sweat and I caress the shifter knob, settling into my zone.

Like Dustin, my instincts take over as soon as Ava's hand drops, and I compensate for my slippery palm within seconds by gassing my way up over sixty in a blink.

I didn't realize how homesick I'd become for the vibrations of the Supra's engine until now. It tickles my chest, and my lips buzz with the pleasing numbness that comes along with the hard ride. I crack one-twenty, and am starting to see separation from Kyle. I quit focusing so much on my competition in my periphery. It slows me down. This world, it's about trusting yourself, trusting your skills. That's something Dustin taught me. Tommy, my brother, honed it for me.

"He's toast," Bailey shouts at my side. The perk of having a passenger is an extra set of eyes.

My chest opens up and my shoulders automatically relax with the knowledge that the pressure is off. Once I make the turn, Kyle won't be able to hang. I wouldn't be surprised if he just keeps on driving. The satisfying smile that lives on my lips every time I conquer something begins its initial stretch, and I sit up and flex my muscles, readying my body for the turn.

"Oh, fuck! Hannah, stop! Stop, stop, stop! Kyle flipped. Kyle fucking flipped!"

It takes my body a few seconds to understand the signals my brain is sending, my mind still unraveling the reality of Bailey's warning. For a moment, I'm not even sure who Kyle is or where we are. I'm simply living the moment and feeling the numb bliss that accompanies driving so fast.

I fishtail to a stop when her words register, and we both fling open our doors and burst out onto the road, hands on our foreheads as our senses take in the clues. The burnt rubber stench is strong, and there's the faint glow of smoke in the moonlight. The road is lit up enough to show that it's clear, which means Kyle is off to the side.

"Get in," I command, rushing into the driver's side and shifting to drive. Bailey climbs in and leans forward, her palms flat on the dash as her eyes scan the roadway. Headlights flash ahead in pairs, and I know others saw what happened. They're coming to help. Someone's called nine-one-one.

"I see him! There!" Bailey points ahead, to the left, and the faint outline of a spinning tire and the underside of a Honda Civic comes into view. I pull to the side of the road and we both rush out of the car, sprinting to the driver's side of Kyle's vehicle.

"Kyle! Are you okay? Can you hear me?" Bailey screams, her voice wavering. We're both in shock.

I tug on the door handle, but it doesn't open. There's movement inside, though, and a smear of blood across the glass. The front windshield is blown out, almost completely. I'm about to snake my way along the ground to reach Kyle when someone literally lifts me in the air and carries me several feet away.

"Bailey, get her out of here! Go!" Dustin points toward the Supra, his eyes glowing, teeth gritting. He rushes back to the flipped car and slides on his stomach through the broken glass until he reaches Kyle. He grips his forearm and pulls, and groans echo in the night air.

"He's okay. Hannah, he's okay," Bailey stammers as she clutches my side.

I take long backward strides, not wanting to leave the scene but understanding what Dustin's worries are. I smell it. Gasoline.

Sirens whine in the distance, and as much as law enforcement looks the other way when it comes to the Straights, it's not a great idea to be hanging around. A few more guys have shown up to help Dustin pull Kyle free, so we wouldn't be abandoning him. We've made it back to the car, and the engine is running. It would be the responsible thing to gain some distance, to make room for the fire engine and the medics.

Something has me glued to the scene, though. Yeah, to an extent I feel responsible. But it's more than that. It's . . . someone.

My head swings toward Bailey, her eyes glued to the now-flaming scene in front of us.

"Take the car."

She jerks her head to face me.

"Not without you." Her lips pucker and eyes draw in tight, but it's no use. I'm not leaving. I have to make sure Kyle is okay.

I have to make sure Dustin is okay.

"Bailey, go!" I bark at her. She blinks rapidly, and I can tell she's torn.

"I'll be right behind you. I have to help." I don't bother elaborating, packing on about my concern for Kyle. She'd see right through it. She must sense my resolve, because she growls out in frustration and rounds the front of the car to the driver's side.

"I'm not leaving until you meet me back at the start." She points at me for added impact. I get the undertone— I'm not going home with Dustin.

"Okay," I agree. I mean it, too. I appreciate her looking out for my heart, but I'm not the frail heartbroken nymph I was when he left town. I've got calluses, hard-earned ones. Painful ones. I don't intend to waste them by letting Dustin gain space inside my heart or my head. I just have to make sure he doesn't get physically hurt. That's all.

Bailey makes a U-turn and stares at me pointedly as she drives by slowly on her way back to the start. I'm sure the crowd has thinned. No doubt Matty has gone. He has the most to lose. Ava's probably holding down the rest. She can't help but feel like the mother of all of us. She'll want to make sure the kid is all right.

I remain several yards away, the smoke building and the smell toxic. I pull my T-shirt collar up over my mouth and nose, holding it to my face with cupped hands. My eyes stay on Dustin as he works to get to his feet, Kyle clutched in his arms. Jimmy and a couple of other regulars out here helped clear out the glass, but blood drips down Dustin's forearm. He didn't wait for it to be safe; he went in and got him.

Firefighters rush from the truck that pulled up, and two of them go to work unraveling hose right away. The others race toward Dustin and Kyle with a backer board, meeting them a safe distance from the overturned car, but not quite to me. My vision tunnels, and my knees buckle a little. I catch myself before I fall, though. Turning my back to the scene, I pace away. I'd like to think it's the smoke getting to me, but I know better.

I was holding my breath.

I was imagining the what if.

I mentally saw Dustin lying there on the ground, medics cutting open his shirt and calling for air transport.

"Hey, they've got this. Come on." A familiar touch accompanies the voice that still haunts my dreams, and I shirk away.

"I'll walk," I say, not bothering to meet Dustin's eyes.

His arm is bloody. If I see it close up, I'll want to care

for it. And I don't want to care about anything having to do with Dustin ever again.

"You're being irrational. Let me take you to Bailey. My car's right here." His steps match mine, and I know if I run I will either look ridiculous or he'll run right along with me—and we'll both look like lunatics.

"Fine. I'm riding in the back, though." I turn on my heels and march toward some family sedan-looking thing that puts a superior smile on my lips. "Nice car, by the way."

Dustin chuckles behind me, but before I can rip open the back door on my own, his arm crosses my path, his palm covering the handle.

"My other car seems to be occupied," he says.

I blink at his hand, hyper-focusing on his knuckles that are only mildly gashed from the glass-covered roadway.

"You lost that car when you abandoned it."

My front teeth come together and my nostrils twitch with my brewing resentment. There's double meaning in my words. Dustin knows it, too. His hand slips from the handle and his feet drag along the blacktop behind me. He moves to the driver's side and gets in, shutting the door but not leaving without me. The engine is still on from when he drove up. My chest heaves twice, the last emotion I'm going to let myself show for this moment. I let the stench of burning oil cover anything alive in my soul then tug open the back door and climb inside.

We're maybe a mile from everyone. Probably less. The distance seems to double every few yards we travel. Dustin is purposely driving slow. Partly because of the situation, I'm sure, but I also think maybe he's prolonging time with me. It's no use. I haven't inhaled once since I got in the car. If I can make it, I'm going to avoid breathing the same air as him. I won't share anything with him. Ever.

"Looks like almost everyone's gone. Have Bailey take you straight home."

My eyes flicker to the rearview mirror and squint. Regardless of the temptation to respond to him with a million retorts, I don't take a breath or part my lips. I'll go where I want. He doesn't get a say in that. I'm not a naïve teenager anymore.

His eyes flit up to meet my gaze and rather than pull away, I keep my focus right where it is. After a few seconds he breathes out a laugh and shakes his head, shifting in his seat and propping his wrist on the steering wheel.

My hand reaches for the door handle as we close in on Bailey, Ava, and the few others remaining, and I open the door before he comes to a complete stop. I stumble a little as I exit, but I cover it with a jog, slamming the door behind me as Dustin shouts, "Hey!" I suck in air, filling my lungs and mentally congratulating myself for holding my breath. Such a stupid victory, but still, one that's mine. Every victory counts.

"Cops are taking statements," Ava says as she steps up to me. Her eyes shift over my shoulder to where Dustin is still waiting in his rental car.

"They can start with him. He's the big hero who pulled that kid out of the car. They know where to find me. Tell them to stop by the mayor's house if they need to talk." I pull down my T-shirt and tuck the front in my shorts, avoiding Ava's returned stare. I can't ditch her glare forever, though, and since she's not the person I'm trying to prove something to, I finally give in and look her in the eyes.

"It's fine. I'll talk to them. I just don't want to do it here.

I can't be here any longer." I let the ache make a short appearance on my face and Ava pulls her mouth in tight, breathing out her nose as she nods.

"Okay. I'll tell them the smoke was getting to you. They'll want to talk tonight, though. Don't screw me over and not be where I say you are."

I cross my heart and maintain our stare. When she gives me a slight nod, I move toward the Supra and signal to Bailey that she can drive us home. My body is too unpredictable right now. Just like my heart.

3

Perspective is funny. When I'm out on the tracks, busting my ass, trying to get respect from some two-bit hot wings king, I don't feel I've climbed very far at all. But Ava was right. In terms of Camp Verde, I guess I'm "famous." At least, famous enough to keep tonight's crash off certain radars.

That Kyle kid's car is totaled. He'll get slapped with reckless driving charges and his parents will probably forbid him from driving—as soon as he can—because his insurance is going to be stupid expensive. But besides a lot of cuts and bruises, he's going to be fine. By the time medics cleared out, he was refusing an ambulance. Seemed a little like his dad didn't want people in their business, But maybe that's just me reading into things.

Almost everyone was gone by then, except me and Ava and a few old-timers, and the cops we have known for years. I'll give the Kyle kid this much—he took the blame and protected the Straights by saying he was only showing off for some car that passed him. Maybe, in a way, that's all he was doing. Because Hannah smoked him, and can't blame a kid for trying to save face in front of a girl as hot as her. He got in over his head, lost tread, and spun out.

It happens.

I did it once when I was a kid. It's actually the *only* time I've done it. The Tucson kart race, when Colt showed up. First time I cried my ass off in front of Hannah. That's when I realized she was special.

Pulling into the motel lot, it's hard not to feel like a loser again. The high from having a few people fawn over me and ask about tracks back east and in the Midwest wore off about a mile away from the Straights. Now, I'm back here, in this temporary hole in the wall, *alone*.

My lungs feel the weight of an elephant sitting on my chest. I haven't been able to breathe quite right since Hannah's eyes met mine in the reflection of the mirror of my rental.

I always knew she'd be angry with me. I even expected the hate. It's that it's so raw, so full of revenge and heat. I could see it in her eyes. The way she said that word, *abandoned*. That's how she feels. That's what I did.

I had to, though. I couldn't stick around only to drag out an inevitable good-bye. And knowing now how fast they got Colt out of prison so they could use him as bait, me lingering around would have only made a dotted line between Hannah and the trouble that is my birthright.

I know it was all for the best. But it hurts so goddamn bad anyway. Best or not, it's hard not to question whether it was worth it.

My hand feels in my front pocket as I limp out of the car, searching for the room key. The cuts on my leg are starting to bleed through my jeans. There's still a lot of glass in my arm, too. I refused to let anyone check me out on the scene. That's the last thing I need is some medical report floating around that keeps me off the track for a month. It means this is going to be a long night, though, because I'm going to have to take care of my own sorry ass, and as far as I can tell, the only tools at my disposal are a few complimentary tea bags and a motel pen.

With my body leaning against the jamb, I finagle the key into the lock and manage to get the door open. Stale cigarette smoke permeates the entry, bringing me back to my youth. I asked for a non-smoking room, but I guess they don't have those at this place. When I complained, the front desk guy politely pointed out that if I wasn't smoking in it now then it's not a smoking room. Pretty sure that's not how that works, but again, I don't need to be making a scene anywhere. The only thing worse than a medical report would probably be a viral news story about some diva wannabe circuit driver throwing a shit fit over his motel room.

I leave the door open behind me and drop the key to the door along with the one for the rental car in the center of the burnt orange bedspread. I feel around under the lamp shade for the switch, eventually clicking it on and casting a dark yellow glow throughout the room. I pause to take it in and laugh to myself.

"Just . . . perfect," I mutter. The aesthetics of this room could not match the way I feel more perfectly.

I tug on the back of my T-shirt on my way into the vanity area, lifting it over my head and dropping it on the countertop. My palm finds the switch for the harsh bulb lighting. It flickers on and I go to work inspecting the wounds on my arm.

"Shit," I breathe out at the first touch of a shard of glass. There are dozens in my skin. That one looked like the easiest. I'm half-tempted to leave them be, let my skin grow over it all and form some weird supervillain trait that can become my calling card. I know that's not an option, though, so I lean forward until my forehead rests on the mirror and I stare at the oozing wounds to give me courage. Rather, to give me motivation. I spend about thirty minutes mostly staring and little else, though.

"Ava said you refused care." My heart beats once at the sound of Hannah's voice, hard enough to wound my ribs, then stops completely. I leave my head where it is and train my eyes on my arm.

It's three in the morning. I have no idea how she found me or why. But I could cry I'm so happy she's here.

"You finish talking to the cops?" My voice echoes off the sink below me.

Keys clank on the dresser top behind me, followed by the sound of something being tossed on the bed. Her purse, I'm guessing. Her shadow mixes with the soft light behind me and the hard glare from above, but it's when I smell her apple-scented shampoo that I accept she's actually here and not a figment of my imagination.

"I did. I wouldn't burn Ava like that. They didn't have a lot of questions, though. Seems they got a good story from their favorite driver and needed me to button down the details." She coughs to show her sarcasm.

"I know, we all lied. To be fair, though, it's the story they want to hear." I roll my head just enough to see her hips. She's wearing dark blue sweatpants rolled up at the waist. They look like men's pants, which has my fist instinctively curling to pummel whatever guy gave them to her.

"Ava stopped by right after the cops. She said I should probably come help you since you're basically helpless."

She sets a bottle of alcohol on the counter and I wince at the sight of it.

"She's not wrong," I utter through a pathetic laugh.

Ava could have come instead. Hannah could have refused. Neither of those things happened, which has my head swimming with hope. Though I'm in too much pain to do more than simply accept Hannah's help.

"Don't be a baby. Sit your ass on the counter and let me see," she orders.

I stand up straight and catch a glimpse of her eyes on me through the reflection. I twist and slide my body up to sit on the countertop as she walks over to her purse. She dumps the contents on the bed and gathers up a roll of gauze, some ointment, and a small first aid kit. I smirk at the familiar red box as she carries it toward me.

"You remember this thing?" She hands it to me then goes to work arranging the other items on the counter.

I run my thumb over the three faded initials written in black magic marker.

T.H.D.

"Your dad fixed a lot of messed up shit with the stuff he kept in this box," I say. I lift my chin briefly and our eyes meet. My chest hollows and my body rushes with the same sensation I get on rollercoasters.

"He still keeps it well stocked. He mostly uses it to fix his own injuries now." She takes it from my hand, our fingertips barely meeting. It was on purpose. I could tell.

"I require a bigger box nowadays." I chuckle.

"Yeah, I can see that." She stands up straight, hands on her hips and eyes focused on my forearms. "But . . . this is the box I've got, so we better hope it gets the job done. Otherwise, I'm hauling your ass to the ER."

"No ER." I'm adamant, and she studies my face for a second, trying to read me.

"I've gotta drive next week," I explain.

Hannah's mouth twists up in understanding. I can't be damaged goods. My sponsor might pull out.

With tentative movements, Hannah reaches for my arm, taking it in her cool palms and holding it over the sink, twisting it gently until she can see most of the gashes and glass bits. Her hair is twisted up in a knot on top of her head and I find myself staring at the strays that float around her face, like dark webs around her pink skin. A light sunburn kisses her nose and the tops of her cheeks, bringing out her freckles. Her lashes are sun bleached too, almost speckled with gold.

"This might hurt," she warns.

I hold my breath and acknowledge the tweezers in her right hand. Our eyes meet again, and there's a thick dose of silence that accompanies the seconds-long pause. I swallow hard, and the slight movement in my throat draws Hannah's eyes toward my bare chest. I draw in a sharp breath under her view. Her initials are like a time stamp on my left pectoral, small but definitely visible. Especially under this harsh light.

"You can look away if you need to," she says, returning her gaze to the job ahead of her.

I nod, knowing I'll watch everything, a part of me enjoying the pain. It feels like something I deserve, like a penance for hurting this absolute gift of a human here with me now. Hannah bends down, bracing her body on her elbows so she can look closely at my skin as she picks out the first piece of glass. It's tiny, like a crushed diamond, and when the tips of her tweezers grab hold it sends a zap through my arm and into every nerve ending in my body.

"Oh fuck, that hurt." I fall back a little, my head hitting the glass. I blink rapidly and mentally calculate how many more of these I have to endure.

"I said you could look away," she reminds me, glancing up with wide eyes and a wry smile.

"I know. You did. I need to see it coming." I tuck my chin so I can maintain my view but leave my body weight against the mirror in case I pass out.

Hannah shakes her head and mutters "stubborn" under her breath.

My mouth ticks up on one side. There's an intimacy to her slight insult. It's the kind of name girls call the loves of their lives.

She goes after the next two shards faster, probably trying to catch me off guard and make the ordeal less traumatic. It doesn't work, though, and by the time she's gotten five pieces out of my arm, I'm begging for a short break.

"You're a pussy. Just so you know," she teases.

"I'm okay with that." I shield her from my arm for a minute. I hold it close to my body and pull up a leg, propping my knee up to help take some of the pressure off my arm.

Hannah takes a few steps back, resting her back on the opposite wall. She crosses her feet at the ankles and clutches the tweezers and the small ball of alcohol-soaked cotton in her palms at her stomach. I recognize the shirt she's wearing. It's one of her dad's, from his dirt bike days. It's torn in a few places from a life well-lived, and she cut off the bottom two-thirds of it so it barely covers her breasts and shows off the slope of her mid-section.

Rather than be embarrassed when she catches me staring at her, I dive right into questions and let my eyes continue to roam. I've missed so many changes to her body.

"How'd you find me?" I ask, only half interested in her answer. I'm lost in the milky skin of her stomach, the small silver hoop accenting her belly button, the slight breeze that flirts with the very loose bottom of her shirt.

"There are only two hotels around here, and this one had that lame ass car parked outside," she says.

I nod and laugh.

"Excellent detective work. I think you're overstating with the word *hotel*, though. This place isn't deserving of the H. It's barely a motor lodge." I let my eyes trail back to her face, and I'm pleased to see her taking the same inventory of my body.

"I didn't want to make you feel bad. I mean, clearly racing is going really well if this is what you can afford." She's always been good at talking shit with me. I've missed this too.

"Yeah, well, maybe Colt left me a secret stash of cash and I can afford the casino seventy miles up next time I'm in town." I laugh at my bad joke, but only briefly. Hannah didn't seem to find that as amusing as I did. Her eyes have dipped to focus on her hands and her lips are pulled in tight.

"I'm sorry about Colt, ya know. I mean, not for your loss, but for—"

"I know what you mean. Thanks," I say, saving her from trying to explain. She doesn't need to. That's why she's Hannah, why she's it for me. She's the only person on this planet who truly gets what's going on in my head in the wake of Colt dying. I'm so fucking happy and so fucking angry at the same time. I resent that he left me a mess, that he existed and had to be attached to me, and that he parted this Earth without me getting the chance to scar him up, as he did to me. The worst scars of all are the ones left by forcing me to leave my home behind—to leave Hannah.

I hate him. I always will. I'll hate his memory until I die.

"I think I can handle more now," I say, clearing my throat and sitting up tall.

Hannah tosses the used cotton ball in the trash and douses a new one in alcohol before getting to work on my arm again. I hold in my reactions better this time. I don't want her to feel as though I'm dragging this out, even if I want to. Every fragment she removes sears my nerves, and some pieces end up gushing blood in their wake, causing Hannah to stop extricating things and switch to pressing gauze into the wounds. It takes about an hour for her to remove everything, and another thirty minutes to glue the two deepest cuts and bandage my arm in a makeshift gauze cast.

"I probably would have bled out if I had to do this on my own, so thanks," I say, sliding from the counter.

"Don't mention it," she says over her shoulder, a nervous waver to her voice.

Guilt crawls around my shoulders and grips at my throat, but I know my words could never be enough to fix the hurt I've caused her. Regardless, I have to try. I have to say something.

"Hannah."

"Hmm?" She's busying herself, packing up to rush out of here. The door's still wide open, so her escape will be easy. Clean.

Her bag packed, she tugs it up her shoulder and straightens her spine, facing me with a deep breath and a heavy exhale through her nose. Her mouth forms a tight, forced smile, and as much as she's faking everything is fine with her wide, blinking eyes, I see the tears welling.

"Han," I breathe out, my head falling to the side.

Her eyes close and she shakes her head in quick movements.

"It's fine. I'm fine." She draws in another breath through her nose and breathes out more slowly this time. When her eyes open, the vulnerable side I saw before is erased, replaced with the hardened version, the girl I made her into when I left town.

"Can I drive you home?" I offer, knowing she probably drove herself here, and even if she didn't, she'd rather walk.

"In that piece of shit? No thanks," she says, a forced laugh accompanying her words.

I play along and smile, shaking my head. "Yeah, I get it. It's pretty bad."

I bend down and grab my T-shirt, gripping it in my fist, squeezing to test my strength on my cut-up arm. It stings a little when I flex the muscle, but it's not impossible.

"I should go. I'll leave the extra roll of gauze and the alcohol behind. I had one Percocet left too, from when I had my wisdom teeth out last year. I know you're not into that shit, but maybe tonight you should take it."

If she only knew. Living in Oklahoma, I've taken those with gin some nights just to get to sleep. I've fallen from grace, breaking all sorts of promises to myself. I don't need to shed light on that for her, though; she already sees a flawed man when she looks at me. No need to up the game.

"Okay. Doctor's orders," I say, saluting her with my fisted T-shirt before I stretch out and move to put it on, pushing my hands inside and carefully sliding the cotton over my bandaged arm. Before I can raise my arms and duck my head inside, Hannah closes in, stepping inches from me and grabbing my wrists.

My lips part automatically, and my eyes move to her mouth. Her plump bottom lip, pale pink and without the red from earlier, quivers and her breath comes quick. Her gaze is down, at the place where she's locked my hands in place. She shakes her head, and I don't think she realizes I can see her doing it. She's warring with herself, and I feel like an asshole for standing here and letting her.

But I'm selfish. I don't want her to go. I don't want her to *let* go.

"I'm so mad at you, Dustin. Just . . . so mad." Her lashes flutter, her eyes still down.

"Okay." It's the only response that I can give her. I can't apologize, and I won't beg her not to feel the way she does. Hannah has a right to whatever feelings consume her. I've always promised myself I'd understand her summation of me after what I likely put her through. I accept it, whatever it is.

When her head tips back and her lashes unmask the ocean blue eyes I've missed with every inch of my soul, my body goes limp and my arms grow heavy, slipping from her hold as they fall against my body. Still tethered by my shirt, I'm unable to react properly when Hannah steps up on her toes, and the shock of her cool lips against my cheek stuns me motionless and unable to speak. Even as she falls back to her heels and stares up at me with an uncertain expression, the kind that accompanies impulsive decisions and regrets, I'm frozen and speechless.

Reaching forward, she places her palm on my bare chest, her sharp nail scratching softly at the three letters that are her name. She must know.

Hannah Beth Judge.

HBJ

It could be nothing else. *No one else.*

"Please be safe, Dustin. Out there? Wherever you go. That's . . . that's all." Her fingertips glide down the center of my chest, slipping away far too quickly. As does she.

I remain standing in that same spot for several minutes, my shirt dangling half on my arms, my chest cut open with invisible wounds that hurt a thousand times more than the real ones cut from glass.

Hannah wants to hate me. And part of her definitely does. But most of her? She just can't. Because we're real, and we're forever. And even the fucking hands of fate with all their destructive power can't undo our destiny. Shame on me for thinking I should give up so easily.

4

I'm pathetic.

It took less than twenty-four hours of Dustin within rock-throwing distance for me to break about a dozen of the vows I made to myself when he left me four years ago.

Damn him.

Damn him *and* those hazel eyes! And his floppy hair that has only gotten longer, more touchable. Maybe softer? And that body of his, lean and toned. His skin golden from working out in the sun, lying flat on his back and sliding out from undercarriages of cars and trucks. And that tattoo. That wasn't fair.

I haven't slept a single second. I took out my sketch pad to work on my shadowing technique and I filled a dozen pages with pictures of Dustin drawn from memory. The sun is peeking over the horizon, the beams finding their way through the slats of my shutters. The chimes Dustin gave me for my seventeenth birthday hang from a thin piece of fishing line above my bed. When the air blows just right, they move with the sunlight, the jagged pieces lighting up like precious gems. As mad as I was—*am*—I couldn't part with his gift. I wouldn't even take it down. I drew the line at taking it to college with me. If I'm being truthful, though, it was less about holding myself accountable and more out of fear that Bailey would destroy it or toss it out when I wasn't looking. She's been good at removing temptation.

She's been my voice of reason. Maybe a little bit my conscience, too. She never tried to stop me from breaking my self-made rules, but she was quick to question them. Like the first time I got absolutely lit at the High Tower Bar after finals our sophomore year and found myself wandering the back alley to decide whether I wanted to throw up or call Dustin and beg him to come home. She held my phone and made me stare at the screen, at his number that I'm not supposed to have, and asked if that was what I really, truly wanted.

"There's no going back once you make that call," she said.

It was enough to snap me out of my manic, drunken state and put my phone away. I threw up instead.

Ava hung around after the police questioned us, long enough for Bailey to go home. I'm not sure even Bailey would have been able to stop me from rushing to Dustin's aid, though. I knew he was hurt. And he's here, in the flesh. It's so much easier to avoid making stupid phone calls or sending texts than it is to avoid an actual living, breathing human.

"You up?" The soft knock at my door that follows my brother's voice jars me, but only a little. I'm so tired that a breakdance crew of zombies could knock on my door and I'd have the same response.

"Come in," I say.

My brother slowly pushes my door open and slips in along with his duffel bag. I'm guessing the rest of his things are still piled downstairs by the front door, or in the trunk of his car. This might be the last summer both he and I are home together. It's strange, and a little sad.

"Hey!" I whisper, sitting up and drawing my legs in so my brother can sit in front of me. I wrap my arms around him the second he does and squeeze him tight.

"How was your drive?" Unlike me, who only went to Northern State about a hundred miles away, Tommy opted for Nebraska. My mom cried fat alligator tears when he finally told her. She'd spent a year preparing herself for him being in New Mexico. Then he went and added a thousand miles to her commute. Doesn't mean she hasn't made it. She's visited my brother at school more times then she has me, and I don't require a flight.

"Long. Not as long as it will be next year, though." Tommy picks up my sketch pad and I hold my breath, afraid he's going to flip through it and see my Dustin drawings. He drops it to the floor instead, though, then flops back on my bed. I stare down at him, the sunlight coming through enough to let me really zero in on his eyes.

"You got in." He applied for a master's program in Chicago. Our mom is going to shit.

He rolls his head to the side and lets his smile break through.

"I got in," he says. "Delayed, because I have one more semester to finish up. Four-year college, my ass!"

"Dude, right?" I laugh with him. I'll be lucky to be done in five.

We both sigh in sync, which makes us laugh. That

sound fades soon, though, and all that's left are the few things we *don't* want to talk about.

"You hear Dustin's in town?" I throw it out there first because I'm sure he has. I know our parents were expecting him. They're acting funny because of it, as though all their words and actions are taken from some pre-approved script.

Tommy lets out a heavy breath. His stare has wandered back to my ceiling, and I don't have to follow the path to know he's staring at my chime. Guilt drips down my throat and coats my stomach as he pulls his lips in tight, stretching out the silence.

"You see him?" He turns to face me enough to quirk a brow.

I gnaw on the inside of my cheek, briefly considering lying. Tommy reads me better than anyone, though, so I nod. He mimics my movement then returns his stare to the ceiling.

"He look good? And no, I don't mean in the way you and Bailey probably discuss him looking."

I stretch out my feet and kick my brother's hip.

"Don't be like that," I say.

"Like what? Honest? Hannah, you've thought Dustin was a—what did you call him, *hottie*, that's right—since fifth grade. I just want to know if the dude looks healthy and shit."

I laugh at my brother's mocking of me then nod.

"Yeah, he seems good. I mean, he cut the shit out of his arm last night out on the Straights, but—"

Tommy sits up and groans. It's not as if I could hide what happened from him. He's home for eight weeks like I am. People around here talk, and it's pretty likely that the

Straights will have to cool it for a couple weeks until chatter dies down.

"You went racing with him?" Tommy's full-on facing me. His tone is less brotherly and more fatherly. It annoys me when he gets like this.

"Noooo." I roll my eyes, but my chest is still tight because I'm omitting details. *Fucking guilt!* "Not *with* him."

"Hannah." I hate his scolding tone.

I sit up and twist so my feet touch the floor, and busy myself with the hair tie next to my bed. It's better to talk and not look my brother in the eyes.

"I was there with Bailey. We were bored. I raced some newbie and he rolled his car. Dustin showed up, and I swear I didn't know." *I did hope he would, though. I've been hoping to see him out there every time I drive.*

My brother runs his palm over his face and grumbles through his fingers. He looks at me sideways.

"Kid rolled his car?"

I grimace.

"Yeah. He's gonna be okay. It was pretty bad, though. Ava said it was handled, but I don't know. This one might be it, ya know?" We've all worried the day would come when officials quit looking the other way, and I can't help this lingering feeling after last night.

"I'm sure we'll be the first to know. Speaking of, how *is* the mayor?" Tommy shifts into my second favorite topic—Mom.

She and I haven't been the same since I dated Dustin. Part of that is my fault, and I know it. I can't seem to help my vocal reflexes when it comes to her. Everything she says sets me on edge, and I react. Not well.

"We were cordial yesterday. I'm sure tonight will be a

great test. Family dinner and all," I remind Tommy. He stands, stretching his arms up until his fingertips dust my ceiling, then beams his signature fake grin at me, teeth and all.

"Wouldn't miss it," he says, moving toward my door.

"That's 'cause you're not allowed. Mom would hunt you down. I bet she can smell that you're here. She's part wolf," I say.

Tommy chuckles.

"You read too much paranormal. I'm starving, so I'm gonna grab breakfast. You want in? Or . . . would you prefer to have an early morning awkward encounter with Mom and really start this summer off with a bang?"

"Uhm, no, thank you. Give me ten minutes and I'll meet you downstairs. I'll drive."

My brother offers a crooked grin, and I know what he's thinking—that he'll beat me to the driver's seat. We both love being behind the wheel of the Supra, but for whatever reason, Tommy usually relents and lets me have my way. I think it started as a way to help me cope with Dustin's leaving. Now, it's habit. Brotherly love.

It takes a twenty-minute drive and a stack of pancakes for Tommy and me to fall right back in step. We take turns stealing bacon from one another's plate, and he does his best to gross me out by showing me his food while he chews. We're obnoxious, and way too old to be acting this way, but it soothes everything that was wrong with me an hour before. I'm almost back to feeling like myself when the front end of the most boring rental car ever crawls to a stop right outside our window.

"Shit," I mumble through my recent bite. Appetite . . . gone.

I push my plate away, surrendering half my stack of hotcakes. Tommy's brow pulls in tight in response and I lean my head toward the window, urging him to look. He does just in time to see Dustin step out. I look up and catch the moment they make eye contact.

"Shiiiiiit," Tommy grits through his toothy, plastered-on smile as he holds up a palm. Dustin gives him a nod through the window, then presses the lock button on his fob, flashing the lights. The burst glows through the window, like paparazzi cameras. As if this is the perfect moment to commemorate.

Tommy leans forward, both palms on the table between us, the same smile still set between his cheeks. "I don't know what to do. I have to say hi." He's muttering his words without moving his lips, which is creepy as fuck.

"It's fine." I sigh, looking down at my lap where I've contorted the cloth napkin into a bowtie.

"Hey, man," Tommy says, sliding out from the booth with open arms. The distinct sound of untied Vans sliding along linoleum floor edges closer to us. Four years later, Dustin is still wearing the same damn footwear and walking like a delinquent about to be busted.

"Han." He pushes his black hoodie from his disheveled hair and gives me a half smile with his greeting, dimple and all. *Damn him for saying my name all hushed and perfect like he used to.*

"Hi." I nod and instantly seal my lips. Tommy will be impressed.

"We were just finishing up, but we could stay . . . if you want company?" My brother's eyes slide to me as he makes this offer, and I'm sure mine are wide and begging him to stop. My stomach twists in anticipation of Dustin's answer.

"Thanks, but nah. It's okay. I'm just gonna get some coffee and wait for this guy. He's supposed to be here at seven." Dustin pushes up his sleeve and checks his watch, his eyes tired-looking, probably from sleeping about as much as I did. Which would be zero.

"What guy?" Tommy tilts his head curiously.

"Lawyer for the state. Guess I'm in for the inheritance of a lifetime. Any interest in a nineteen-eighty-something trailer that's probably had crack stuffed in its walls?" Dustin squints one eye and dips a brow while Tommy and I chuckle at his joke. On its face, though, nothing about what he said is funny. That's where Dustin grew up. In a crappy trailer that was used to cook and hide drugs for most his life.

"Alright, well, if you're good. I guess we'll pay our tab and see ya later, maybe?" Tommy again shifts his eyes to me as he extends the olive branch. If I weren't in Dustin's line of sight, I might shake my head, pleading for him to stop or make an excuse.

"Yeah, I don't know how long I'll be here. As soon as this is wrapped up, I should probably get back. I'm already missing a race for this, so—"

"Sure, no problem. Next time maybe." Tommy drops two twenties on our messy table then leans in with stiff arms to hug Dustin. It's not the same two boys who hugged like actual brothers most of my life. This is an embrace of two strangers.

"See ya," I hum as I shift to step through the tight space between my side of the booth and where Dustin stands. I only glance up for a second, not wanting to make eye contact longer than a breath. In my foolish haste, though, it isn't my gaze that gets caught on my way out. Our hands like magnets, drawn to connect, whisper against one another as I leave two steps behind my brother. Our touch is painful, and lasts long enough for my pinky to hook with his then slip away. I shudder silently and suck in the hot morning air as soon as we get outside. It bakes the threat of tears and keeps me whole, but my hand will never be the same.

There was longing in that touch. In a fragment of a second, our bodies told the truth—we aren't done with each other. Not even close.

I sink into the driver's seat and glance to my left while my brother gets in. Dustin's rental seems even more pathetic now for some reason. Nondescript, and washed of identity. Maybe I'm projecting the way I feel. I worked so hard to make myself into someone without the title of being *Dustin's girl.* But who did I become? Not the girl I wanted to. I'm still taking business courses, like my parents wanted, and I fill my free time with anything that gives me a taste of that same rush I always felt being near Dustin. I'm no better than his mom or dad in my addiction, only I'm addicted to him.

"You should go with him."

"Huh?" I clearly took Tommy by surprise. I chew at my thumbnail as I study Dustin's form where he sits inside the diner, back to me, alone on a stool. I swivel my head and meet my brother's twisted expression.

"I thought you didn't want to get too involved. Han, I'm so confused—"

"No, you're right. I don't want to get involved. But I have this bad feeling, Tommy. Dustin knows his way around a race track and a pit and an auto shop. But who knows what Colt put in his name? I don't think he should be there without someone with a little legal savvy. And you and I both know it can't be Dad."

I let my pleading stare soak through Tommy's armor, until his eyes soften and understanding settles in his posture. He sinks back against the passenger door and his eyes dip to the space between us.

"Fuck," he grumbles.

"Yeah, fuck," I agree.

His eyes fall shut and he nods a few times, forming his hands into fists on his knees, as though he's pumping himself up. He probably is.

"All right. But if this gets messy, you're bailing my ass out." He points a finger at me and pushes open the door. I lean forward to meet his eyes before he shuts it.

"You planning on getting in a biker fight or something?" I tease.

"Hey, with Dustin? Anything is possible." He shrugs out a laugh and flings the door closed. I crank the engine and wait while my brother marches back inside. Even through the glare, I can see the smile spread on Dustin's face when my brother steps up next to him and they clasp hands. Tommy takes up the stool to Dustin's right, and Dustin leaves his hand on my brother's shoulder for a few long seconds—long enough to glance my way and stretch his grin a little wider.

5

I'm glad Tommy came back in and met the lawyer with me. Not because I don't think I could handle it on my own. I do. I've learned a lot about business and legal shit the hard way. But after Hannah's hand brushed against mine, I lost my ability to focus. Even after all this time, Tommy wouldn't let me sign everything the lawyer reviewed with us if something in there seemed risky. It meant while the man from the state rattled on about tax liabilities if I decide to keep the trailer—*as if there's a chance in hell I would ever do that*—I was free to recreate that millisecond over and over in my mind. My own personal animated gif.

I'm out of fantasyland, though. There's nothing soft or supple about this place. If anything can wreck a memory of Hannah, it's my old home.

"You didn't have to stick around for this part, dude." I kick at a rusted coffee can in the middle of the dirt lot in front of the trailer. It leaks sludge as it spins, probably old tobacco Colt spit in there for target practice.

"You're my ride. I felt guilty asking you to drive me home only to come back out here." Tommy kicks the can harder, sending it onto the neighboring property that's junked up as much as this place. He shoots me a grin.

"Well, thanks anyway. I appreciate the company." I draw in a deep breath, the act difficult, like sucking air through a straw. Hands deep in my pockets, I pace around the property, making a mental list of what I might be able to sell or use, and what needs to get hauled out for a fee.

"If you're lucky, Colt left just enough cash in that safe deposit box to cover the dump fees," Tommy jokes. He knocks a metal lid off a crate, and mice scurry out. We both leap back and scream like little girls.

"Shit!" I laugh out.

Tommy climbed up on Colt's old picnic table and he's hugging himself tightly but laughing almost as hard as I am.

"Hannah would call us out for being pussies," he says.

"No doubt. She'd probably trap the mice and make them pets," I say, edging my way closer to the crate to peek inside. Nothing else escapes, and judging by the few droppings, I don't think that's the nest. *I mean, with so many options around this place, why would they settle on the rickety crate?*

While Tommy and I may have been the ones to take to cars and engines first, Hannah was always the wildlife nut. There wasn't much in nature that frightened her.

"Remember when your sister tried to feed that coyote she saw roaming your street when we were kids?" Tommy rocks his head back, laughing at the memory.

"She put leftovers at the edge of our driveway after our parents went to bed. Dad was so pissed when he woke up to a whole pack. And those fuckers kept coming back for more!"

I fall so far down the memory rabbit hole, I lose myself for a moment and forget that the last four years happened at all. Tommy and I pick our way around the outside of Colt's trailer, reliving our favorite memories. And despite the nauseating task in front of me, I'm genuinely happy for the first time in years.

"God, I've missed you, dude," I finally admit. I stare at my former best friend across the mounds of junk as he kneels and picks through a pile of nuts and bolts mixed with gravel. He pauses long enough to squint up at me and shield his eyes from the sun.

"Me, too, man. Me, too."

He means it. I can tell. His gaze sticks on mine long enough for a silent agreement to pass between us. Whatever the bullshit of our past, we're still us when it comes down to it. And he knows I left to keep Hannah safe. He might not know all the details or agree with my ultimate decision, but he respects it.

Hannah is family.

"Well, should we check inside?" Tommy pats his hands together, making faint dust plumes in front of him.

"No sense putting this off. Like ripping a Band-Aid, right?" I reach in my pocket and fish out the key the lawyer gave me.

"Like pulling of an oozing, disgusting Band-Aid, you mean," Tommy says, preparing himself as he steps up to the door behind me. He's pulled his shirt up over his nose and is practically burying his face in his elbow.

"Bit dramatic," I tease, knowing full well I'll be doing the same thing the moment I push open this door.

I turn the key, jiggling it as I remember from when I

was a kid, then brace myself for the impending, assaulting odor. Even through my shirt, the smell permeates. It's different from before. Worse, maybe. There's definitely sickness in the air.

"How long was he in here before they found him?" Tommy coughs after talking. I should have warned him that merely opening your mouth comes at a risk in this place.

"I don't know. Two, maybe three days." It's my turn to cough now.

I never thought this place could look less inhabitable, but when I compare the before to now, I realize how wrong I was. The amount of rotten food items outnumber cigarette butts tenfold, and it's clear that the mice outside were only getting a dose of sunshine. The scurrying action that happened when I opened the door was unreal.

"Yo, I love you like a brother, man, but I can't. I've gotta cut loose and save myself." Tommy draws a line across his throat, his other hand palming his mouth.

"Yeah, I get it. I won't be long. I just need to see what I'm dealing with." I nod toward the door, giving him permission to leave. That he said he loved me and called me brother means more than he probably realizes. I use his words as motivation to keep going through this hellhole.

I can't fathom Colt was totally clean while he was wasting away in here, even on cancer meds, yet so far, I've found nothing from the *old* Colt's days. The bottles of scripts on the coffee table are under his name, and the medication names aren't anything of his usual variety. I'm guessing most of these are antibiotics or some shit like that.

A stack of boxes lines the wall on the way to the bedroom. I pull my pocket knife from my jeans, slice open the box on top, and unveil basic care products like swabs and bandages. The one underneath is more of the same, and a quick glance at the shipping address shows the stuff came from some home healthcare company.

"Fucker had insurance?" I shake my head. I can't imagine that's the case, so I assume the government took care of basic needs in return for Colt snitching on a few cartel connections.

I riffle through various drawers in the kitchen and bathroom and weave my way through the mess and filth into my old room. It seems all the hate and resentment Colt had for me, he took out on this room. There are holes pounded in at least two of the walls, and the carpet, where it's not worn thin, is stained with what I'm pretty sure is urine. Nothing remotely resembling me or the boy who grew up here is visible, so I shut the door and close that chapter of my life.

I make my way down the hall to Colt's bedroom. I am not ready for the scene I encounter, and I wobble on my legs a little at the doorway. It's still gross as fuck in here, but I'm hit with the evidence of Colt's final days in this room. Some monitor-looking thing is bound by its power cord and pushed into the corner, next to the dresser. A drip line for fluids, and I'm guessing pain meds, is stashed away in the opposite corner, and the bed is made as if someone proper lives here and expects to come back home for a night's rest. Saline packs sit unused in a large, gray laundry basket, and the nook under the night table is stuffed with adult diapers.

Not to be outdone, Colt filled the ashtray on top of the night table to the point of overflowing. And his wastebasket is filled beyond the top with empty bottles of his favorite piss-cheap beer.

"You son of a bitch," I mutter to myself.

I slide open the closet door, ready for anything but the neatly hung dresses and women's blouses that fill the right half of space. A definitive line is drawn, a place where the woman my mom liked to pretend she was, or maybe hoped she would become, existed and then a chaotic disaster that was her and Colt's truth. Two white V-neck T-shirts, large enough to cover Colt's belly, dangle on wire hangers. A cigarette burn punctuates the sleeve of one of them, and I can't help but wonder if my mom put it there while Colt was in it.

The floor is a pile of other things, mostly T-shirts and button-downs I've seen Colt in over the years. He had a gray and black bowling shirt with his name stitched on the back, and I catch a glimpse of the fabric under the pile. He used to say he bowled before I was born, that he had friends and a life. Hard to imagine that looking at the pile of scraps and dirty laundry, literally, at my feet.

A small box on the top shelf catches my eye, so I grimace and brace myself for something I'll have to report to the authorities, like a gun. I don't want to keep anything Colt ever touched while doing something bad. I know better. That shit will become a link straight to me for some heinous deed he probably got away with when he was alive.

The box is generic enough, scribbled on and probably saved from some stupid thing my mom ordered in the mail. The lid is flimsy and falling apart, so it tears when I pull it back and toss it to the floor. The first thing I notice on the inside is a small plastic bag with what looks to be baby teeth. I bet these are fucking mine. I hold it up to get a closer look and count five of them, only one of them a molar. I bet these suckers were full of cavities when they fell out. I've been to the dentist a few times out in Oklahoma and got an earful each visit about the neglect my parents must have had for my teeth. Thankfully, only two fillings in my adult mouth.

I flip up a few photos of me as a kid, mostly before I started school and met Tommy. My bowl haircut makes me laugh. I can actually remember my mom giving it to me while I sat on the kitchen counter, her favorite mixing bowl on my head. My hair's a little curly, so the look didn't come out quite as she expected, though a bowl cut looks like shit no matter what the expectation.

I come across a folded newspaper clipping under the photos, so I move to the bed and set the box down so I can inspect it. The date at the top is nine years ago, almost to the day, and the photo on the main story is of me and Tommy hoisting this giant gold cup above our heads. We were kings back then, and after winning a dozen races in a row, the local paper did a story. My mom must have saved it.

I rummage through the remaining things in the box, three more newspaper articles and a ticket from the drive-in theater down in the Valley. It's too faded to tell for sure, but I think I was four based on the date I can read. I wonder if we all went to the movie or just me and Mom. I wonder if she was sober then, or if she drove me around while drunk. Hard to be sentimental when the reality is so goddamned ugly.

Once everything is back in the box, I work the lid back in place as best as I can and take the box and its contents out the door with me.

"Anything good in there? Like, cash?" Tommy's leaning on the front of the rental car, eyes constantly scanning the property for critters.

"Found my baby teeth," I say, holding up the box.

I round the car and get in, and Tommy does the same.

"Wanna see them?" I offer him the box and he wrinkles his nose at it.

"Trust me when I say my old teeth are the least disgusting thing in that place." I toss the box on the floor in the back seat. Tommy might like seeing the old news articles too, but I'm not really feeling it. Besides, I'm pretty sure his parents have actual albums filled with our photos and achievements. And I bet there aren't any goddamned teeth lurking around.

I drop Tommy off at home, not bothering to kill the engine or ask questions about who may or may not be home. The Supra is there, and that's all I really care about. My heart squeezes as I drive away, but I have a safe deposit box to visit. I don't know why, but my gut tells me I need to be alone when I see whatever's inside that thing.

It takes about ten minutes to get to the bank. I was kind of shocked to find out this place actually had safe deposit boxes. It's rinky-dink, and maybe the most small-town thing about this place. It's called Mountain Bank, because it's on a mountain. Really, more of a hill. Thanks to modern-day criminals, though, the two bankers on staff finally have a wall of bullet-proof glass between them and the public. There was a gun drawn here in a robbery when I was in high school. Nobody was shot, and the only thing taken was the candy machine in the lobby. Because of that, I have to lean down to talk through the holes in the glass so the woman helping me can hear my request.

"I have a key for one of those," I say, pointing toward

the heavy safe door behind her. I pull the paperwork from the lawyer from my pocket and unfold it, flattening it against the glass. I feel as though I'm in prison, though she's the one inside.

It takes her several seconds to read my paperwork, so I use the time to figure out her name. Her tag reads BETINA, SENIOR BRANCH MANAGER. She finally says "okay" and closes her drawer before sliding one of those rubber key bracelets on her wrist. She hits a button on the wall and waves for me to step through the door to my left.

"Arms out," a security officer demands, popping up from a chair after I enter. I startle, and his muscles twitch, probably finding that suspicious. The man scared the crap out of me, and the first thing I saw was his Taser. I've been shocked before. That's one of those things I only care to experience once.

Overzealous high school resource officer.

I let the man wave his wand around every nook of my body, and when he's satisfied, Betina takes my key and guides me to the vault, opening the door and revealing a tiny room lined with even smaller doors that lead to boxes. She bends down, close to the floor, and pushes my key into box one-thirty-four.

"Hit that buzzer when you're done," she says, pointing to the bright red button on the wall.

"Or I could just yell 'ready,'" I joke.

Betina is unamused and straightens the tight salt and pepper bun knotted at the base of her neck as she rolls her eyes.

The moment the door clicks in place, I find it harder to breathe. It's cool in this space, so I know the AC is working in here. It's not an oxygen thing. But this room is small, and I can't help but sense secrets are hidden inside.

There's not much to the box. Even when she set it on the table, I could tell it isn't packing gold or family heirlooms. It had no weight to it. I flip the lid up and am instantly disappointed. There's an envelope inside, the kind people's bills arrive in, with the small see-through window for the address. It's not sealed. In fact, the top where it was ripped open is folded over a quarter inch. Whatever's inside must be pointless.

I pull the envelope out and lean back in the metal folding chair, expecting an even more underwhelming letter or bill inside. That would be just like Colt to leave me some overdue IRS bill. Good thing he never made shit, according to the government.

It's not until I feel the raised crest from some official seal that I sit up and take this business seriously. My eyes aren't sure what they're reading at first. It's my name. The letters typed on the document, Colt Bridges listed below on the line labeled FATHER.

My birth certificate. I've never actually seen it. I partly assumed I was born in the back seat of my parents' car, or worse, in that fucking trailer.

And then I read the line for MOTHER.

Alysha Solerno.

Not Patricia Miller.

Trisha Miller.

The woman I watched overdose and survive three times.

The woman I never looked like but wanted to just so I didn't look like my dad.

A stranger. A liar.

A deserter and an addict.

Trisha Miller is not my real mom. She's some fraud.

So who the fuck is Alysha Solerno?

I close the box and sloppily fold my birth certificate into a square, stuffing it in my back pocket and leaving its half-hearted envelope on the table to be thrown away. I press the red button, but impatience has me holding my thumb on it two seconds later. I can't get out of this room fast enough, and my manic distress earns me a nasty greeting from Betina. I don't care, though. I need air —*outside* air.

"I feel sick," I announce, making sure to calm the security guard before he can get his hand on his stun gun. He opens the secondary door for me and I stumble my way through the lobby and onto the sidewalk outside.

Fingers threaded across my forehead, I press at my thumbs into my temples and will this reality away. It won't work. It never has. I tried so many times when I was a kid to wake up and be somewhere different, to be one of the Judges, or even live in Bailey's house. My life was always the same, though. Cursed. Branded by Colt Bridges and stained by Trisha Miller.

Only neither of them are to blame at all. My fate was sealed by some woman I never met. I mean, I guess I met her once—*when I was fucking born!*

Wound up and ready to fight, I pace between the bank's door and the front of my car until my mind is spinning so much I start to feel lost. I get in the car and peel out as I back away, my hand numb against the steering wheel. I'm driving too fast, but my speed feels impossibly slow at the same time. I roar over the highway, cutting through the ranch land on the dirt road marked private and come out at the end of Hannah's street. It's barely two, so I know she's home. The Supra is there, like it was before when I dropped Tommy off. I pull up next to it as my mouth salivates.

I'm actually going to be sick.

I hunch over where the Judges' gravel meets their driveway and hurl bile onto a cactus. My head is hot, beads of sweat growing large enough that I feel them slide along my skin. At the same time, I'm shivering. I'm near passing out when Hannah rushes out her front door, Tommy not far behind.

And that's the last thing I remember.

It's dark in Hannah's room. Too dark for it to be from closed shutters alone. The sun's gone down, which means I've missed a good amount of time. It takes my eyes a few seconds to adjust to my surroundings, and my body is sticky with sweat. I prop myself up enough to work the hoodie from my arms and toss it on the floor. I'm about to test my vocal chords to see if I can manage uttering Hannah's name when a soft hand on my torn-up arm stops me.

The touch of an angel.

She must have changed the dressing while I was asleep.

"*Shhh.*" Hannah holds a single finger to her lips while her other hand gently presses the surgical tape in place along my arm.

I mouth *thank you* when her eyes lift to mine. And that's when I see it—the break in her walls I've been praying for. It isn't a smile, but rather the soft curve of empathy. Her eyes don't run away from my stare. They remain fixed on my own. She stays wordless.

She stays.

All through the night.

She stays.

6

The only thing I could think to do was bring Dustin inside. Instinct took over and grudges were put on pause. Seems that's a constant pattern for me when it comes to Dustin Bridges. Only now that I've done it, I've fallen down the slippery slope letting him back inside my heart.

Self-control was never our strong point. I'm willing to admit I was usually the bold one. I pushed for every kiss, each touch. I felt it, as I do now—that assuredness that tells me all I need to do is step in close enough and part my lips and four years of heartache and nightmares would be thrown to the side for a moment of bliss.

Addict.

Like I said.

I don't know what was wrong last night. I only know that Dustin seemed disoriented. He wasn't on anything; it was more like a mental snap. He never told me what was at the heart of his torment. *I never asked.* I'm not sure I should. That line of communication between us that once felt so easy to cross, that bond? It broke. Now the space between us is a canyon. I can't be his home like I used to be. It's too hard, no matter how natural it feels in my soul.

Whatever the cause of his troubles, I can't imagine the scene he's about to walk into this morning is going to make it any better. It's definitely not doing much for me.

Right now, I could do without my mom's passive aggressive line of questioning. She keeps trying to get at the root of why he's here. I don't have answers, and that infuriates her—like most of my choices since the day he left. She should be glad I'm going to the school she wanted and getting the degree she pushed me toward. That's enough.

"So are you and Dustin . . . *talking?*"

This one actually makes me roll my eyes, like my teenaged-self kinda roll. My mom uses that special tone, as if she's an insider on the way youth talk these days. I had told her there were a few guys at the university I was "talking" to as a way to get her off my back about dating. I went on four dates. Four, and they were all awful. So awful they made Michael Bosa, my senior prom date, seem suddenly appealing. My mom's big takeaway from my dating recap, though, was that hip term—*talking*. She has dropped it at least a dozen times since I've been home for the summer.

"Mom, stop," I reprimand her, lifting my focus from my phone long enough to hit her with my dead-serious eyes.

"I'm sorry, honey. It's just . . . I don't understand. I thought you never wanted to see him again, and now he's suddenly sleeping in your bedroom? I think your father and I are being pretty cool under these circumstances. That boy—"

"Amanda." My dad stops her free flow, shaking his head. "He just buried his father. Lay off."

A suffocating quiet fills the room, eating up all the oxygen. It makes my skin itch, and both my dad and I shift in our chairs at the kitchen table.

"I'm pretty sure he was cremated."

I cough out a laugh at my brother's remark. My dad moves his scornful look from my mom to his son.

"What? I'm right," Tommy adds.

"He is," Dustin affirms.

My dad skids his chair across the tile as he darts to a stand. I think our collective pulses are probably drumming in sync at Dustin's sudden entry into the room.

Dustin has his hoodie pulled up, his messy hair peeking out, and his Vans are on his feet, though the laces are undone. My guess is he just woke up and can't wait to get out of here. I've been up for an hour, and I can't wait to leave.

"That lawyer I met yesterday gave me instructions on where to pick up his ashes. I guess I have to or they charge the next of kin some sort of fee. I'll probably throw them in the garbage."

Dustin's mouth forms the briefest and tiniest of smiles. It's gone in an instant.

"Son," my dad says, stepping toward Dustin. His endearing approach catches us all off-guard, Dustin more than any of us as he jerks back and drops his hands deep into his pockets. His head tilts to one side and his eyes narrow.

"Dustin, I mean," my dad immediately coughs out, trying to recover from his misstep. He hasn't called Dustin son around me since we started dating in high school, despite that he used that term often and affectionately when we were growing up.

"I should actually get to the funeral home. Apparently,

it's going to cost me two hundred and seventy-five dollars to pick up a bag of my dad's dust." Dustin makes a wide path around the table toward the door. My eyes connect with Tommy's as he does. I feel lost in this situation and I'm looking to my brother to help. We can't just let him leave, but I can't be the one fighting for him to stay. It can't be me. *It can't. It can't. It . . .*

"Do you need money, Dustin?" my mom stammers out her offer, trying to stop him before he reaches the door. Dustin's palm flattens on the wood above the door-knob and he bows his head, his shoulders shaking with what I'm guessing is silent laughter. He stands up straight and drops his hand from the surface, turning slowly to face my father.

"I've got my own money." A straight, indignant line marks his mouth as he holds his gaze on my dad, almost as if he's proving something to him. I'm sure Dustin feels he has a lot to prove to everybody. He's making it on his own, despite who he is and where he came from. Broken-hearted or not, I can't deny that he has persevered beyond anyone's expectations. Anyone but me, that is. I knew he would become exactly the man he wanted, down to his own design. I didn't know he would have to break my heart to get there.

"Oh." My mom's meek voice breaks and she leans back in her chair. Her eyes dart to my dad, then to me. I see through her charade. She's ridden with guilt. It's never really been about the fact Dustin broke her daughter's heart. She likes that he's on the outs with me because it means she doesn't have to own up to the horrible way she treated him before he left. This brief interaction, though . . . *my God.* It's a little delicious to watch her squirm.

The deafening silence overtakes the room again, and

Dustin must feel it, too. His shoulders bunch up and his mouth pulls into a tight line as he nods and glances to the floor. We've all let him down. Probably as he expected. That's what that nod is for.

"I'll go with you," I announce, surprising myself along with my family. I stand from my seat and whip through the kitchen to grab my mini backpack with my keys, wallet and phone. I ignore the burning stare coming from my mom as well as the loud warnings inside my head, and move toward the stunned expression on Dustin's face.

"Hannah, I thought—" My mom suddenly stops her protest. I turn to understand why and see my dad has stepped into the space between me and them, his palm up, urging my mom to let me be. He shifts on his feet, glancing to me over his shoulder, and we share a silent pact, something we haven't done in years.

Dustin needs someone. You're that someone. You need to be careful.

I will. I promise.

I walk out the door behind Dustin and make it only steps before my heart skips and a smile flirts with my lips. This isn't a happy moment, not for Dustin. And I also shouldn't feel soothed being the person he leans on through it. This act, it lets him in. It exposes me and risks my still-wounded heart.

My scars aren't nearly tough enough. And my heart . . . it betrays me. More than I ever thought it would or could. The thousands of times I imagined our inevitable reunion, I was always strong. In my mind, I was cold and stoic. That was always the plan, and I carried it out perfectly when I first laid eyes on him out on the Straights.

There is no such thing as training a heart to behave, though. For me to survive this, I need to remind my head what to do, will it to be stronger. It's the only antidote I have for my weak and all-too-willing heart.

Being guarded does not mean I have to be cold, however, and as we near Dustin's rental, a thought takes over my actions.

"Hey," I say, halting him before he reaches the driver's door of his rental. He turns to square himself with me, eyes sagging with wear. *He needs this.* "Let's take the Supra."

I toss him the keys. His hand swallows them from the air as if a piece of him has come home. I know it has. That car will never belong to anyone else, regardless of who drives it. It doesn't mean I'm giving it back, though. Owning that set of wheels gives me power. Yeah, it's a bit like revenge. *Okay, a lot like it.* But I need to hold on to something harsh. That's how I remain vigilant and safe from ever feeling the way I did when Dustin left again.

"You sure?"

I like that he asks for permission. *Good boy.*

"I'm sure." I march to the passenger door and wait impatiently for him to push the unlock button on the fob. I tap my nails on the roof of the car as he stares at me, dumbstruck. Slowly, his hand raises and he presses the button that blinks the lights and makes the doors click. For a hint of a moment, the two of us mirror our crooked smiles.

"Get in," he says, and I shake my head, letting out a *tsk.*

"You know I don't like taking orders," I say, getting in anyway. He's still chuckling by the time he lets himself in the driver's side.

"I remember. I've got a permanent Hannah Judge's fist-shaped bruise on my arm from all the times you told me to shove it.

"To be fair, I punched Tommy *way* harder." I buckle up

and drop my backpack between my feet, folding my hands in my lap. I turn when I sense Dustin isn't moving, and our eyes meet. His smile inches up a little more.

"To be fair, Tommy always deserved to be punched harder," he says.

I pucker my lips, trying to hold my smile at bay, to keep it from growing. I waggle my head side-to-side and shift my gaze to the windshield. "You're probably right," I say. That grin, though? That fucker breaks through wide.

I've heard my dad talk about the way certain things in life simply fit. I guess that's where the "like a glove" saying comes from. I've never fully gotten the significance of that feeling until now. Dustin's hands wrap almost tenderly around the Supra's wheel. With the precision of a surgeon, he layers his fingers around the tightly bound leather one at a time, then rolls his knuckles forward, flexing his hands to feel the grip. I can almost hear the *ahhh* that I know he is saying in his head.

"Wow. You've never looked at me like that." I can't believe I uttered that out loud. I was openly jealous of a car, which—granted—I have been before. I've always envied the way Dustin loved this thing. I suppose that's why I kept it. It was like forbidding him the one thing I knew could replace me.

My face is hot and I continue to look away, waiting for him to rev the motor and move on from what I said. But instead, he brushes my bare shoulder, and I turn to look just in time to catch his thumb and index finger gently tug on the beaded tie on the sleeve of my shirt. My breath catches and gaze flits up as Dustin's does the same. Our eyes . . . they dance.

"You have no idea how many times, how many ways, I have looked at you." Dustin rolls the beaded tassel between his fingers and his eyes dip to where his knuckles tickle against my skin. His lips part and he inhales a fast breath, but quickly exhales, dropping the bead and returning his focus to the car.

I remain rigid, my heart racing, not even deterred by the roar of the engine as he starts the car. I don't sink back into my seat until he plows into reverse and jets us down my street. That's when an entirely new sensation takes hold of my body.

It's been years since I've seen Dustin drive. He was always a wonder to watch. But this? It's different. This is art. With deft movements, he's seamless in the way he shifts, taking us up to eighty then back down to ten for a quick turn on one of the back roads. He wants to really open it up, to feel the road that groomed him under the will of his hands and the pressure of his foot—pedal to the floor. He doesn't have to ask. He knows I'll say yes. And with a single breath, we're flying.

"I can never drive her like you do," I admit.

He shifts his gaze my way and smiles on the right side of his mouth, leaning in.

"You drive her pretty damn well." Our eyes flicker for a beat before his return to the road.

My shoulders relax at what is perhaps the highest compliment Dustin Bridges can give a soul.

We are in town within minutes. The coroner's building to our left, Dustin shoots past it and cranks the wheel, drifting a one-eighty only to race back to the location on the right side of the road.

It's not quite eight in the morning, not that there is ever much traffic in our tiny downtown, but the streets are exceptionally empty this morning. Dustin kills the engine and relaxes into the seat, his hands slipping down to the base of the wheel as a satisfied smile takes over his face.

"Show off," I tease.

Laughter pours from his lips like piano bar jazz, the notes full and drunk with whiskey. I feel my head slipping, my guard dropping. So much about Dustin has always been disarming. Even as a young teen, he had natural charm and charisma. He also had an innate compass for right and wrong, perhaps forged from his upbringing. He was so determined to be the opposite of what he knew, what he saw in Colt and his mom. I suppose while the dimples and hair and hazel eyes captivated my eyes, it was all that inside stuff that made me fall for him in the first place. I'm a fool to think it can't overcome me again.

"Ready to go get my dad?" Dustin points his thumb over his shoulder as he opens the door. He's approaching this in a satirical manner, and I'm not quite sure whether it's because it's painful or because he really doesn't give a shit. Maybe it's a bit of both.

"This might be the most pleasant interaction I've ever had with him," I pile on.

Dustin chuckles, then holds up the keys to toss back to me as I meet his gaze over the hood of the Supra. I shake my head, deciding selfishly to enjoy being his passenger a little while longer. Letting him drive is an indulgence I think I can handle.

"If you insist." He grins and pockets the keys.

Dustin waits at the edge of the sidewalk for me to catch up, and I swear for a moment his pinky finger reaches out as if prepared to take my hand. Such a natural reflex that I almost give in and finish the connection. When he quickly sinks his hands into his pockets, I wrap mine around the straps of my backpack, holding it at my shoulders.

"Ladies first," he says, pulling the heavy metal door open for me.

This building used to be the jail; I remember it from when we were kids. The county built a new one on the other side of the freeway, larger capacity to house more criminals. When this place was abandoned, the town seized the opportunity to get the coroner's office out from the back of the police station. My mom was so proud of the move, since she led the charge of the town council to get it done. Tommy and I had to come to the ribbon cutting. Glancing around now, it looks like the same damn building as before, only instead of cots in the jail cells, there are metal tables and scales. I guess the big change is the freezer in the back for the bodies. It still amazes me that there are whole companies that do nothing but make freezers to store bodies in.

I take a seat in one of the yellow plastic chairs lined up near the entrance while Dustin steps to the window to tap the bell. He dings it twice and we glance at one another and quietly laugh. Such a cheery noise for such a dark business.

"Yeah?" A small woman with short gray hair curled tightly against her head steps close to the glass and turns her ear toward Dustin. She looks to be in her sixties, maybe older. She wears scrubs and has a mask pulled down around her chin.

"I was told to come here to pick up Colt Bridges' ashes." Dustin reaches into his back pocket and pulls out a folded paper. He slips it through the opening at the bottom of the window and the woman on the other side tips her glasses down from the top of her head to read it.

"Ah, right. He was a well-check. Shame. Sorry for your loss. That'll be two-seventy-five."

She slides the paper back to Dustin and rests on her palms, leaning forward enough to scan the lobby where I am the only person waiting. She nods toward me and Dustin glances over his shoulder, a wry smile on his lips when our eyes meet.

"Oh, she's with me," he explains.

"Good. I've got a body on the table," the woman says.

I can't contain the distance my eyebrows travel up my head, so I look down at my knees and purse my lips, trying to contain my laughter. This woman has found her calling. I think it probably takes a certain level of detachment to work in a place that is about nothing but loss and finality. She has it in spades.

Dustin unfurls two hundred dollar bills from his wallet, then counts out the rest in twenties and fives, sliding the cash to the woman. She doesn't even bother to count it, instead typing in a key code that unlocks what looks like a cash box on the small front desk. She drops the money inside and closes the lid again before holding up a finger and heading to the back of the building, presumably to find the bag of Colt.

"This is funny, right?" Dustin says under his breath, his chin tucked against his shoulder.

I nod and pull my lips in for a tight smile. It's good that he finds humor in the moment, because I have a strong feeling that when we walk out of here with his father's remains, the reality of this all is going to hit him. His father is dead. Hate him or not, it's a dark milestone in anyone's lifeline. It forces one to think, and Dustin doesn't like to spend time in his past.

"Here you go. Now if you'd like to look through our urn book, I can get you pricing on anything you might want." The woman slides a clear plastic bag through the notch in the window, then moves to grab a binder from the desk. Dustin waves her off before she can dive any further into her pitch.

"I think we're good with the bag. Man lived his life in them. Seems . . . *fitting*." Dustin holds the bag up, his fist curled around the top the same way a child holds up a bagged goldfish from a fair. The woman blinks at him, a blank expression fixed on her face.

"Suit yourself," she says, whistling as she puts the binder back in place, then dutifully heads back to work.

Dustin turns toward me slowly, his arm holding the bag of ashes out and away from his body. His eyes meet mine then dart to the bag.

"You wanna hold him?" He quirks a brow.

"What, like a puppy? Nah, I'm good. But thanks." I move toward the door and hold it open for Dustin. He keeps the bag out from his body and I find I'm giving it a wide berth as well.

Dustin pops open the trunk and tucks the bag inside the spare tire well, then glances to me for approval. I step beside him to pay my respects and reach behind him to pat his shoulder.

"Seems secure enough," I say. I sure as hell am not holding that thing.

Dustin drops the trunk lid and we climb back into the car. We both buckle up, and Dustin revs the engine. I'm settled in and ready for him to peel out of this strange place, but instead, his hands drop from the wheel to his lap as his eyes seem to haze out into the distance.

"It's weird how very little I feel, isn't it?"

This is what I expected.

"Yes, and no. Colt was never much of a father to you. You shared an address, and the man abused you your entire life. So while it's sad when someone dies, it maybe also feels like he deserved it?" I'm not sure if I overstepped with that last part, but it's the truth. There's a part of Dustin that believes it, and I think he needed to hear it said out loud.

His head rolls to the side and his eyes flit up from my waist to my chin, then my eyes.

"He did abuse me. I was abused." He blinks as he takes in the words uttered by his own mouth, in his own voice. This universal truth has always been a thing we simply accepted—that *Dustin* accepted. That's different from *actual* acceptance, though. To really understand the impact of what abuse can do, you need to pair it with self-awareness. Dustin's doing that now.

I nod, a dozen awful moments flashing through the back of my mind. Dustin getting slapped with an open palm out on the track in Tucson. Dustin coming over late at night to shower and wash the blood from his favorite T-shirt. Dustin burying his face in my pillow so he could scream without anyone asking him why.

"You were. And you didn't deserve any of it." A flutter passes through my chest, different from the nervous rush that happens before a kiss. I recognize this feeling all the same. It's my resolve melting. It's the bridge rebuilding. My need to love and care for Dustin is as great as his need to be loved and cared for. Our souls are reaching toward one another.

This time, there is no mistaking the twitch of Dustin's hand. His palm inches from his thigh toward the center console, giving me a second, maybe two, to make my decision. My heart's already abandoned its mission and has started to drum steadily in my chest, calling out to the broken parts inside Dustin. My head is caving quickly, too.

The invitation unfolds on the console between us, Dustin's wrist turning up and his palm opening, begging for its partner. I stare at it. I look on long enough for Dustin's fingers to curl inward and form a loose, rejected fist. Before his hand recedes, though, I reach forward with both hands and unbend his fingers one at a time before pressing my hand flat against his, like two kids comparing hand sizes. He has me by a full knuckle.

I brush my palm against his and stop when my thumb meets the center of his hand, on his lifeline. I rub that spot lightly as I decide whether to travel up or down the wrinkle.

"I found out Trisha wasn't my real mom."

My decision is instantly so simple. Palm to palm, our fingers accordion together, and my other hand encloses Dustin's completely before bringing it to my mouth. I press my lips against his dry knuckles, recognizing the scent of my pear hand soap.

I press his hand to my cheek and meet his eyes.

"How?" I ask.

He holds my gaze for what feels like several seconds, then licks his lips as he leans to the side enough to reach into his pocket. He pulls out another folded piece of paper, this one thicker than the one that said he had a right to the ashes we have in the trunk. With one hand, he presses the document flat and rotates it for me to read.

His birth certificate. Proof of his existence. The makers of his life.

Trisha Miller is nowhere to be found—not in real life, and not on this piece of paper.

"Alysha Solerno?" I'm both not sure I'm pronouncing that right, and have no clue who this person is.

"Apparently," he utters. He spins the paper back toward

him and runs a finger over the mystery woman's name before refolding the paper and dropping it in the cup holder.

I lean in to match his angle, his hand still held close to my face, and as if no time has passed from when we last sat like this, our heads fall together in a peaceful reconciliation. I still hate him so much. I hate how he made me feel, how much I cried when he left, and how broken he left me before his return. But damn, do I love him just the same.

I love him *too* much.

"I'm sorry." It's the only thing there is to say.

He shrugs and a cool breath falls from his lips. His eyes are closed. I know it because I peeked before closing mine. I bring my other hand up to his face and run my thumb along his cheek, a day's worth of beard shadowing his jawline.

"Where do you want to take Colt?"

Our noses touch when I speak.

Dustin shrugs again.

I guess he doesn't have to be put to rest right now. Maybe not ever.

"Hey, Hannah?"

"Hmm?"

I feel his lashes kiss mine. I don't dare open to look.

"Can we stay here a while? Like this?"

I surrender.

I nod, my forehead moving against his, and soon I'm lost to the soft brush of our noses and the palpable temptation numbing my lips.

"Yeah, Dustin. We can stay right here for as long as you want." I tilt his head down and press my lips to the space between his eyes. Our hands unclasp, both of us suddenly wanting nothing more than to touch each other's faces. We hold on to one another, a breath away from total forgiveness; a breath away from walking through the door to reclaim our past.

Teetering in two worlds, the before and the after.

For now, it feels like enough.

7

I forgot how good it felt just to hold her. To be held *by* her. If I could have ended our day there like that, I would have. But per his usual timing, Colt wasn't having any of that.

As comforting as Hannah's embrace is—*was*—the reality of that damn plastic bag full of Colt's ashes was too loud in my head to feel the absolute peace that I want when alone with her. I won't be able to rest until I get it. Hannah must know, too, because she's been so willing to go along with me today.

As much as I want to throw Colt's ashes in a dumpster, I'm pretty sure the universe would punish me tenfold. I don't have to respect the man, which is good, because I never will. But I will respect the life—the one he gave me. My sperm donor.

The hiccup is Colt never really had a place. Other than his money and his high or buzz, I don't think much mattered in that man's life. The only place I could think of spreading his ashes into the wind was at Sunset Point. It's basically a rest stop between our town and the Grand Canyon.

"You're sure you don't have anywhere to be? I know I'm asking a lot." I glance to my right, where Hannah sits in the passenger seat, older but still here. This is how I always imagined life. I've had glimpses of our future, and she's always in that seat right next to me. Only, I missed a lot of years of this. And *this* is fleeting. I realize that. Hannah might not stay. She probably shouldn't. She has an entire life, a year left of college, and who knows . . . maybe an MBA to earn and some big world to conquer.

Some guy who will treat her right.

"You know I like it when you drive." A rebellious smirk paints her lips and I hold her gaze, not looking at the straight and empty road ahead of me as I press the pedal and climb us over a hundred miles per hour.

Maybe I *can* have her now, have that life. Colt is gone. His legacy is dangerous, and there are probably plenty of people out there he left broken and screwed, but it's not as if they'll punish him by coming after his family. *Not like he ever gave a shit about his family in the first place.*

The wide open road before us, my hands find their favorite spot on the wheel and I punch the gas as we become a blur through the desert brush and jagged mountain cliffs. I glance to Hannah a few times, her eyes always on the road, her expression sure and steady. It was like that the very first time she rode with me.

Fearless.

I almost wish our landscape was dotted with challengers. I'd love to show her what I'm capable of now, dodging through narrow lanes and passing opponents. Peacocks love to strut their feathers. Mine happen to be high octane.

My eyes scan the sides of the road as we soar along the blacktop. I might be able to talk my way out of a ticket in Camp Verde, but not on the highways out of town. One day, though . . . people will know me. Everyone will know me. And when they do? I'll come back to this stretch and assault the road with the same kind of speed, looking for cops to pull me over. They'll want my autograph or a picture. And I'll oblige.

I slow us down when I see the first sign for Sunset Point. Five miles away from the place where I intend to forget Colt forever. Something about it feels empty. I should hurt, maybe. Or grieve? But instead, my chest is hollow, my heart beatless.

Traffic is finally picking up. There's a junction nearby for the interstate, and this is the only rest stop for miles. It's the ideal place for that quintessential road trip photo, which explains the rows of RVs and family cars pulled up near the canyon. I veer off the highway an exit early, taking the less-traveled utility road that runs along the back side of the restrooms and visitor center. There aren't parking spots over here, so I peel off into the dirt and tuck the Supra behind the brush, away from onlookers.

"Ready?" Hannah's wide eyes take me in, glossed with worry that this moment is going to be hard for me. I can tell. She's worn this same expression for me so many times. She's always been my home, and maybe I took advantage of that, showed her too much pain. It's only that I didn't know where else to turn with it. When Colt made me feel small, she was the only thing that could remind me I was significant.

"Guess so," I say with a casual lift of my shoulder.

I step out of the driver's side and join Hannah at the back of the car to flip open the trunk. The bag has slid to the far corner, lodged where the carpet has started to pull away from the floor. It may as well contain leftovers or trash.

"Let's do this," I say, reaching in and grabbing the bag with my hand.

I shut the trunk and hold Colt at my side the way a construction worker holds his lunch break sandwich. Hannah shades her eyes with both of her hands and gazes out across the deep cavern a dozen feet away from us.

"He's going to blow right back up in our faces if you toss him down there," she says, her finger drawing a line across the horizon. She's right. The wind gusts out here can be pretty wild. I didn't count on that.

I chew at my lip and spin slowly in search of the next best thing. It needs to be appropriate for the job and that's it. There is no meaning assigned to this. I'll never come here to visit and stop to talk to my long lost dad. I'll come here to take a piss on my way up to the Grand Canyon or Utah, which really is the most fitting tribute I could ever give Colt.

"There's a wash over there. When the monsoons come, Colt can go for a ride." I point to the dried gully carved through the rocks and sand. Hannah nods in agreement and we hike down through the boulders to the dry riverbed. The ground already looks like ash, so Colt should blend right in.

With a quick glance around to make sure nobody is watching, I break the seal on the bag and cup the bottom with my palm.

"You want to say something?"

I stare at Colt's remains, give Hannah's question some thought, and finally nod. She steps in close then weaves her arm through mine, hugging it close to her body. I'm glad she's here.

The wind is steady but not strong where we are. It will carry him along the silt and scatter him for the coyotes to smell and the vultures to circle. Then, come late July, when the clouds build and the rain soaks the earth, he'll be washed away for good. A smile tugs at the corners of my mouth.

"Fuck you, you son of a bitch," I say, tilting the bag and letting the contents pour into the air.

There's nothing magical about this. No big release in my chest. The vise I've always felt around my neck? It's still there. I don't think I will ever outgrow it. Colt tattooed his hands around my throat. He seared his boots into my belly and his fists on my face. This is just a pointless ceremony to get rid of his remains. To follow through with what humanity expects. To respect life, but not the man.

My fist gobbles up the empty bag as Hannah's cheek falls against my arm where she hugs it. My eyes deaden on the scene, the earth so dry and hungry for water. He's already gone, his ashes the same color as the scorched sand and desert fauna. I allow my head to fall to the side, resting on top of Hannah's, and I indulge in something selfish as my lips press a kiss on top of her head. Her hands squeeze my bicep harder and I breathe her in.

"Ready to go home?"

She nods against me. I shift so my arm circles her body and we walk, side-by-side, back to the car. On our way, I toss the empty bag in the trash can behind the bathrooms.

There isn't any fanfare to it. No talk about what just happened or how I feel. Hannah knows better than to ask. She already knows the answer. This is nothing. And it's done.

I roar the engine back to life and we crawl our way back to the highway where I let loose on the road once again. It's different this time. I guess more melancholy. It isn't anything to do with Colt, though. This feeling, it stems from knowing we're going back, that Hannah will get out of this car and so will I. And once my business here is done, that's it. I'll go. She'll stay.

My pocket has been vibrating since the rest stop. We're halfway back to Hannah's house, though, and I'd rather wait to deal with whoever is incessantly calling me when I get there. But it's roughly the twentieth round of buzzing, and I can't take the nagging anymore. I lean to the side and pull my phone from my pocket, handing it to Hannah.

"Can you see if whoever that is left me a message?"

"Sure," she says, holding my phone in her palm and waiting for the passcode.

"Zero four one seven," I say, forcing my eyes to stay on the road. I don't think I'll be able to handle seeing her face.

"My birthday," she whispers.

"Uh huh." I nod. I can feel her eyes on me, but I manage to avoid meeting them.

She types the sequence in and swipes to my list of calls.

"Who's Virgil?"

I chuckle and nod, a little relieved it's him and not the lawyer about Colt's things or the landowner who is anxious for me to get the trailer off his property.

"He's Tommy's replacement. Well, sorta. He's actually a pretty shitty mechanic, but he's a lot nicer to me than your brother ever is." I lean in and peek at the screen, noting the dozen or more messages, several of them over the last thirty minutes. Before I can tell Hannah to play the most recent one on speaker, my phone buzzes in her palm.

"I got it," I say, taking it from her and swiping to answer before pressing the phone to my ear.

"Virg, hey. Sorry, I've been tied up all morning. What's up?"

I brace myself for one of his usual code red phone calls. Virgil tends to panic when things don't go smoothly. If a part we ordered comes in late, or worse, isn't the right part at all? Virgil spins out. If the sponsor doesn't like something I said in the local paper? Virgil goes into full-on crisis mode. And if I blow off a race? Well, I must be dead or have the plague. It couldn't be that I just wasn't interested in driving for two hours to bring home a fifty-dollar prize and a month's worth of chicken wings.

"This is that call, Dustin. *That. Call.*"

For a moment, my ears mute. It's beyond that rush of blood that comes with adrenaline, and it's not the usual ringing from tinnitus after a dozen hours out on the track. I slow the car and pull over, stopping near a fruit stand with zero customers and run by an old man who seems to be selling nothing but jerky. Not a fruit to be found. I step out of the car, leaving the motor humming, and walk across the road, my fingers dug into my hair and the butt of my palm pressed against my disbelieving forehead.

"Don't fuck with me, Virgil."

"I wouldn't fuck with you, Dust."

Virgil doesn't use that word. He wouldn't say it unless the moment absolutely called for it—unless he wanted me to take him seriously.

I laugh out and spin, my gaze landing on Hannah, who is looking at me over the roof of the car as she stands on the chassis of the open door.

"When? Where?"

Hannah's mouth hangs open, her eyes eager for details. I hope she can tell this isn't bad news.

"That's the thing. You're in Arizona, and the Phoenix series is in two weeks. The fact you're in town and could make it happen . . ."

"Son of a bitch," I mutter. I run my hand down my face in disbelief.

"Gorman Truit had to pull out," Virgil continues.

A spot opened. My time is good enough. My wins are good enough. I'm in the area. Local. Colt did one thing right by me. That fucker died at the perfect time.

"You tell them yes?" I smile across the road at Hannah, holding my thumb up. She hops down from her perch and hustles to the other side, waiting while a station wagon passes by.

"I did, but they need to know your address. You've got some contracts to sign, and you probably need to get yourself representation. And you're gonna need to smooth things over with Tulsa Wings since you have to take on Gorman's sponsor, and—"

"I got it, Virg. I can handle it. I'll text you my info and then you work on getting your ass to Phoenix." I hang up before he has time to rattle off more to-dos. I'm too excited to handle his lists right now. I'm too much in shock.

"Well?" Hannah holds her palms out to her sides. I stare at my phone screen for another moment then slip it in my pocket before holding my palms to my face. Everything is numb. My skin, my bones, my veins. Can blood be numb?

"I'm racing at Series!"

Hearing my own voice utter that statement feels like a dream.

"Hannah, I'm fucking racing at Series!" I repeat.

Her eyes widen as the corners of her mouth tug up to meet them.

"Shut up!" Her hands cup her knees as she stares at me across the dotted yellow line.

"Han—" Tears prick at the corners of my eyes and I let them take over. A wave of triumph engulfs my chest and I shudder at the overwhelming reality of what is about to happen. Years of dedication, of sacrifice. *My God.*

I bite at my fist just as Hannah sprints across the road. I catch her when she leaps at me, and she pushes her hands into my hair, fisting it as she presses her forehead to mine and utters "yes."

"Hannah," I croak out her name. My eyes close as I spin us, tethered together. There is nobody I would rather experience this moment with, nobody who could possibly understand the gravity of it all the way she does.

I'm not sure who moves first; perhaps we do it together. Whatever gave us permission, it happens equally and with abandon. My lips find hers; hers mine. A thousand days lost disappear in one kiss. Four years of suffering—of trying not to want and trying to forget—disappear in a single press of the flesh. Teeth graze familiar places on lips. Tongues remember how to caress. Hannah moans and I hold her tight.

I did right by the life that made me. And now the universe is rewarding me by giving me back the love I lost. The one that matters. *Hannah's.*

This is more than a big break. It's more than *that call.*

This is the pivotal moment in my making. How I walk this path will dictate my future, and there is no way in hell I'm not coming away with it all.

8

W hat am I doing?

I knew the minute I got in that car with Dustin that it would end up like this. If I'm honest with myself, I wanted it to. Every piece of me misses every piece of him. It's been like this since he left, and I've tried to cut the feeling off. But Dustin has infected me. He's in my blood, a poison and a cure.

It would be so easy to give in completely. My inner voice, though, is somehow still loud enough to remind me why I can't. When this chapter of his life is done, when the chapter on Colt is closed, he's going to leave. It's what he does. What he did. And now that everything he's ever wanted is on the cusp of happening, he'll have to.

So while I hold his hand as we turn down my street, I'm overcome with the sense that I am a fraud, to him and to myself. I pretend nothing is wrong in my heart. And as good as it felt to be the one to hold him up and to celebrate with him, it is literally killing me right now, knowing none of this is real.

It helps to find my parents leaning on Dustin's rental car with their arms crossed as we pull into the driveway.

"Why does it look like they want to ground you?" Dustin jokes.

I unwind my hand from his and note the way his palm turns up, lost and wondering where I went. He must realize how temporary this all is.

"Because they do. They hate that I'm an adult now and they can't." I unclick the seat belt and lean forward enough to see my parents in the side mirror. They haven't moved, but damn, are they staring at me with fire in their eyes.

"I'm pretty sure I'm the one they have a problem with," Dustin says as he shifts to park and kills the engine. His eyes linger on the rearview mirror and a cold, distant frown takes over his mouth.

"They don't have a problem with you. Seeing you makes them feel terrible about who *they* are . . . how they treated you."

His eyes shift to me, and the temptation is there to take his hand again. I don't. If I keep giving in, it will be harder to stop.

"You get why I left, don't you?"

My muscles twitch at his question and I instantly fall into one of my many rehearsed reactions. Instead of being cold, this time I will be flippant.

"Yeah, sure. I get it. It's . . . fine. That was forever ago. It's fine."

Fine.

"Hannah—"

Before he can launch into the root of our end, I climb out of the car and ready myself to face my parents instead. Somehow, in the moment, this feels easier. The truth is, no, I don't get why he left. I mean, on the surface it makes sense. His dad was a danger and Dustin was a connection between me and his dad. But why he left the way he did, in the middle of the night without explanation? Without a word, or a note, or any form of contact for four long years? No—I don't get that. And hearing him try to explain it will only rip open the wounds I worked so damn hard to close.

My mom's face is stern, a far cry from the tortured worry lines she usually wears on her forehead and around her mouth. I've learned the way to disarm her is to cut her off before she can get started.

"It's taken care of. Colt had his send off, so you can all quit worrying about that." I want to remind them that while they're in the midst of being angry with me over who knows what, I went to support someone they once treated like family deal with the death of his *actual* family member.

"When were you going to tell me you gave a statement for a police report?" My mom flings a small stack of papers at my chest. They don't make it all the way to my body and land at my feet. I recognize my signature on the bottom of my statement and let out a breathy laugh.

"Um, when it's your business. Which it isn't, since I'm an adult, and I wasn't the one getting a citation. I was only a witness." I flutter my eyes as I speak, a tell that seems to accompany my lies. I wish I could break the habit.

"Hannah, your mom is up for re-election. This is the kind of thing her opponent is going to climb all over. You know how his constituents feel about the drag-racing problem in this town," my dad explains.

Dustin spits out a laugh that he quickly stifles when my father's glare moves to him.

"Sorry," Dustin says, holding up a hand.

"I'm sure you are," my dad grunts back. He paces toward the house and back again, his eyes hovering between the front door and the Supra, which he helped tinker with when the boys were in high school. His finger-prints are all over the racing scene in this town as much as Dustin's are. So are mine and Tommy's, for that matter. Hell, I've become a bit of a legend out there on Friday nights.

"That's not necessary." Dustin's response to my dad catches me off guard. It must needle at my father, too, because he pauses mid-step and jerks his head up until he's staring Dustin in the eyes. He stomps close to him, his hands balled in fists at his side and his nostrils flaring.

"What was that?" My dad's head tilts and Dustin's does the same. While my father's mouth is a hard line, Dustin's shifts into a soft smile. His eyes flit to me, and my hand twitches just from his look. It's already becoming hard to let go.

"I should leave." Dustin reaches into his pocket, every-thing about him calm and not at all like the teenager he was before he fled this place. I wonder when his last fight was. He always respected my dad, but it didn't stop him from talking back to him when he was provoked.

He holds out the Supra keys and I wrap my hand around them while his grip lingers for an extra second. The ache in my chest grows, and when he relents and tucks his hands in his pockets, my hand is left hovering in the space between us.

"Dustin, you don't need to go," my mom says, taking us all by surprise, Dad especially.

"He doesn't?" my father snarks.

I crane my neck and glare at him, and though my dad tries to ignore my scornful expression, he sees it. Our eyes meet, a few times, and I hold steady with my gaze, not willing to let him off the hook.

"No, Tom. He doesn't. It's been a hard day for him. For all of us. I'm just . . . stressed. That's all. And the police report was a surprise. My assistant brought it over, and I'm just glad I saw it before they put a story in the paper."

"Wait, there's a story coming out?" My heart is picking up speed. I don't want to be a part of some controversy. Even though only seventy people read our local press, that's seventy people I don't want in my business.

"They want to shut down the Straights. There's a motion to install roundabouts every half mile."

This time, Dustin and I both spit out a laugh.

"I'm sorry, but they can't do that," I protest.

My mom's easy-going façade tightens, and I can tell I've worked her up again.

"Actually, *we* can. I'm part of the council, you know. It's hard for me not to support this measure when some kid flipped his car there a few nights ago and is in a coma."

"What?" My eyes fly wide and I rush to pick up the police report from the ground. It's only been a couple of days, less than forty-eight hours, but from what I last heard, the kid was going to be fine. What changed?

I scan the various notes and flip pages, noting additional information added to the report yesterday and again this morning. "Internal bleeding?" I shift to look at Dustin and hold the report out for him.

"Don't worry, they mentioned your heroics in there. I'm sure you'll get a call from the reporter. Should be great for your image," my dad says.

Dustin doesn't react to my father's tone, and frankly, I'm impressed at how well he's holding back. I don't know what my dad's deal is, but this has to be deeper than some overprotective fatherly bullshit.

"They flew him to Phoenix yesterday?" Dustin glances up to get confirmation from my mom.

"I believe so," she responds.

His fingers massage his forehead as he reads and I step to his side to follow along at his shoulder. Under his long sleeve is a bandaged arm, a dressing that probably needs to be changed again. Dustin's heroics *are* the story. That's what people should focus on. The council should name that road after him rather than plot to destroy its nature. But the powers that be in this town don't get it. The Straights is a part of Camp Verde's story. It's a part of Dustin's story. And one day, when people come from far and wide to see where the world's greatest driver came from, they're not going to be impressed with a bunch of well-landscaped roundabouts.

My mom is worried about her legacy. Being the mayor of this town is what defines her, and I used to think it made her so special. I bragged to my classmates and reveled in the fact that when I was sixteen I got to drive to city hall to have lunch with her, in her very important office. Now I see how empty the title is. She wants to cling to this job because that's what my grandfather did for thirty years. It's a town without term limits, with a handful of families who have been here for decades, and a budget that has finally started to grow as the state gobbles up land and development looks northward. But what is a legacy if it's not one that fights for things?

"I'm going to go visit him today, in Phoenix. I'll come back, though. I have an idea I'd like to run by you, but . . . I need to make some phone calls." Dustin hands the papers back to my mom and meets her gaze as her mouth hangs open. He's being vague, but there's a sparkle in his eyes that seems to fill my mom with hope.

"You should take the Supra," I say, holding out the keys for him. He stares at them for a second, hesitating, so I jingle them emphatically. "Damn it, Dustin. The damn thing belongs to you anyway. Always has."

A smirk peels up the corner of his mouth and after another second or two, he gives in. While technically my dad pays the insurance and the tags, and the title is in his name, that car was merely being babysat at this house. I'm not stupid. The only reason my dad let me drive it was because it made me feel better after Dustin left.

"I can fix this. All of it. I promise," Dustin say, skipping backward toward the driver seat. I'm tempted to rush to the passenger side and ride off with him . . . again. But I can feel the unfinished business here, the conversations waiting to be had. The air is thick and vibrates to the same beat as my heart, pumping blood behind my ear drums.

As soon as the Supra fires up, I turn to face my father. He's usually not the one I have a problem with, so confronting him doesn't come as naturally as it does my mom.

"What happened?" It's the only question I can think of starting with. It's what comes out. My dad ignores it as I expect him to any other thing I asked, with a grumble and a wave of his hand.

"Don't do that," I demand. I catch up to him as he marches toward our house and tug on his arm, jerking him around.

"Hannah, now's not the time," he says.

Vague, like Dustin.

Mom scurries into the space between us, her palms out in front of her chest, motioning as if trying to calm sparring children.

"Don't defend him," I shout to her. She drops her hands

as her forehead divots. "Your behavior I can at least understand. You were afraid of your daughter dating a 'bad boy' and now you feel guilty for labeling him. But *you!*" I spin and poke my finger in the center of my dad's chest. "You actually used to *be* the bad boy. I know about the cars you drove, the motorcycle, the fucking weed down by the river when you were in high school. And you loved Dustin. You would have done anything for him. And ever since we dated in high school, you've been so hot and cold. First you want to help him, then you want to block him out of our lives. You say you're his lawyer, then you want to erase his existence and give away his car."

"Hannah, there are things you don't understand." Before my dad can pull out his lawyerly smooth talk, I counter him.

"Oh, I'm aware, Dad! That biggest being the fact I can't tell whether you love Dustin or hate him." I step up on my toes and while my hands ache to push against my father's chest, I keep them balled at my sides. We're too close to look him in both eyes at once, so I shift my focus, left to right. My teeth grit, and I feel like that seventeen-year-old girl again, trying to force her parents to accept that she's growing up and has a boyfriend. Only, I don't have one.

I'm too grown up to think anything with Dustin is easy. And I'm too scared he'll hurt me again. It doesn't mean I don't love him, though. And it doesn't mean I'm not proud. I believe in the man he's become. I'm just terrified of being left wondering where he went and why.

I swallow hard as my father's jaw relaxes, his eyes falling. Shame, or perhaps guilt, settles in.

"He got the call, by the way. Dustin Bridges is racing in the Series. In Phoenix. There was a time when you would have been in his corner. But don't worry, Dad. I got this one on my own. Me and Tommy will cheer him on. Team *Eat My Dust* and all."

I shake my head and leave my dad stunned with the news. I caught the smile trying to break into his hard features before I turned my back to him. He might even be tearing up by now. It doesn't matter, though, because I'm sure he'll be rooting against Dustin by dinner time. Seems to be what he does.

Fickle motherfucker.

9

I have no clue whether I'll be able to pull any of this off. But if there's a shot—if I can fix things for Hannah, for the Judges, and maybe make something special while I'm at it—I have to try. Something that is mine, that I can leave behind, that will make me feel proud to come home, to tell people where I'm from.

Something that isn't about being Colt Bridge's kid. A timeline beyond that trailer, and that pathetic bag of ashes I scattered on a dry river bottom because I literally have nowhere to call special when it comes to my dad.

My heart kicks with excited energy at the potential brewing in my head. Building a real track in Camp Verde, a place for young people to train and forge memories, has always been a fantasy of mine. I would go there in my head when was little and things at home got bad. The old Carney Raceway, an abandoned structure and tumble-weed-filled oval on the outskirts of town limits, has been deserted since the sixties. In its prime, horses ran up there. Some of the most storied thoroughbreds in the history books pounded the dirt track at Carney on their way to triple crown glory. As modern tracks became more appealing, Carney was converted into a dog track. In the nineties, someone bought the property and attempted to pave it. They got halfway around before running out of money, and it's been falling apart a little every year since.

In my young mind, the place was magical. I envisioned grandstands filled with fans all chanting my name. Fuel-soaked air and a constant rumble of engines. Smaller tracks for kids on the inside, ringed by a banking roadway for the big boys. I could almost talk myself into believing it was real before Colt jarred me back to real life with a knuckle to my face or a jerk to my arm.

Something clicked when Hannah's mom talked about shutting down the Straights. It's as though my fate and fortune aligned and I knew in my gut that this is the time. It's a crazy plan, really. I hardly have a savings account, and while I've made a pretty tight amateur name for myself, I've got a lot to prove. Hell, I could burn out in this first race and never get a shot again. That narrow window, though? Those odds? I thrive on that shit. And that's why I have to try.

Carney. That's how we save what makes Camp Verde special. It's how Hannah's mom gets her legacy. And it's how I build my dream. I'll need Tommy's help to make it work, but I'll cross that bridge of begging once I get that far. Step one, before anything, is to make things right for Mrs. Judge.

And for Hannah.

That means making sure Kyle wakes up and that he's taken care of completely. And, as heartless as it sounds, it also means ensuring he and his family don't torch everyone who has ever raced out on the Straights as a way to get even. It's part of the code one accepts when they burn rubber out there: racing is dangerous, but it's never the road's fault.

I've missed the ease of cutting through traffic in the Supra. I've had a few cars come close to this feeling over the last four years, like the Honda I traded in for the last stock truck, but this car, my baby? It's special. Maybe it has something to do with being my first. I lost my hundred-mile-per-hour virginity behind this wheel. I'm making better time than I expected, which means I have to get my thoughts in order and quick.

About thirty minutes out from the medical center, I slip my phone from my pocket and put it on speaker in the passenger seat, pressing Virgil on speed dial. I figured he would answer quick. Today's news is still fresh in both our veins, and being the overly organized type that he is, he probably wants to know if I've taken care of the nineteen bullet-point items he texted me the moment we hung up. I won't let him know that I haven't yet read his full text.

"Dustin, thank God. I'm spinning in circles here. I don't know what to do first." I love how genuinely excited Virgil is for me. I will keep him on my team for as long as my ride lasts, shitty mechanic or not. I simply need his energy.

"Look, Virg. I promise I'll get everything taken care of. But right now, I need you to do two things for me. Life or death things." I might be being a bit dramatic, but it gets Virgil to calm down on the other end of the line.

"Okay, yeah. What do you need?"

I swear I hear him click a ballpoint pen and rip off a paper from a notepad. I love this man.

"Sell the truck."

He audibly gasps at number one. I sorta expected that.

"I know, I know. Nothing is guaranteed, and one Series

race doesn't mean I'm leaving the truck circuit behind blah blah blah. But Virg?"

He gulps.

"Yeah, Dust."

"I'm not going to fail. I'm leaving the truck circuit behind. And this thing you're in with me? It's about to get big. *Real* big." I probably sound manic to him. Hell, I might *be* manic right now. But this thinking—manifesting a destiny—is what got me where I am. I'm not about to give up on the only method that seems to have worked.

"Sell truck. Got it. What's number two."

I grin, loving that even though he probably thinks I'm nuts, he's all in for the ride. If he's still this committed after my second request, I'm giving him the first piece of real hardware I win.

"I need you to talk Mr. O'Keefe into coming to Arizona with you this weekend. Oh, and he's gonna have to pay for your flights because I'm about to be broke."

My second request is initially met with silence. I lean my head against the window, ready to knock it against the glass a few times, when Virgil finally pipes up.

"About your sponsor. . ."

Shit.

"Let me guess. He's not my sponsor anymore." I commence with the head banging.

"I'd prefer ya focus on that positivity you were spoutin' a second ago. Remember? How it won't matter because bigger and better things, and you've got bigger sponsors lining up already."

Just like Virgil to throw my own words back at me in such a damn nice-guy way. I grit my teeth and fake a grin, not that he can see it.

"You're right. Well, then, how about you drive down

here. We'll sell the truck in A Z. Get a better price for it." I keep the chipper tone up for Virgil's sake, but the second he hangs up I pound the steering wheel and growl out, "Fuck!"

As if somehow she knew I would need it, a glimpse of teal blue leather catches my eyes where the passenger seat meets the console. I feel in the crevice and tug on what turns out to be the strap of Hannah's small backpack. She must have forgotten it under her seat. I pull it free and rest it on the seat, leaving my hand on it as if I can somehow draw power and encouragement from it. Hell, maybe I can.

Ridiculous or not, by the time I exit the freeway in the heart of downtown Phoenix, I'm renewed with hope. Virgil is right. I'll find someone better—deeper pockets. Sometimes, all it takes to get someone to believe in your dream with you is simply to ask. And I'm good with people. I mean, not the ones I think are dicks. I've got a long history of juvenile delinquency in Arizona, and young adult bar fights in Oklahoma that prove contrary to my people skills, but those were truly *almost* always the other guy's fault.

I fill my chest with the swagger power of Hannah's purse one last time after I finally find a spot in the hospital garage, then tuck her bag back under the seat and head inside. One thing that has always surprised me about hospitals is the complete lack of security. It's easy to walk just about anywhere as long as you keep moving and don't look too much of anything—happy, distraught, lost. I navigate my way to the intensive care unit, park my ass on a chair, and pull out my phone. The rest of my afternoon is going to be spent observing everyone who comes and goes.

I used to play this game when I waited for my mom after an overdose. *The woman I thought was my mom.* Given enough context clues, you can usually match visitors to patients in a hospital. This trick is harder in an ER, mostly because of the constant turnover. Up here, on the third floor of one of the nicer hospitals in the Valley, the puzzle pieces are few and well-matched.

The first couple to pass through the visitor doors is too old to belong to Kyle Procter. I got his last name from the report, and I know his mother's name is Myra. There wasn't a father's name on the report, but that doesn't necessarily mean there isn't one in the picture. He showed up at the track. He came and left with his kid. My fake mom never put Colt's name on anything when she was sober enough to take me to doctors' offices or appointments. Maybe this is a lot like that.

Twenty minutes into my wait, a woman in her early forties with shoulder-length blonde hair steps into the lobby where I sit, her cell phone pressed to her ear. She fits the profile physically, her traits match up with Kyle, but I'm going to need more before I know for sure.

"Maybe if he had a father who gave a shit—" I catch the last bit of her gritted words before she slips through the lobby door and into the hallway. Her bitterness is familiar. Sometimes, fake mom showed glimpses of that kind of fire.

I follow her into the hall and hover near the lobby doors until she finishes her call. She jumps when she turns and sees me.

"Sorry." I hold up my palms.

"I'm just frazzled. I didn't hear you come out," she says, her hand on her chest, fingers gripping the puckered center of the blue T-shirt she's probably been wearing since she had to rush her son here. I'm guessing dad, who refused the ambulance ride, didn't think Kyle needed to get checked out. *I wonder if Kyle has other injuries his dad doesn't want people to see.*

"I swear to God I'm not being creepy . . ." I trail off because that intro, in and of itself—it's creepy. She rightfully takes a step back.

"I'm from Camp Verde. I'm the one who pulled Kyle out of the car? I'm . . ."

Before I can utter another word, the woman slings her arms around my neck, her hand clutching the back of my head and her body trembling.

"Dustin. Oh, my God, you're him!" Her voice is already hoarse from sleep deprivation, but the new tears she's shedding on my shoulder make it worse.

"I am. Hi." My arms instinctually hug her back, and a warmth soothes my chest. I recognize the withdrawals of affection as soon as they hit me. It's been a while since I've felt someone need me like this—like family. Like a parent. A part of me instantly needs her back.

"I wanted to call you and thank you, but the police said you were only in town for a few days. Everyone seems to know you, though." She pulls away from our embrace and we both take a step back. She's comfortable with me. I can tell by her relaxed shoulders, and that sets my nerves at ease.

"I grew up there. I had some family stuff to take care of and I'm thinking of sticking around."

"Dear God, why?" She cups her mouth, realizing her gaffe.

I chuckle and wave off her apology before she can fully articulate it.

"I get it. Unless you grew up in Camp Verde, or really like small towns and nature and, well, nature, it seems like the worst place to live on Earth."

She nods in agreement.

"My husband's family left him land. He wants to stay."

Her eyes tell the rest of the story. She would give anything to leave—*to leave him.*

"I'd like to help out however I can. I mean, I don't have much, not yet. But I'm racing in the Series race in a few weeks—"

"You're . . . you're a driver!" Her eyes light up more than a woman with a kid suffering from car crash injuries should at the news of meeting a race car driver.

"I am, yeah."

"Come with me," she says, taking my hand and leading me back into the lobby with her. We're through the unit's doors seconds later and soon inside Kyle's room. She presses a button on the main monitor, turning down the regular beep.

"I finally had to ask the nurse how to do that. I'm always staring at that thing when I'm in here, so I don't need to hear it. The sound—"

"It's the worst," I finish for her. I think back on the times my fake mom was in a hospital bed with machines making the exact same noise. It's weird how it both haunts you one moment and you're used to it the next.

She moves to the opposite side of the bed, where she's made the chair more comfortable with blankets and a pillow, and takes her son's hand.

"I'm Myra, by the way." She glances up and gives me the softest smile. I don't tell her I already know her name.

"It's nice to meet you, Myra. Not under these circumstance, but . . ." My cheeks flush from the massive foot-in-my-mouth moment, but she quickly laughs it off.

"It's very nice to meet you." I can tell by the calmness that seems to relax her cheeks and slow her breath that she's being earnest. Sometimes, it's simply nice to not be alone in moments like this—in rooms like this.

I give in to the silence and for once, it isn't hard. It actually gives me time to think. Virgil's news about O'Keefe pulling his backing threw a hiccup in what felt like a fairly plausible plan, despite the fact that most of it is dependent on me winning my ass off this weekend. I have a back-up option. It's been a while since we talked, but I've remained in contact with the guys I know in Vegas. It's one thing to make some bets with them, maybe fix a desert race or two, or hit the strip hard with them over a weekend. But getting into business is a lot like getting into bed, and I've always had this strong suspicion that Alex Offerman sleeps with a loaded gun.

I tuck that option to the back of my mind and focus on what's present. I'm not sure whether it's the fact I'm in a hospital and getting pummeled with memories or if I'm nervous about how to approach my next conversation with Myra, but I'm suddenly sweating my ass off. I lean forward and pull my arms free from my hoodie, forgetting the bandage wrapped around my arm that looks as if it's been through a war on its own. Before I can hide it to my side, Myra notices and reaches across her son toward my arm.

"You were hurt? Is that from helping Kyle?"

I grimace because the divot in her forehead is undoubtedly from guilt.

"It's nothing," I lie. I've already caught a glimpse and saw that the blood soaked through pretty good. It honestly doesn't hurt that bad anymore. Redressing this thing is going to be a bitch, though.

"Dustin, that is definitely something. Let me get one of the nurses to take a look—"

"No. It's fine," I cut in, standing to match her posture. She stares into my eyes for a few hard seconds, and my eyes pain. Truth is, I don't like doctors. And I've gotten good at healing on my own. This isn't even the first time my arm's been cut from glass.

I don't have to say it out loud. Sometimes, when you're a victim of abuse by someone who is supposed to love you, you're given this superpower. It lets you look inside others and see how you're alike. Myra, Kyle, and me? We're alike.

"Can I at least take a look at it?" She reaches forward with both hands and for the first time in a while the skin on my arm burns.

After a deep breath, I relent, holding my arm out so she can inspect it more easily. Her hands are gentle, stripping away the loose end of gauze and unwrapping my wounds enough to get an idea of what's underneath.

"Dustin." She sounds like Hannah's mom.

"I know. I'll get it cleaned up." I try to pull my arm away, but her hold on my hand tightens. I lift my chin to meet her parental stare. She's cleaning this up, and she's doing it now. I sigh but laugh a little through it.

"Okay. Let's go to the bathroom." I follow her lead toward the small bathroom attached to Kyle's room and slide into the space between the wall and the sink so she can stand opposite me. When she steps out to search the small nursing station in the corner of the room, I unwind the gauze and wince when it sticks from the dried blood. By the time she comes back into the bathroom, I'm nearly done. The arm looks better than I thought it would, honestly. Probably because someone else cared enough to help me with it the first time.

"Can we clean it up?" She nods down toward the sink and I relent. She tests the water, finding a temperature she deems "luke," then guides my arm under the stream. The sting isn't nearly as bad as I thought it would be, and I relax my weight into the wall behind me, letting her take over.

She rolls my arm slowly and runs her fingertips a few times over the deep scratches.

"You really should get some antibiotics on this," she says, turning the water off and pressing a hand towel on my arm in sections to dry it off. I nod, knowing that Hannah will insist on it too.

Hannah.

My chest suddenly burns. This is the first time I've thought about Hannah in a future sense in so long. We kissed. She kissed back. It was so sudden and I was lost in this euphoria over my news. I haven't had a chance to process what it means, but it has to mean something.

Hannah will want to take care of my arm—*take care of me.* I shiver, and I know Myra thinks it's from the new wrap she's affixing to my arm, but it's not. That shiver was from my lack of control. I want Hannah, all of her, forever. But I'd be a fool to think that one excited moment in reaction to some big news meant more than it probably does.

"Myra, I have a favor to ask, and it's uncomfortable and probably . . ." I pull my lips in tight and brace myself for the shitty thing I have to ask. "It's definitely inappropriate, especially here in this room, where your son is recovering."

"What is it?" That dent is back in her brow. She's finished dressing my arm and the space in this bathroom feels about a million times tighter. I hug my arm against my chest, my other hand feeling her handiwork. *This is how a mother takes care of a child.*

"That news article they're writing on the crash, and your push for the town council— Don't shut down the Straights. I know it's a lot to ask. And you have no reason to trust me or believe me, but I'm working on a solution. But until I can, that road is too important to too many people. A lot of identities are made on that road, and for a lot of people, it's the only place they have to feel, well, anything. So, while it's a lot to ask, I have to."

I meet her eyes for the first time since I began my ramble, and I'm not prepared for the confused expression pulling in her brow and flattening her mouth.

"I'm sorry, Dustin, but I don't know what you're talking about."

My stomach sinks while my chest breaks open. I'm both relieved and panicked by her answer. If Myra doesn't know, then who does?

"Would your husband be pursuing—"

"Trust me, he doesn't want to pursue anything that makes him have to talk to people," she says. I get the secondary message; he doesn't want people in their business, nosing around and giving Myra ideas about deserving better.

"Okay. Well, that's good, then. I'm sorry I had to ask."

"Dustin, I might not love that I was dragged out there, but I get the idea of wanting a place to escape. And Kyle? He's going to absolutely flip when he wakes up and realizes he was saved by a real circuit driver."

I bite my lip on instinct, overcome with this odd bashful sensation. I smile through it and look down at the blood-stained bandage left behind in the sink. I am a real driver. Not just any driver, either. I'm the best, the best that ever was.

I follow her back to the main room, tossing away my old gauze as she settles into her visitor chair for a long afternoon and night. I pick up my hoodie and slip it back on, reaching for her hand one more time before leaving. She gives it to me willingly, and for a tiny moment, I imagine she's my mom, and that our hands are the same.

"Kyle's a really lucky dude, and when he gets out of here I'm going to have a job waiting for him, if he wants it."

Her smile spreads and tears prick the corners of her eyes.

"He would like that."

We both nod a silent agreement and I let her hand slip from mine, then find my way back to the garage. I'll make the call to my Vegas friends on my drive home. I'll get Tommy on board with the idea when I get to the Judge house. And then, I'll win Hannah back completely, leaving my heart without ache, without question.

I'll do it because I'm Dustin *fucking* Bridges.

10

I wonder how many hours of my life I have spent staring up at Dustin's wind chime? The fact I'm having that thought while hugging my knees to my chest sitting in the center of my bed, my head tilted back, and my focus blurring in and out on the jagged twists of metal, is not unusual. And here I always thought *I* was the artist.

He was such a kid when he made this for me. I mean, yes, he was almost eighteen and on his way to independence, but he was also this scared boy who only showed his fears to me. His hands made that. Hands that have grown to match his soul. Dustin finally walks around in a body befitting the man he is inside.

My God, he's glorious.

My mouth falls into a seduced smile as I close my eyes and think about our kiss, my fingertips trailing down the curve of my neck to my shoulder, my breast and between my legs. I swallow hard and stop myself, blinking my eyes open and dropping my chin to my chest as I stretch my legs out to rid myself of this growing need. It's more than simple temptation when it comes to Dustin. It always has been.

A soft rapping at my door is followed by its slow opening. Bailey looks in with only one eye, exaggerating the way she peeks through the crack in an effort to make me laugh. I do, but not very hard. She's gotten used to my ups and downs. I had a lot of them in the beginning, right after Dustin left. Fewer in recent years. I'm not sure what I'm riding right now, a wave or a dip.

"So, are you hiding from me in here because you're getting back together with the guy who broke your heart? Or are you *that* in love with your bedroom?" She looks in now with both pleading eyes. I nod to the end of my bed and encourage her to come revel in my epic childhood bedroom with me.

"Definitely the bedroom thing," I say, flipping around to look up at the ceiling while my legs dangle off the side of the bed.

"I miss our dorm room," Bailey says.

I breathe out and try to imagine that's where we are, someone's music blaring down the hall, the smell of burnt popcorn wafting from the common area.

"Me, too," I sigh out.

College has been this perfect in-between, and to be honest, it scares me a little knowing I only have one more year left to shelter there with Bailey. I'll finish my fifth year of college alone because, unlike me, Bailey's graduating on time. Probably because she *likes* her degree. I had to drop three of my courses over the last three years because I was failing them so bad. I just can't get excited about supply-chain theory. At least in the marketing classes I could work in some design.

"I kissed him." I know she can tell. Besides Dustin, nobody reads me so well.

I roll my head slightly to my side to meet her eyes. I figured she'd be staring down at me, and I was right.

"Was it as good as you remember?" She shrugs.

I spit out a laugh and slap my hand over my eyes.

"Well? Was it?" She's not going to yell at me. She doesn't have to. I'm torturing myself enough over this decision, and she gets that.

"Oh, Bailey . . . it's gotten better." I touch my fingertips to my lips, tracing the faint feeling I can still conjure from memory. It wasn't even the *right* kind of kiss and I felt it in my toes. It was a kiss of the moment, a celebration out of habit. But now that we've done that, I can't stop thinking about the other kinds of kisses.

The other kinds of everything.

"He got called up." The bed moves as my friend jolts at the news.

"When? Where?"

"Two weeks. Here. The Series race in Phoenix." It warms me to see her smile. I know she called Dustin and let him know about his dad. I saw the call record on my phone. She's a terrible criminal, fingerprints and a trail of evidence everywhere. I'll let the two of them keep this secret, though. They need to have something, too.

"I know your dad didn't kiss Dustin," she breaks in. My lips contort into a confused smile. Bailey shrugs a shoulder and glances to my window behind her. "I figure Dustin's got something to do with all of that fishing gear he's sorting out in your garage. He planning on escaping up to the lake?"

So that's where my dad's been hiding.

I lift myself to a sitting position and adjust the slats of

my shutters to look down at the driveway. His project is spilling out of the garage, tackle boxes with rods and lures lying in piles. He has so many. It's been a while since I've gone out to the lake with him. I used to be his buddy when I was a kid, before I turned sixteen and started going out to the Straights. *Before I got in the Supra with Dustin Bridges.*

"I should go talk to him," I groan. My heart wants to but my stubborn-ass gut is anchoring me in place. Any conversation we have about Dustin is going to be hard. We've never really had the tough talk. First, Dad was angry that we were dating, and then he was mad at Dustin for breaking my heart. There was never much in between.

I pause at my door, turning when I realize Bailey is still sitting on my bed, her feet dangling off the edge. There's a heaviness to her eyes, the kind of expression she gets when she's overwhelmed. She looked like this during finals, and when she took that Shakespeare class.

"I'm sorry, you probably came here to see me. My head is such a mess." I thrust my hand into my tangled hair for effect and Bailey breathes out a short laugh. She's still unsettled. I see it in her eyes and my stomach aches with worry for my friend.

"Nothing really. It's hard to be home after feeling all that freedom. I'll come by later, hear more about that kiss?" She rocks her feet to the floor and slaps her hands to her side, forcing energy and life into her body and face. She's faking it, but I understand the need. We all need to fake it sometimes.

"Promise?" I hold out my pinky and she hooks hers with mine. We give each other a tiny shake, a move we perfected in fourth grade while making plans behind the teacher's back.

"Don't kiss anyone until I come back," she says,

waggling her fingers over her shoulder at me on her way down the hallway and down our stairs.

"Oh, fuck. You kissed?" Tommy is rubbing his face and hovering in his doorway, having just woken up from a nap. He seems to have settled into his old routine nicely, his pile of dirty laundry waiting on the floor behind him for our mom to magically swoop in and take care of. She'll totally enable him, too.

"Why is everyone so interested in all things me and Dustin?" I hold my hands out to my sides and roll my eyes before leaving my brother behind to deal with his wrinkled-ass shirt and uncomfortable-to-look-at boxer situation.

"Because when things go wrong between you two it's bad for all of us!" he shouts as I skip down the stairs.

"Blah blah, can't hear you," I joke back. I laugh at his reaction but my smile falls by the time I reach the first floor. He's not wrong. Dustin and I have chemistry, and sometimes chemicals explode.

I push those thoughts to the side and ready myself to face my father. Things have been put off long enough, and I can't keep holding back my words with him. I won't dive right in, though. I'll ease him in. Don't want him getting all flustered and tangling his fishing line.

"You really should think about a yard sale, you know?" I shield my eyes from the setting sun and scan the contents that are now spilling into our driveway. "It's a ridiculous amount of fishing gear."

"You sound like your mother," he grumbles.

I clutch my chest.

"Ouch! Wow, low shot," I tease. *Really, though? Fuck, do I sound like Mom?*

"You going to the lake tonight?" It's a weekday, and my

dad has been spending long hours at the office. Land acquisitions have been at an all-time high, and he's had a lot of tough contracts to work through. There's a fine balance between developing and over-developing. I can't believe I'm about to acknowledge this, but I'd kinda hate to see this place lose its small-town charm.

"This weekend, probably. Why? My old fishing partner interested?" He looks up from the last of the old metal tackle boxes he's knelt over. I'm sure he thought he was clear and free of the signs, but his eyes are as red as Satan. My dad doesn't have allergies, and he's been sick once in the last five years. Those puffy eyes? They're from crying.

"Dad," I level my gaze at him, my head falling to the side. He falls back on his ass and runs the back of his hand over his eyes.

"Damn it all to hell," he grumbles.

I nudge a few boxes out of the way so I can sit next to him on the floor of the garage. He waves his hand at me to avoid the attention, but I'm as stubborn as he is. We both don't like crying, and when we do, we sure as shit don't like getting caught.

"Come on," I say, pulling his wrist from where it rests on his knee and weaving my hand into his. No matter how grown I am, his hand will always swallow mine.

"This about Dustin?" I know it is.

He shrugs. No need to voice his answer.

"He's gonna make it, Dad. You shouldn't be crying. Forget the last four years, too. You're allowed to be proud of him. He's going to race in a Series race, Dad. He's using all of the things you taught him." I shake my dad's arm at my side before hugging it.

My dad blubbers out a mixture of happy laughter and tears.

"He's a million times better than I ever was. I was a hack," he says, rolling his eyes at the memory of his youth. "That kid . . . he had it when he was ten. Hell, seven! He was born . . . for . . . this."

My father's last few words come out with sobs and he lowers his head, pinching the bridge of his nose as if that will somehow stop the flow. It won't. It never does. I would know; I try the same damn techniques.

As he lifts his head enough to meet my eyes, all the rawness on display, I see how distraught he is.

"You think he knows I'm proud of him?" he utters, and I instantly fall apart.

"Daddy," I cry, throwing my arms around my father only to have him squeeze me right back. It's been too long since I've hugged him like this. Tucked inside the walls of the garage, we shed our armor and give in to emotions that we've kept bottled way too long.

"Oh, Hannah. I failed that boy. I failed him, I failed him." My dad is rocking in my arms, and hearing his anguish makes me cry more.

There were times, as recent as this morning, that I hated my father for his casual dismissal of Dustin. He was never giving up on Dustin at all, though. He was giving up on himself. He was masking guilt. He was putting up walls and building a front, the way us Judges do.

"You didn't, Daddy. Dustin . . . he's amazing! He's going to be something spectacular. He's going to be one of those guys old farts like you sit around and reminisce about over your boxes of random car parts."

My dad spits out laughter over my shoulder.

"Garage sale, Dad. It's time," I tease.

His arms relax around me, and when the tears finally stop, I nestle in against my father's chest and listen to the steady beat of his heart. When I was really young, maybe four or five, I used to pray before I went to sleep, and I always asked God to take care of my dad's heart. I never met my grandpas on either side of our family; their hearts quit too soon. My dad's, though, it has always been strong, the beat loud and present.

"Did you know Trisha wasn't really Dustin's mom?" I let my words slip out casually, lulled by the comfort of the moment. I've been dying to talk to someone about what Dustin showed me, and I thought maybe my dad was the perfect sounding board. As he peels back from me slowly, though, his body suddenly rigid and his eyes wide and fearful, I realize this conversation isn't going to go the way I thought it would.

"Dustin knows this?" he croaks.

I nod slowly, realization hitting me as I do.

"You already knew." My mouth instantly goes dry, and if I could breathe, I'm sure I would choke. My father's face is guilty, frozen as it was the moment I first broached this subject.

"Hannah." The guilt drizzled throughout his words since I came into the garage has become the main ingredient in his voice. He looks fallen, unable to gasp for enough air to cry any more but also too stricken by this new reality to elaborate.

"Dad?" I feel my anger renewing in my belly. I don't want to be angry at my father anymore, not about Dustin.

"Dad!" I shout, pushing my hands into his body, hoping it will force him to let me in on his secrets.

His head falling forward, the first movement in nearly a minute, I catch a glimpse of the wrecked man before me— the heartbroken soul under a mask he's worn far too long. The tears come hard and fast, and this time, there is nothing I can do to stop them. All I can do is wait. And hope he lets me in so I can understand too. Without his part of this mystery, I'll never be able to put either of them back together again, and other than Tommy, Dustin and my father are the only men I ever want in my life.

This cry is different. It's silent, and it causes my dad to shudder when I can tell he's reaching back for memories, old thoughts he must have thought he buried for good. Nothing stays dead forever, though. Not even Colt Bridges, scattered in a dry river bed. That man's legacy is somehow alive and well right now, haunting us. And we aren't even blood.

Minutes pass, threatening to turn into an hour, but finally, my dad's eyes meet mine and they're clear. They're ready. *He's* ready.

"You know I wasn't always a land attorney, right?"

I nod. *This is a weird route for this topic to take.*

"Did you know I worked with Bailey's dad, Rob?" *He knows I don't. He hates Rob Tingle.* It's half the reason it's been so hard for me and Bailey to have a friendship. There's this weird, ages-old grudge between the two men over some case they were involved in. I never knew the details, but something tells me those details are at the heart of this moment—of Dustin's birth certificate and his real mom.

"What kind of law?" I brace myself for his response, but he takes the same roundabout path he began with, despite that my gut is certain of where this is all going.

"We were both trying to get into the land side of things. It's not easy to break into, and Carl Ridgeway, remember him?"

I shake my head, stunned with wide eyes, circling my

finger in an attempt to motivate him to get to the fucking point! "Uh, yeah. Carl. Get to the point."

"Carl had a lock on the land business, but he was retiring. Rob and I knew we'd have to act fast to stake our positions. Rob and I never liked each other much." Dad's focus wanders out to the expanse of the driveway. I'd clap in front of his face if he wasn't still talking.

"We were handling family law," he says, and my gut sinks.

"It was our last case. A simple one. A junkie, prostitute mom—just a teenager. She'd gotten pregnant and took off without the baby right after the birth. When she showed back up six months later, the kid had already been introduced to another female figure, and the father had a job and could pay for the baby's needs. She wanted custody, but she hardly had a case to stand on."

"Something in my gut said not to take it on. Something spoke to me, and I don't know, Hannah, I tried to listen." His eyes meet mine, the tears hanging on the edge. His pupils dilate and even though he's looking right at me, I know my father sees a life from more than twenty years ago.

"I helped that man keep his son. I took that boy away from a life that might have been a hell of a lot better than the one he ended up with. I did that, because Rob said it was a 'slam-dunk.' A 'no-brainer.' It was a quick close, and then we were free to move on our separate ways, gobbling up the land business all the way up to the county line. We were rid of each other. And Rob never once flinched with regret."

I want to tell him to stop. I shake my head because I've heard enough. I'm sick, too sick to cry. So much pain Dustin could have been spared. No matter how much I don't want to hear the rest, I need to. I need to lend proof to my heart that what happened was real, and that on a large level, my father thinks he's to blame for Dustin's abuse. Right now, I want to blame him, too. It's not fair, because he's only one of so many variables, and Colt is responsible for his actions. Yet still . . .

"When you and Tommy brought your new best friend over, I ran upstairs and puked my guts out. I saw it written all over his face, even as a child. The cuts. The bruising. The way he got in fights at school over the littlest things. I fed Dustin to a monster, and since I was the one who did it, I didn't have a way to undo the damage. Rob certainly wouldn't support it. As rotten as Colt Bridges was, Rob always saw Dustin's real mother as the ultimate sinner. I'd have to climb that battle alone, and I still probably wouldn't win. Dustin would get sent into a system. He'd be lost to you and Tommy. I wouldn't be able to take care of him."

My dad wouldn't be able to take care of him.

"You thought of him as a son," I hum. My dad's eyes snap to awareness, and he nods emphatically.

"Always. I still do. And it gives me so much shame. I'm no better than Colt." His eyes flutter closed, and for a moment I think he might pass out from the wave of guilt and sorrow crashing into him.

I want to ease it, but I'm not sure how. The only thing I can think to say are all the truths.

"Dustin is such a good man, Dad. He's so driven, so talented. He's independent. I mean, look what he's figured out on his own. He's made it so far. He's destined, too. You know it. I know it. You were behind that, Dad. You were the one who was there. We all were."

"Except when I looked at him and all I saw was Colt," he

admits. His eyes melt, heavy tear drops cutting down his unshaven cheeks and landing on his T-shirt.

My dad was afraid I'd fallen in love with Colt. He was afraid I was going to fall in love with someone who couldn't help but turn into a monster. I shake my head.

"No, Dad. He was never going to be Colt. Never at all," I say.

A pathetic laugh slips from his lips and he shrugs, defeated and ready to let me rewrite history for him.

"I fell for him because of you. Girls love their fathers. I love my Daddy."

"And you love Dustin," he whispers the truth for me.

I pull my lips in tight, a pained smile stretching them as more tears sting my eyes. I won't say it out loud. I may never be able to say it again. That's the damage I have to contend with. Dustin isn't Colt, but he did hurt me. His absence hurt. So sudden. I won't correct my father's words, though. Because as far as he's concerned, yes. Yes, I do.

11

I t's strange how a person can love driving to their very core yet absolutely hate road trips. I blame the Valley traffic. By the time I cleared the city and opened up the Supra, my body relaxed. My knuckles are still sore from clenching the wheel through the city. If race drivers were as idiotic as business people heading home at five o'clock, I would never win a damn race.

So unpredictable.

So . . . moronic!

By the time the Supra's wheels hit the Judge driveway, my body is near collapse. I've packed a lot of emotion into one day, and I'm starting to feel it. My body is begging my head for relief, but my mind is too busy working, negotiating, convincing. I have to get the Vegas guys to buy into this, but that means giving up some control.

Our transactions over the years, though technically illegal, have always been professional. They book the best races for making actual cash. I've gotten it down to one or two visits a year out in the Nevada desert. And when I need to lose, I lose. It's how I pay for parts; how I bought the truck. Race winnings alone wouldn't buy shit, and I don't feel close enough to Uncle Jeff to ask him for money. I see how hard he works, and to be honest, I don't think he has extra to spare.

I'm so mired in my own thoughts that I don't notice the pile of lures and hooks I somehow managed to miss with the Supra tires as I pulled into the driveway. I'm not so lucky with my feet, though, and a hook from some glowing minnow lure punctures my right shoe.

"Oh, shit!" I hop on one foot while grabbing my injured one.

"Dustin?" Hannah comes rushing out of the garage, earbuds stuffed in her ears. She reaches me just as I'm able to lean my weight on the back of the Supra and pry the hook from my sole.

"Weird time for a garage sale," I say, wincing from the wound that's probably soaking my sock as I speak. I'm pulling off my shoe as Hannah's dad wanders toward us from the house, two lemonades in his hand.

"Did you hear him? Garage sale," Hannah says.

"Yeah, yeah. I heard him. I'm sorting. Can't you all tell the difference?" Mr. Judge shoves one of the lemonades into my chest, splashing me with a third of it, then pushes the nearby scattered lures out of our way with his work boot.

"Let me see." He grips my shoe in his palm and my toe throbs from the sudden movement.

"Toughen up, son. You think the eleven car is going to be gentle with you out at the speedway?" He slides his glasses from his head down to his nose and removes my shoe. In his distraction, I let myself study his face.

"No, sir," I say, not able to help the grin forming on my lips. "Hannah told you, huh?"

"Uh huh," Mr. Judge grunts.

My gaze slides over to Hannah, and when our eyes connect, I swear I hear her thoughts. *My dad is proud of you.* My chest warms. He hasn't called me son, other than his one slip up, in a really long time.

"Han, can you run in and grab the first aid kit? Oh, and the alcohol?" He glances sideways to his daughter.

"Oh, that's not neccess— Oh, *wowawow!*" He's barely squeezing my toe and I'm literally reeling.

"It's necessary," he emphasizes.

"Gah!" I let my head fall back and my arms fold over my face. I can take a punch. Heck, I've been stabbed! Why is it that a toe injury can literally cripple me?

Hannah rushes toward the house, leaving me alone with her father for the first time since we met in a diner and he told me I needed to leave. His focus is tunneled on my foot, despite that there isn't much for him to do until Hannah comes back with bandages and alcohol. He's avoiding eye contact, which is fine with me because I'm still not sure how to fit in here. It used to be so natural and easy, but life fucked everything up.

"How was the drive?" he grumbles.

"Oh, you know, your typical landscape of sedans and minivans all holding steady at sixty-five."

Mr. Judge coughs out a laugh, but he still doesn't look up. He pulls my sock down and folds it over my toes to soak up more blood.

"That sucker went right through, huh?" I twist my ankle in his palm and he grips it steady, holding me still.

"That lure and hook was for big fish," he responds,

pulling his glasses from his face and hooking them on the collar of his shirt.

"Welp, caught one," I joke.

His lip tugs up on the side I can see, but he doesn't laugh. That's okay. It was a pretty stupid joke. I'm uncomfortable and can't think of anything to say.

"Dustin, listen—"

"It's fine. Really," I cut in. "Whatever it is, don't worry about it." My chest is so tight. As uncomfortable as it is to sit here in either silence or forced banter, I don't know if I can handle whatever direction Mr. Judge is planning to go. Unfortunately, I don't know that I have a choice as I look down and into the eyes of a truly broken man.

"It isn't fine," he says, the corners of his mouth drawing down, his shoulders falling.

Sucking in my lips, I breathe in through my nose and widen my eyes as I shake my head at him. A short laugh slips out, and the dam I've worked so hard to build cracks in my chest. I squeeze my eyes shut tight, then lean my head back when I open them. The sky is purple, caught between sunset's pink and dusk's blue. This sky . . . it makes me think of the Straights, of rolling up and seeing Hannah there, of winning.

"It's not fine. You're right. But what does that matter? It's done. All of it. I can't go back and get the last four years as a do over, and even if I could, I wouldn't want to put your daughter in danger. I see the mess Colt left behind. It wouldn't have been good here. Who knows what kind of man I would have turned into. I would have felt obligated when he got sick, and then I would have felt even more cursed than I already do. So yeah, Mr. Judge. It isn't fine, but it's also over with. I'd kinda like to focus on the future now if that's all right with you?"

I don't meet his gaze until my last few words, but I can tell by the way my anguish is reflected in his eyes that he understands. I see the respect. He hasn't looked at me like this in a while—*like a son.*

His brow draws in slowly, the lines on his forehead growing deeper with each breath as his eyes flit from our connection and away again.

"Whatever it is you think you need to say to me, Mr. Judge, don't. You don't have to. I don't really want to know. Unless you truly think it's a matter of life or death, my safety, Hannah's safety, Tommy's? If it's not, then seal it up and forget it yourself." *There are a lot of things I'm locking away and forgetting when I can.*

Torment clouds his eyes, and for a moment his lips part as if he's going to counter my request and force me to listen. Eventually, his teeth clamp down and he grits out a forced smile, nodding his acceptance.

"How about you start calling me Tom again. That work for you?" He looks up at me, one eye squinted.

Everything in my chest aches to call him Dad, like I used to when we were little. I tried that name out for a while and I liked it, but using it only made it harder to go back home to my real father. Tom came easy, though. I suppose it could again.

"I can do that," I agree as Hannah rejoins us. She wrinkles her face when she spots the state of my sock.

"That's a lot of blood," she says, her lips soured.

"Nah, it's nothing. Right, Tom?" Her dad chuckles and shakes his head before going to work on my injury.

"I've seen worse," he says, tossing my blood-drenched sock to the ground. He pours the alcohol on my wound and I brace myself from the burn of it before leaning forward enough to get a good look at the piercing on the outside of my big toe. If it didn't hurt so much I'd think it was pretty cool.

"Maybe I can put one of those septum rings in it," I joke. Hannah lightly smacks the back of my head, but her dad laughs. It's a genuine, unfiltered, unforced response, and this little glimpse into a possible future where life could be normal is what I need. It gives me the courage to ask my big question.

"Hey, Tom?"

Hannah's gaze snaps to me. She's probably surprised to hear me call him that. I shrug and give her a half smile before returning my attention to her dad.

"Yessss?" He drags out the word teasingly, knowing I'm having fun with his name, but also perhaps suspecting I'm going to hit him up for help with something. He's not wrong. And what I'm about to ask? It's a big deal. From a guy like me to a guy like him.

"You think Hannah, Tommy, and I could borrow your truck for a little road trip to Vegas along with my mechanic Virgil when he gets to town?"

I'm not surprised when his first reaction is to laugh out loud. But after several seconds of me not letting him off the hook, his hands still where they press a square patch of gauze to my wound. His head pops up, and I can tell by the way his eyes pull in that he realizes I'm dead serious. He also knows that after that big speech, he can't say no. I may not know the details of his burning confession, but I'm savvy enough to get that Hannah's dad feels guilty about a lot of things having to do with me. Maybe it makes me a jerk, but I need a better vehicle to make that drive to Vegas. One that can comfortably hold the four of us and some luggage.

He's about to say yes.

"This have something to do with this grand plan of yours to fix things for Amanda? This about the Straights?"

He's no dummy.

I tilt my head and lift a shoulder, pulling my bottom lip up over the top to let him know he's in the ballpark. He studies me while his hands go back to work rolling gauze around my toe and foot. At this rate, I'll be in a full body cast by next week. I really hope that thought isn't prophetic.

"You the only one driving it?" He lifts a brow.

"Yes, sir."

"Hey!" Hannah protests. Her dad waves his hand and chews at the inside of his mouth, keeping his focus on me.

"Honey, I love you, but you've taken off that passenger mirror twice now," he says. I smirk and Hannah not-so-playfully punches my arm.

I rub it and hold my breath while Tom looks down at my foot to finish his treatment of my injury, tearing off the roll of gauze and clamping the end down with a small metal fastener.

"She doesn't go over eighty. And you scrape the bugs off and give her a nice hand wash when you get back."

I smile and nod when he looks up, accepting his verbal contract.

"When you going?"

"As soon as Virgil gets here with my race truck," I say, news that sparks a glimmer in Tom's eyes. "Maybe I leave those keys behind in case you need to take it somewhere?"

He simpers then leans back rubbing his hands together, no doubt already imagining the donuts he's bound to do out in the desert. Finally leaning forward, he holds out his hand and we shake.

"She's yours."

Hannah squeals at the news, and I'm not sure whether she's excited about Vegas, a road trip with me, or both. But I note the subtle clue her dad just said there, and I'm kinda glad she missed it. He's giving me his blessing to try again, to try to win Hannah's heart completely. And he can say she's mine all he wants, but that doesn't mean a damn thing until she declares it herself.

My brother is still pissed that he was the last to know Dustin's big news. It's all he griped about during the three-hour drive to Vegas. Thank God for hot strippers and showgirls, because he seems to have moved on from chirping about it now that we're on the strip and his eyes are being assaulted by flesh.

"Maybe I'll get a job here. My parents would love that," Bailey says, picking up a card from the sidewalk with a topless woman pictured on one side. She flips it over as if she's really reading the phone number and considering giving this place a call.

"I'm pretty sure they would hire a hitman and take me out of your life for good," I joke, knocking the card from her hand and back to the ground. I loop our arms together and hold my friend close as we all make our way into one of the casinos.

I begged Dustin to let Bailey join us for the trip. She and I haven't had a lot of time together since the whirlwind of getting home and Dustin crashing back into my life. I can tell she's off, too. We had talked a lot about this summer, about her maybe staying up at school and getting a job. I toyed with the idea of doing that with her, but it was the Straights that lured me back. I missed the vibe. The culture. *Dustin's ghost.*

There's a part of me that's always looked for him out there, and it's why I picked coming home over cutting the ties a little more and trying full independence. I'm ready for it, to be my own woman without my parents' input. But Amanda Judge is running for mayor. Again. And "family is family, and we support each other" *blah blah blah.* My dad's rah-rah speech has grown truly tiresome. I quit pointing out that nobody seems to support my desire to study art. All I get is the polished line "art is more of a hobby; you don't need to go to school for that." I don't even paint for fun anymore. I have a useless portfolio of work buried in one of the boxes I brought home from college. My parents and their weird penchant for practical life goals ruined it.

Practical. As if there is anything practical about me graduating in a year or two and then going to work at some hedge fund, or in human resources at some company, or whatever the fuck it is I'm supposed to do with a business degree. I have the distinct feeling I will be fetching coffee. *How inspiring.*

The five of us pile through a huge set of heavy glass doors. Virgil holds one side open and insists Bailey and I enter after him. I like Virgil. I'm not sure he appreciated being stuffed in the back seat of my dad's truck with two college girls and their playlists blasting through the speakers, but he took it like a champ. He's got this gentleman quality about him, and I can see why Dustin trusts him. Too bad Virgil couldn't have been Dustin's father. I guess

Dustin wouldn't have been Dustin then, and I like him as he is. I like him a lot.

"You guys hang here and I'll check with the concierge, see if Alex is here yet."

Dustin keeps rolling then unrolling his sleeves. I can tell he's nervous, but I have faith in him. I know Alex does too. They have history on the track, back to our high school days. He's one of the very few who never treated Dustin like he was some punk kid. He's far from a kid. Always has been, really, but looking at him now—he's so mature. He put on a black button down in the truck when we pulled into the garage. It looks nice on him, fitted to his chest, the top button open, the silver chain he's worn since he was a high school freshman reflected in the casino lights. My parents bought him that chain, and I remember feeling embarrassed that it wasn't gold; it was silver—*cheaper.* But Dustin loved it instantly. He's grown up with it and grown *into* it. "Silver," he always said, "is faster. Like a bullet."

It's crazy how such a tiny outfit change can shift an appearance. It's the same black jeans, the same skate shoes. Even his hair is the same. But those arms, that chest, his waist and hips, his jaw—*his lips.* Maybe I'm intoxicated by the lure of Vegas as a twenty-one-old. The last time I was here I used a fake ID, and Bailey was too scared to cut loose. Perhaps I'm looking forward to a night at the clubs, dancing with Dustin's eyes on me. I'm flirting with danger, but my body is drunk on allure.

"Better pick your chin up before you drool on the floor," Bailey teases at my ear.

I glare at her, but I know my cheeks are red from getting caught. My skin burns when I'm embarrassed.

"Doesn't he seem, I don't know, *older* to you? Like, gah! Sexy older?" I fidget with the small metal tag hanging from my chain, pressing my thumb into the Latin stamped on the surface—Semper Fidelis. *Always faithful.* I bought this for my eighteenth birthday. I liked the sentiment, and on some level, I liked that it made me feel superior to Dustin. It let me be angry at him for *not* being faithful. For leaving. But standing here now, seeing the man he's become, the effort he is putting into a really crazy plan to create something for a town that's never been very nice to him, I realize what perhaps drew me to this charm in the first place.

Always faithful.

Maybe this is what that looks like.

"You forget, Hannah," Bailey says at my side, bringing me back to the present. I turn my head to meet her eyes and concentrate on her cunning smile. "You've grown up a lot too."

My friend winks at me and steps away to join Tommy and Virgil on the set of chairs nestled around an ornate fountain. I linger on my brother, my friend, and the man who's become an anchor in Dustin's life for a few seconds before turning my gaze back to Dustin, to the near future playing out in my mind—when his hands are on me. Yes, I have grown up. So much.

I hardly recognize Alex when he slips out from a door behind the desk. He was always a few years older than us, but that gap seems greater now. His beard-covered face and clearly expensive suit scream of a man who has moved beyond street races and daddy's money. But I trust Dustin, that he knows what he's doing. It's clear Alex is in a position to invest. What's not clear is why he would want to.

"Guys," I say, waving the rest of our crew over as Dustin waves to me.

I feel the heat from Alex's eyes as we stroll up, and I

think Dustin does too because his hand finds mine in the space between us. I manage to mask the flinch in my reaction and play along, weaving our fingers together and letting Dustin go as far as to bring our tethered hands to his mouth to kiss the back of my hand. The gesture makes Tommy roll his eyes, but it seems to do the job in warding off Alex's unwanted attention.

"Welcome, welcome!" Alex stretches his arms wide, then greets each of us with a handshake or a kiss on our cheeks for Bailey and me. His breath is warm, tainted with expensive cigar and whiskey, and something about him feels predatory. My eyes meet Bailey's and I catch the small flash she gives me, lifting her lids in warning. She feels it, too.

"I've reserved a table for us for seven. And I have your rooms in the tower. We can talk business over drinks and dinner, but I'm sure you all are tired from the drive. I mean, except this guy, right?" Alex slaps Dustin's chest with a heavy hand, his palm stretching across his heart in a possessive, dominant way. Dustin's jaw ticks, but he forces his tight lips to smile through it.

"Actually, I'm pretty tired of weaving through hungry gamblers," he says, cracking a wider smile. Alex plays along, laughing. Still, this all feels scripted, as if there are things *not* being said.

"Do you need help with your things? Hannah?" Alex's attention turns to me and I instinctively squeeze Dustin's hand, relieved he's still holding on to me.

"We've got it. Thanks," Dustin answers for me. He puts his hand on Alex's shoulder, fingers wide as he pats with that same show of strength Alex used. The testosterone fumigating the air around me is toxic.

"Excellent," Alex says, playing out a mini stare-off with

Dustin that ends in the both of them chuckling. It's less humorous when you're the prize of some male pissing match.

"Are those our keys?" I say, nodding toward the five separate cards laid out on the concierge desk. Alex glances over his shoulder.

"Yes." Before he can reach to take control over them, no doubt taking pleasure in doling them out to us—to me—I grab the two on top and unravel Dustin's hand from mine, replacing it with Bailey's.

"Great. We're going to freshen up," I say, pulling my friend from what feels like seconds away from becoming a sword fight. I'm glad Tommy doesn't pipe up. He's less nuanced than Dustin, and would kill any possibility of convincing Alex to invest in Dustin's idea. As it is, I'm not so sure I like the idea of Alex being involved.

Bailey and I escape to the elevator with our small travel bags, and when the doors close without anyone following us, I let out the breath I've been holding and sink against the mirrored surface.

"That Alex guy is intense," she says, pressing the twenti-eth-floor button then falling into the opposite corner and kicking the heels from her feet. Both of us got a little excited about coming to Vegas and maybe didn't dress car-ride comfortable. My feet are killing me. I'd kick my heels off too if the straps didn't wrap around my legs four times.

"Be careful." Bailey's quiet warning draws my gaze to hers in a snap. I blink a few times through our stare. We're barely into our elevator ride and she hits me with the first lecture of the trip. It's coming from a good place. And she's not wrong. I just don't want to hear it right now.

"I'm being careful," I say. *Am I?* A closetful of clothes, and I wore black shorts with a deep red halter top and strappy heels. I can't even say I just threw my hair up in this messy bun because the truth is I re-messy-bunned my hair seven times before I was satisfied with how the loose hairs fell around my temple and neck.

"I don't want to see you get hurt."

I nod at her explanation and smile with tight lips. My chest is literally caving in on itself with the growing want I have for Dustin. Physical, for sure. But deeper than that. I want to be his anchor again, to not miss any of the moments coming for him. As he's turned to me over the last few days, it's been so natural. Our partnership syncs, and I love being the person he turns to. *I still love him.*

"What if I don't care if it hurts?" I can't look my friend in the eyes because I don't want to see her disappointment. I was a mess when Dustin left. Thing is, I still am. I'm a mess just having had a piece of him, and it doesn't matter how careful I am from here on out.

"I care if it hurts," she says, crossing the small space between us and taking my hand in both of hers. I offer a pitiful smile and twist my lips in my effort to hold back sappy tears. I hate crying.

The doors open and Bailey and I navigate our way to our rooms. She's across from me, which is perfect. We make plans to get ready for dinner and the club together, then retreat to our own spaces to rest. I wheel my small bag in a large circle behind me as I take in the expanse of my room. I've never lived anywhere alone, and even though my friends are all just a room away, it's still striking to have this much space all to myself.

The entire wall is glass that overlooks the strip and the mountains beyond. It's not yet evening, so the air is dusty and the busy world twenty stories below looks messy and cluttered. The sun is starting to light the mountains, though, a crisp orange line detailing the jagged edges. By sunset, this scene is going to be spectacular. If I were a better friend, I'd trade Bailey so she could see it. I'm pretty sure she's looking at the airport.

I lift my bag and set it on the couch across from the enormous king bed. A copper-colored rug fills the center of the room, a table under a chandelier set perfectly in the middle. A bouquet of fresh flowers in a vase with orange-colored marbles arranged in the water draws me in to smell. They must change these every day. The money in this place is insane. Every detail oozes luxury, and not the fake kind like the bag of knock-off designer dresses I brought for the club scene tonight. Things in this room are legit.

My fingertips run across the billowy satin bedding on my way to the sliding glass panel that leads to the balcony. Warm air embraces my arms and chest as I slip through the door and step out into the open sky. I breathe in the desert and close my eyes as I grip the railing. Lifting my chin to the sky and closing my eyes, I tug my hair free from my hardly effortless bun and shake it into loose waves down my back.

I've grown up, too.

"You've got some fantasy brewing in your head right now," Dustin says.

I don't even realize I'm smiling until he calls me on it. I wonder if my body knew he was near. I open my eyes and let my smile grow before dropping my chin and meeting his gaze. Our balconies connect. How . . . convenient.

"You plan this?" I glare at him with playful suspicion.

He holds up a key card.

"It was the last one left after Virgil and Tommy grabbed

theirs. They're down the hall, corner rooms. I bet their views—"

"Aren't anything like ours," I fill in for him, my insinuation clear by the way my eyes rake down his chest. I blush at my overt flirtation, but I'm not sorry I said it.

"Han, this trip. These guys?" He grimaces for a moment, seemingly trying to work out his words, before shaking his head and looking down. His hands slip into his pockets, his body closing off.

"It's business. I get it," I wave him off. I feel stupid for hoping for more, but maybe a little relieved that I won't disappoint Bailey. It used to be so easy to draw him in and push his buttons. I felt his desire, and maybe it was because the idea of us seemed so forbidden when we were teens. It's still forbidden, but for entirely different reasons now. And he's grown more disciplined.

"I should shower so I can get ready for later," I say, making my way toward my glass door. Dustin hasn't moved.

"Hannah . . ."

"Dustin, it's fine," I say, beaming my best smile over my shoulder. Our eyes lock and I know he can see right through my façade. My ego is bruised, and I hate that I feel it.

"I want to get this right," he says, his head tilting a little to the side. I imagine my hand running up his jaw, but only for a second.

"I know you do. I'll see you for dinner." I shut the glass behind me and draw the curtains before I sit on the end of the softest bed I've ever seen and fucking cry. I let it all out —the irrational thoughts, the memories, the fantasies, and more—and then I seal it up and promise I won't ever let him see me do that. Nobody will. Not ever again.

13

I should get a different room.

I've marinated on that thought since Hannah stepped back into her room, which is on the other side of this wall, a room I could be in after taking a dozen steps. Yet here I remain, on the end of my bed, feet on the floor, hands clasped and elbows on knees as if I'm waiting for someone to come get a different room for me. I can think it as many times as I want—*or don't want*—and it's not going to change the fact there is no way in hell I am getting a different room.

Temptation is the devil, but better to know where it is, right? I laugh out loud and lower my head, pushing my hands into my hair. I took the coldest shower of my life an hour ago and I'm still searing from my one minute alone with Hannah on the balcony. Red suits her. Any color, really, but something about that blood red shirt against her bronzed skin, the light sheen of sweat on her sun-kissed arms and chest. The swell of her breasts. The stud in her belly button. The curves from her hips to her calves.

"Fuck," I grumble.

My phone vibrates on the bed next to me and I flip it over to read the text from Tommy.

TOMMY: *Dinner's comped, right?*

I breathe out a laugh and rub my palm over my eye before typing back a shrugging emoji. Of course it's comped, but I like that I can still fuck with my friend. Some things you don't outgrow.

Knowing he'll stew about this and march down the hall to my room in seconds, I stand and roll up the sleeves of my shirt, then tuck the hem into my pants. I have one nice semi-suit and I packed it in a roll in a backpack. I left the jacket because my arms don't fit anymore, but the shirt and pants still look nice. I was supposed to take Hannah to prom in this outfit—black dress pants and a crisp white shirt. The fit is a little tighter than when I was almost eighteen, but I think this suit was always meant for a man anyhow. I got it on clearance.

It's hard to look the part when I'm with Alex. Anything he owns is about a thousand percent more expensive than everything I own added together. I do a decent job of faking it, though. I clasp the watch my uncle gave me on my wrist. It's a vintage Rolex, and it hasn't kept time since the seventies, but who checks to see if a watch is ticking? I rip one of the cologne ads from the magazine left on the night table and rub it against my wrist and the side of my neck. The only thing I'm missing is a solid stack of cash to roll up in my money clip. The few hundreds I have left will have to do if any bets are made tonight.

I'm hoping we can get right to business. The longer I'm in that place, the more I'm going to want to pound a few Jack and Cokes. A week totally sober is not a very long time, and I only halfway committed to veering off the bad path I was on until I saw Colt's trailer and the mess he left behind. I don't want to become that—*become him.*

I slip my room key in my pocket and take a deep breath, then head into the hall. I beat Tommy's knock on my door by about half a second. I lay my hand on his chest as his mouth opens and I hold a finger up to stop him.

"Of course it's comped," I say.

He grimaces and shakes his head.

"Asshole," he spits out, tossing my hand from his body.

I laugh, loving that I can still get under his skin like old times, when my breath is literally ripped from my body and all sound and time halts.

Her dress is red, gathered in these touchable strips around her breasts and hips, skin exposed at her back and her sides. Her hair is straight and silky, and the ends flirt with the peaks of her breasts in the front and the small of her back as she turns after checking the handle on her door. *And...* Tommy is staring at me.

"You legit never change, do you?" He furrows his brow and shakes his head, but for some reason doesn't punch me.

"What's that?" Hannah steps closer to us. While her brother stews I laugh through my crooked, very guilty smile.

"I was checking you out and Tommy wants to kill me for it. Same story, different age." I shrug, accepting that I'm going to have to let myself admire her at the very least.

"Well you can look, but ..." She mouths the rest. *You can't touch.*

There's a devious flicker in her eyes and a slight snarl to her candy red smirk. She's still angry about the balcony. Good. It's easier if she's angry. When she's forward with me, I'm a weak-ass puppy.

Hannah knocks at Bailey's door just as Virgil ambles down the hallway to join us in his Stetson hat, formal jeans, and black vest. Born and raised in Oklahoma, Virgil has two sides to his story—mediocre mechanic and mediocre cowboy. He dresses both parts well, and this is about as fancy as I've ever seen him.

"You on the prowl or something?" Tommy teases him.

Virgil gives him a wink and tips his hat as Bailey exits her room to join us, wearing the blue version of Hannah's dress. Tommy chokes a little when he sees her and I tuck that fact away for later, grinning to myself as I lead our crew down the hall.

Virgil didn't really want to come out with us tonight. He's not much of a club-scene kinda guy. He's widowed; his wife was his high school sweetheart and she died in a car crash. When he's not in the garage with me, he's at home watching sports and eating TV dinners. I don't begrudge him his existence. I get it. Add in drinking alone and I was exactly the same my first couple of years in Oklahoma. Virgil has a way of keeping me out of trouble, though. Again, there's surely some father issues at play here. It's why he was all right tagging along to Vegas. It's why I need him at my side while I talk to Alex tonight. And it's what will keep my glass filled with water instead of whiskey.

We pile into the elevator and use a special key to take it to the top floor where Alex owns a club. The music possesses my internal organs the second the doors open, and my heart syncs with the rhythm. We weave through the throng of bodies, past the bar, and into the more secluded back area shielded by tinted glass walls. Alex and his partners are already several glasses deep into the night at a large round velvet booth, and when he spots me, he stands on the seat and opens his arms wide, shouting my name.

"Dustin Bridges, you motherfucker! Get your ass in here." He hops over the back of the booth and I paste on my best smile. Meanwhile, my insides twist with the force of someone ringing out a mop. We pat each other's backs through our bro-hug, then Alex motions for his friends to slide around the curve of the booth to make room for us. Virgil and Tommy drag over a couple of chairs to sit at the open end of the table.

"Ladies, you are lovely tonight. What are you drinking?"

"We're all good," I say, waving my hand. *Assuming. Yeah . . . ass . . . me.*

"Suit yourself, bro. I'd like whatever's on tap," Tommy says. I shouldn't answer for everyone, but damn, I wish we could all just be sober tonight.

Alex holds up his hand and snaps a few times, calling over one of the servers. He orders Tommy's beer and one for Virgil, along with several plates of hors d'oeuvres and a round of some drink named after him. I'm sure it's mostly vodka. *Fuck.*

"Listen, Alex . . ." I do my best to get right to business, but before I can, he slides over a fat stack of papers, all bound together with a binder clip with his club's logo.

I flatten my palm on it and slide it toward me, but meet his gaze.

"What's this?" My heart is racing. I've never heard of a business deal getting messy with Alex, but I'm savvy enough to realize there are things he keeps out of the public's eyes and ears. His entire family does.

"Dustin, you doubt yourself too much. I know what you're capable of, and if it's something you're behind, I'm in. It's a contract to be partners in this . . . this . . . track thing you proposed over the phone. I had my lawyer dig into it and get the ball rolling. It's a good idea, lots of potential. And who knows, maybe there will be one here in Vegas someday."

The waiter delivers a tray of drinks just as Alex finishes, and I'm too stunned to move. He winks at me and chuckles, then passes me a drink. I take it, but don't bring it to my lips.

"Now, relax tonight. Enjoy yourself. Enjoy . . . the view," he says, letting his eyes rake over Hannah. I set my drink down and push it a safe distance away.

"Mind if I have my lawyer look this over too?" I hand the contract to Virgil, though it's probably pretty obvious to every person in this room that he isn't a lawyer. His combover is on point tonight, though. As are his Wranglers.

Alex's head falls back in a laugh but he brings it back up and steps out of the booth, holding his glass in the air. "You review whatever you like. Send me the signed version and we'll get started. Now, drink!" He downs his drink in one smooth gulp, as does Tommy. The girls sip at theirs, and I roll the stem of the glass in my fingers before taking a modest sip.

The burn is good. It's been a week since I've tasted it. I can feel the alcohol's claws working down my tongue, warming my body and fueling my desire for more. I put the glass down and push it a safe distance away, enough to make it an awkward reach but not so far that it's an insult to Alex.

I should be happy. I should be thrilled, relieved—ready to celebrate. But all I can think about is the way his eyes lit up when they drank in my girl.

My girl. She's not my girl, and that's the problem.

Conversation picks up and for the next hour, I find myself dipping in and out of the various pockets, trying to talk about my race prep with Alex's guys but losing focus halfway through. I reminisce a few times with Tommy, Bailey, and Hannah, but swapping stories only makes me think about the past, the one I left and the massive chunk I missed out on.

Virgil's probably going to head up to his room in twenty minutes now that he's nursed two beers, and if I had any sense, I'd go with him. But sense has never led me to what I want. And what I want? It's now grinding against Alex Offerman out on the dance floor.

"You okay with that?" I say, elbowing Tommy. My mouth waters, wanting a drink. I wave down the waiter and ask for a water.

"Nope." Tommy's eyes have not left his sister since she went out there to dance and Alex followed. If it weren't risky to my deal, I'm pretty sure he'd tear through the crowd and choke the man out on the floor with the weight of his body.

"Go on. Get her out of that," he says, his eyes meandering to me and rolling briefly.

A smile touches the corner of my lips.

"Don't get cocky and think this means I'm all right with you and her starting up whatever the fuck you do again. I'm just a lot more all right with that than I am with this fucking shit show." He waves his hand out toward the dance floor.

"Bailey looks like she could use a rescue, too," I say, taking the water the waiter just dropped off and swallowing it in one gulp. I step out from the booth and meet Tommy's eyes. He gives me a middle finger and I laugh.

"What? You're saying you *don't* have the hots for your sister's best friend?"

"Fuck off. That's your thing, Bridges." He sinks back into the banquette, stretching his arms along the back and returning his glare to Alex and Hannah. I leave him be, but give him one last chuckle before I go to get further under his skin.

When I turn my focus to Alex and Hannah, it becomes all I see.

She's always been a temptress when she dances. We messed around dancing a few times in high school, but I never got to move with her the way I wanted. The fact Alex is indulging in some of those movements right now has my blood boiling. I hook my thumbs in my pockets and make my way through the bodies around them. Alex smirks as I step up, and I know he's not looking to fight. As much as I love to mess with Tommy, he loves fucking with me about a million times more. He always has. It started out on the Straights when he put Hannah in the car with me. He knows my weakness, and while I hate that he does, I won't deny it. I would do anything for her. Even walk away when I don't want to. But right now? I'm staying right the fuck here.

"Mind?" I step between them and lift a brow to Alex. Quiet laughter shakes his chest and he runs his palm through his beard. He eyes me for a few seconds, his body still moving with the heavy thumps vibrating the club.

"Yeah, all right," he says, leaving his eyes on me as he steps forward and kisses Hannah's cheek. I could crack a molar I'm biting down so hard.

I don't wait for him to fully pull away before I slide my hand across her midsection, letting my fingers possessively scratch at her bare skin, then the crisscross of fabric above her navel. She turns under my hold and flattens her back against my chest before arching it and laying her head back on my shoulder. She lifts her chin toward my ear and I wrap my other arm around her, both of us swaying to the beat.

"I thought this was a business trip," she hums at my ear.

"Ah, yes. About that." I inhale her scent. She smells of fresh fruit and honey, like a dessert I want to devour, and I'm no longer able to be shy about that. I bend my head lower, pressing my lips against the crook of her neck, allowing myself a single taste. The alcohol I was able to refuse, but Hannah is a different type of addiction. She's embedded in my soul. My fingers are on fire where they meet her skin.

"I lied." I breathe those two words against her ear and she melts into me.

All of my innocent intentions disappeared the moment I saw her in that dress. We roll together as I inch us to the center of the room, cloaking us in an endless sea of bodies all grinding and filling the air with lust. Hannah reaches up, her hands twisting in my hair as she leans into me, her fingers dusting against my neck as she draws out the hungry beast inside me. I run the backs of my fingers up her sides, skimming the curves of her breasts until I make my way to her arms and hands. Our fingers twine and she moves my hold back down her body to her hips. On the beat, she bends down, her ass barely concealed by the bottom of her dress as it presses against my aching cock. I grip her hips and hold her to me tight as her body forms a wave. She glances at me over her shoulder, her hair sticking to her skin, her teeth playfully gripping her bottom lip.

Unable to wait, I turn her so she's facing me and hold

her wrists against my chest as our bodies continue to move. Her eyes are fixed on our hands, her lids heavy, lashes dark. The faint sprinkle of freckles that I've memorized on her nose glistens under the soft powder on her face. She doesn't need any of this, but I love how powerful it seems to make her feel. Hannah is beautiful in all ways. A vixen no matter what she wears. My beginning and end whether she's in a pair of sweatpants or a red dress in the middle of one of Vegas's hottest clubs.

I let go of her hands to touch her face, but she leaves them clutched to my shirt, her thumbs flirting with the button and my bare chest underneath. I smooth away the stray hairs interrupting my view of her eyes, then lift her chin with my fingertips until she blinks her gaze onto mine.

"You have to know how sorry I am," I say. She falters a step, so I move my hand to the small of her back to hold her steady. "About all of it. I wish he wasn't my dad. I wish it wasn't dangerous. I wish I had stayed even though I couldn't. Your birthdays. I missed four of your birthdays. I'm sorry for that."

She sucks in her lips and her eyes glaze over, reflecting the myriad lights glowing, beating, flashing around us. The music mutes in my ears. All I hear is her. I hear her breath, the way it catches when our eyes flit away and reconnect. I hear her heartbeat, feel it in her body as it sinks into mine. I hear our past, our pain, our future.

I take her hand in mine and turn her wrist, pressing my lips on the small tattoo that Bailey helped me understand. I close my eyes and whisper "I'm sorry" against her skin, against the word painted on her body as a mantra.

Her fingers inch up my jaw, caressing my unshaven face, moving into my hair as her eyes search mine, her lips stunned and the damage I left behind too much for her to power her words through. I know she feels it though. This palpable feeling between us is undeniable. It always is. Always has been.

She lifts up on her toes and pulls my head down until our lips meet, and the second they do, everything over the last four years fades into the distance and we are undone. I clutch her back, holding her to me, dipping her with the beat and pulling her leg up against my hip. My cock pulses against her heat, and her teeth grip my bottom lip. She breaks our kiss but doesn't pull away completely, just enough to make room to speak. Then she calls the shots in a whisper against my lips.

"Balcony," she says. "Now."

And I obey.

14

I 'm disappointed when the elevator isn't empty, but not so much that I'm willing to wait for another one.

Dustin grips my hand and leads me to the back of the small space filled with intoxicated frat boys and what looks like a group of women out for a bachelorette party. This elevator smells of the potent mixture of perfume and too-heavy-cologne, and a whole lot of Vegas, but I swear my senses are locked in on Dustin's scent. His cologne is light, but that's not the fragrance that infects me. Underneath it all, my body has found that faint note of oil, the burnt tenor of rubber, the sweetness of his sweat, and the fresh cover of his shampoo. It's a recipe that is entirely and uniquely him, and my God, have I missed it.

The trip to our floor is slow, stopping on what seems to be every floor between the club level and ours. Dustin let go of my hand and moved his palm to my back, his thumb flirting with the draped deep-cut back of my dress and my bare skin underneath. With every floor we stop at, his hand grows bolder, at first teasing me just underneath the fabric, then tickling against the ribbed lace of my thong, and now hooking his thumb under the thin strip of material at the crest of my ass. He pulls it snug, and it intensifies the deep swelling between my legs to the point that I have to cross my ankles and squeeze my thighs together so I don't come undone right here.

By the time we reach our floor, only two people are left in the elevator with us, and they're too drunk to be aware of anything other than what is right in front of them. Before the doors open and we step past them, Dustin slips his hand down my dress completely, his palm cupping my ass and squeezing hard—*not hard enough*. I pant out a faint cry and bite my lip quickly, desperate to be alone with him.

Once in the hallway, Dustin turns to walk backward and untucks his white shirt from his pants as he saunters. It's the sexiest fucking thing I have ever seen, exactly as I've imagined so many times. I catch up to him and grab the ends of his shirt in my fists and let my bottom lip slip from the grip of my teeth as I look up into his hooded eyes. His sinister smile taunts me, as does every backward step he takes, each time barely out of reach to kiss him like I want. Unable to stand it, I rush at him and slide my hands up his chest and around his neck, and trust he will catch me when I leap at him.

He does, swinging me as my legs wrap around his waist. I giggle, my head hung back as the glorious sound of his husky laughter floats across my throat before his mouth tastes its way up my jaw. When I bring my head up, that same intoxicating smile is waiting, along with eyes that zero in on my lips. His tongue peeks out from his teeth, and he bites the tip of it as he smiles and shakes his head at me.

"What?" *I know what.*

He doesn't answer until we reach our doors and he lets me slide down his body. I leave my hands against his hard ab muscles as my pinkies flirt with the waistband of his pants. His back falls against my door and his hands run up my arms to my shoulders, hovering along the thin satin strap that holds my dress up on each side. He slides the right strap down my arm, his gaze focused on his small, steady movement. His thumb caresses the curve of my shoulder before his eyes flit to the tight space between us where my hands are slowly inching down, the tips of my fingers clawing at the V that leads to his hardness.

"It's like a dream." His eyes seem lost to the moment, his smile faint but forever present.

"What is?" My eyes flit up to meet his before I close them and let my head fall to his chest, my lips pressing in the very center. My fingers curl against his tight skin, and a ragged breath precedes his hard swallow. His head falls back against the door.

"Here, with you. Touching you, and getting to say things I've wanted to say. I didn't think . . . I never. . ."

I step up on my toes and press my mouth to his before he can say more or too much, the kiss soft and chaste as he suckles my upper lip. My mouth escapes his grip with the stretch of my smile, one I let spread the width of my cheeks. I show my joy, allowing him to see behind the walls I worked so hard to build and maintain. I choose to be vulnerable, right now, here with him. This isn't the kind of careful Bailey warned me to be, but it's honest and it's inevitable. I have to honor my heart.

"I never thought we'd get our time either." My eyes blink slowly as I look up at him, his hands traveling back up the curve of my neck and to my jaw so he can cradle my face. I've missed his hazel eyes, the way they bewilder up close, never quite blue and never quite green. I fall into them now. I fall into him.

I reach into my dress, into the red strapless bra where I tucked the small key card for my room, and press it against the reader on the door. It beeps and Dustin pushes down the handle, swinging open the door into my room. I run my hand along his body, from his stomach to his chest, then along the length of his arm as I step inside. My fingers catch on his and I tug, urging him to follow. The door clicks shut behind us and now it's my turn to walk backward.

"You mentioned . . . *the balcony,*" he says, his voice deep and mouth hung open after speaking.

"I did." I take another step away from him and slip the left strap from my shoulder. He hovers near the entrance, sinking his hands into his pockets as his head tilts slightly. His lip ticks up on one side, and for a moment, I glimpse the boy I once seduced in my parents' kitchen when nobody was looking.

"I'll meet you out there," he says as I reach behind my back to find the zipper. I lower my chin and raise a brow.

"You don't want to be late for this," I tease.

"Oh, Han. I'm not late, sweetheart. I'm right on time for the show." He rolls his shoulders and widens his stance, his hands still casually slung in his pockets as he watches me work the zipper down my spine in the center of my hotel room. He seems emboldened, almost arrogant, and it's so damn sexy.

"Never pegged you for a watcher," I say, my body radiating heat under his stare. I could come undone simply from having his eyes on me, I swear.

"I'm both. I like to see, then I like to sample."

A nervous laugh slips from my mouth at his dirty talk,

just as my dress slips from my shoulders. I hug my chest to hold it up and continue to step toward the sliding glass doors. The curtains are still drawn from earlier, but they're sheer, and with the room dim and the city bright, he'll get the picture.

I push the glass open and slip through the silky white curtains. Dustin shifts his feet and lifts his chin, but remains where he is, still watching. I wonder how experienced he expects me to be. This part of the dance, the seduction? I've mastered this. And for the other guys I've dated—*briefly*—it's only ever gotten about this far. I've never been able to allow someone else in completely, to trust them with my heart and my body. In my mind, I convinced myself it was because I wanted to protect myself from ever getting hurt again, but now that I'm here—now that I'm opening myself up for Dustin to have, completely —I realize I wasn't guarding myself at all. I was *saving* myself. For the only person I ever wanted to have me.

My body quakes as if it's chilled, despite the warm summer breeze passing over my skin. I'm nervous, but also ready. Dustin is all I have ever wanted. And now he's here. He's here because of me. He could have left after dealing with Colt's matters, could have paid someone to simply clear out the trailer and lot, or let them keep whatever profit they could squeeze out of that place. He could have left the Straights behind, too, because based on where he's going, he's never going to need that place again. He should be in Phoenix, near the track for his first race, training and perfecting the nuances with his team. But instead, he's here, fighting to make something of our town, attempting to help my mom keep her ego intact and keep her post as mayor, and hoping I'll let him love me.

I will. *I do.*

My fingers loosen their grip on my dress enough to let it fall down my body and pool at my feet. Still balanced gracefully, somehow, on very high heels, I lift one leg behind me and unbuckle the leather strap that wraps up my calf, kicking away my shoe when it loosens. I repeat with the other, my gaze glued to Dustin's silhouette as he stands inside. He shifts his weight a few times, but still hasn't made a move to come closer.

I recede a few steps until my body meets the back of one of the outdoor chairs. In my periphery, I can see the other balconies, but I'm fairly certain we're alone on our level. At this point, I wouldn't care. I'd welcome the audience. I grip the iron frame and let myself breathe in deep for courage before stretching out my arm and curling my finger, beckoning Dustin to me. I shudder at the sight of his first step in my direction.

His hands move up the length of his shirt, unbuttoning along the way until his chest is bared. He slips his arms from the shirt and tosses it to the side while taking slow but steady paces toward the balcony. My hands squeeze the metal bars and my knees grow week. I bought this lingerie set on a whim, born out of a fantasy that someday maybe I would wear it for this man. I never actually thought I would, and until this trip, it still had the tags on it. Red silk and lace that barely covers where it should, and I'm still not a hundred percent confident that I'm in shape enough to wear it. But under his intense stare, I feel empowered enough to hold my chest up high and spread my legs as he steps through the gauzy curtains.

Dustin's measured steps make his travel the few feet between us seem to draw on forever. By the time his finger lifts my chin, I'm quivering with nerves and need. My eyes rake up the perfect lines of his chest to my initials over his heart and I nearly break seeing them, knowing they're there. He lifts my chin more and soon, our gazes lock.

"I want you." Warmth coats my body at his declaration.

"Take me," I respond, arching back a fraction and exposing my neck as my eyes close. He bends and softly kisses my throat, leaving behind the coolness from his tongue. His fingertips glide from my jaw to my collarbone, then stop at the tight line where my bra binds my breasts.

"I like this," he says, letting his thumb graze over the gathered satin.

"I picked it for you," I admit, my eyes fluttering closed as his thumb brushes over the hard peak of my breast underneath. I arch more, wanting him to touch me there again.

"And nobody else?"

I swallow, knowing the meaning behind his question. My lips quiver, my fear of getting hurt echoing in the depths of my head. I push that voice away, mute it if not erase it, and shake my head slowly as I let my eyes open on his.

"Nobody." I lift my chin with pride, not expecting the same from him but hoping still. Our breathing grows heavy, chests rising with thick draws of air, in and out, while our eyes meet in silent communication. I can see in his that he can't offer me the same gift, the same purity of experience, but I never expected him to. I know what he and my brother did in high school. I wasn't ever going to be his first, but I wanted to be his last. I still can.

Guilt is tearing at his insides, and it draws his eyes low, pulling at the corners of his mouth, but I refuse to let the last four years of our lives take any more from us. This time—this *now*—is ours.

"Dustin," I whisper his name, calling his gaze back to

mine. His eyes make the slow trip up my body. I lick my lips when he reaches my face.

"Have me. All of me. *Please?*" My voice breaks with part emotion and part need.

"You are the only thing that has ever mattered," he says, and I know he means it. I'm what makes him fight to be good. He isn't Colt, and I'm aware of the part I played in his life that kept him from following darker paths. I'm also not naïve to the pull those temptations probably had on him when we were apart. What matters is our now, and our days ahead.

"Show me," I beg.

His lids grow heavier and his hands bolder as he returns his attention to my lace-covered breasts. My nipples are so hard that the floral pattern scratches against them as I breathe. The abrasive sensation makes my breath shudder, which seems to bolster Dustin's touch, his fists forming around the material at both sides, gathering it and rolling it down to my midriff.

I've always felt my tits were too small to be sexy, but under his attentive stare, I feel like a femme fatale. Dustin's hands slip down the sides of my body to my waist, and he lifts me enough that I'm sitting on the back of the massive chair. Without pause, his mouth covers my right breast, his tongue swirling circles around my nipple until he sucks it in so hard it becomes instantly raw. It throbs at the feel of the warm air when he lets go, his attention now on the other one.

His hand slides behind my back, allowing me to arch more, allowing him to take more of my breast in his mouth. I can't get enough of the release he gives me with each suckle and graze of his teeth, and eventually he bites down, just enough to pull my pale pink skin toward him.

"Ah." I whimper, my hands letting go of the chair back and reaching forward to the button of his pants.

He steps in closer, my thighs widening, then closing in tight around his hips. I yank his button free and rip down the zipper, his mouth never once leaving my skin as he devours me from neck to breasts and back again. If it weren't for his strong hold around me, I would fall over onto the chair.

My hands wrap around the band of his boxers and I lift myself enough to be even with him, but still having to look up to see his face. His mouth moves to mine, his kiss ragged and hungry as one hand remains firm behind my back while the other cradles my jaw. I slip his pants and boxers down his hips, the tip of his cock peeking out under my touch. I run my thumbs over the ridged skin and he trembles under my power. I can't help but smile, proud of my effect on him.

"Not fair," he whispers against my mouth.

I'm about to quietly laugh, feeling superior and completely in charge, when his hand leaves my face and soon his knuckles graze the small strip of satin between my legs. I shudder in response and squeeze my thighs around him. Now, he's the one smiling.

"Are we even now?" I say, opening my eyes to see his hot gaze staring down at me. He presses his entire hand against my wet center and I erupt immediately, my hand automatically flying to cover his, to keep his pressure sweet and hard as my swollen sex spasms over and over again. I have never had one of these that I did not give to myself.

Dustin bends down enough to bring his mouth to my ear.

"Not even close," he whispers against me, and in the

next breath his hand has tugged my thong to the side and his finger has sunk into me.

"Oh . . . oh, God," I gasp out in a meager voice, my breath failing me. His hand moves against me, his finger sliding in and out. My hips feel the urge to rock with him, and eventually, I can't help it and they do. My hands return to his pants, to his hot length that is now almost completely exposed. My hand grips his width and he flexes under my touch. The sensation causes him to press his finger into me deeper, adding a second and stretching me wider. It burns, yet I crave it.

"You're so fucking wet." His forehead presses into mine, his eyes squeezed shut and his jaw rigid with self-control that is hanging on by a thread.

I'm overcome with a desire to wrap my mouth around him, to taste him and bring him to his knees, so I slide myself forward enough that my feet find the ground and his hand falls away from my center. Before he can refuse, I kneel in front of him, dragging his pants down the rest of the way as my lips wrap around the tip of his cock.

"Oh, fuck. Hannah," he groans.

"You better," I tease, before taking more of him in my mouth. His hands fall into my hair, twining strands around his fingers but never pressuring me to move more than I already am. I coat him with my kisses, caress him with my tongue and suck as I reach his tip, driving him to near breaking points before slowing down and lightly kissing his sensitive skin.

Unable to take it anymore, he lifts my chin and coaxes me to stand. He steps away from his clothes, plucking a condom from his pocket, then walks me backward toward the railing. We're on display now. There's no doubt someone isn't seeing this, and my body aches at that notion. Dustin tears the package open with his teeth and rolls the condom on as I lean back against the rail.

"I'll be gentle," he says when our eyes meet. And though the part of me that's on fire wants to tell him "don't," the nervous girl inside who has never done this before knows better, so I nod.

Dustin slowly rolls my thong down my hips, slipping it past my calves and tossing it to the side when it hits the ground. His fingers trail up the inside of my leg as he stands, stopping against my swollen center. He presses the most sensitive area with his thumb, rubbing circles against my slick skin before sliding his fingers inside me a few more times. Eventually, he steps in close, holding himself in one hand while his fingers still work me with the other. I hold my breath as he guides himself to my entrance, and with one thrust, his fingers are replaced with his cock.

My teeth bite down on his bare shoulder, his skin salty with sweat. My hair clings to my body, and he slides it from my neck as he suckles my skin.

"Is this okay?" he asks.

I nod, my mouth still muffled against his body. He moves into me more and my body stretches, the burn more intense than before, but the reward as gratifying. While Dustin pulls out, my breath returns, and as he pushes in again, I whimper. His hands move to my face and he lifts my chin until our eyes meet, but I nod before he can ask. *Yes, I'm okay. Yes, I want this. Don't stop.*

I lick my lips and he moves his hips again, this time my hands roaming to his hips. My body leans back, still safe against the high railing, as Dustin bends his knees enough to slide into me completely, his length filling me more than before. Everything inside me swells, every nerve on heightened alert, my pulse beating around his swollen cock. I grow bold enough to lift my knee and as I do, Dustin reaches to my thigh and holds it against him as he continues to rock his hips.

I glance up to see a few lights flicker on and off in the various windows above. Anyone seeing this right now is seeing love. They see a young lifetime of yearning and waiting, two souls meant to finally collide. They are seeing my heart break open to let this man in, let him own me. *Again.* And as the tension builds and my body quakes under Dustin's control, four years' worth of heartbreak dissipates, washed over by passion and heat and a connection I will never have with anyone other than this man.

15

She's always been beautiful when she sleeps. Something about the *after* has made her blossom under my gaze overnight.

I didn't sleep. How was I supposed to after what we did? It's not that I feel guilty for taking something so precious from her, but rather that I feel honored. I feel responsible. I feel *chosen.*

I've loved Hannah for so long that I don't know how not to, but now—now that I know her intimately, now that I've marked her as mine—the protective nature that made me leave her in the first place makes leaving feel impossible. I hope she knows that. I hope she believes it and trusts me. I'll prove it to her, earn everything she's given me. That's what this trip to Vegas is all about.

I'm sure it seemed rude that we left the club after Alex comped us, and I'll have to smooth that over, but deep down, I also know he understands. It's why he flirts with Hannah. He likes to toy with my weakness. It's a dangerous part of his fabric, and it does make me question this partnership with him. But there isn't any other way to make things happen. Not now, at least. It would take me a decade to turn that track around and save Camp Verde's soul. I also hope it makes Hannah's mom look like a hero. She'll get full credit for the venture. I'll tell everyone it was her idea. Whatever it takes for her to see that I'm one of them, that I love her daughter, that I am committed to this family for life.

The soft knock at the door draws my attention and I roll over in the bed to see the time on my phone. It's barely nine, early by Vegas standards. I'd worry it's Tommy but I know he had more than a few beers last night, and I'm sure he found a way to spend his time. He's not waking up early for anyone. It could be Bailey, since this is Hannah's room, and that thought makes me wince a little.

When Hannah's phone buzzes from a text, I decide to check the door rather than snoop on Hannah's privacy. I have a sneaking suspicion I'll find Bailey waiting outside, staring at her phone. I slip on my pants from last night and run my hands through my hair enough to look semi presentable, though probably totally obvious, and peek through the hole on the door.

As expected, Bailey is standing outside, chewing at the inside of her mouth, her eyes moving from my door to the one in front of her. She's putting it together.

I glance over my shoulder to Hannah's body, still wrapped in expensive sheets and completely asleep. I take a deep breath and ready myself for condemnation and judgement, then crack open the door.

Bailey's eyes widen fast and her mouth forms an O. I look back over my shoulder to Hannah, then turn back to her visitor and hold up a finger, begging her to wait. I shut the door gently, search the floor for Hannah's room card key, spotting it just under the end of the bed, then snag it before slipping back into the hall where Bailey and I can talk a little more freely.

"Dustin Bridges," she says through gritted teeth. She's smirking a little so I know she's not entirely angry. She's distrustful, as all best friends should be.

I hold up my hands to plead guilty and her eyes zero in on Hannah's card key, as if she's spotted evidence. I shake my head and drop my hands into my pockets and gesture my head to the right, urging her to follow me a few steps from Hannah's door.

"I'm not gonna lie, it's totally what you think it is, but Bailey—it's Hannah." I lift my shoulders in a guilty shrug and own my stupid grin. Her eyes soften from their glare and her smile breaks through.

She points at me, her finger not quite touching me but coming close.

"If you fucking hurt her—"

"I know!" I whisper shout, holding up a scout's honor sign. She wraps her hand around it and jerks it out of the air, tossing my own hand at me.

"I mean it, Dustin. That girl just about broke completely."

I swallow at the gravity of her words.

"I know," I repeat in a croak.

An awkward silence settles in, and when Bailey looks to my waist, her cheeks redden and she looks to the side. I think she probably gets the picture that I'm not wearing anything under these pants, and these pants? They were picked up in haste from the floor.

"Let Hannah be the one to tell you, okay? She'll want to. Don't tell her you came by." I don't want to *lie* to Hannah, but I want her to be in charge of her narrative.

Bailey nods lightly, but when her eyes flash to me, I see tears are threatening to fall.

"Bails, what's wrong?" I lurch toward her but she steps back, shaking her head.

"It's nothing." I know a lie when it's told. Especially the kind trying to cover pain.

"Tell me. At least tell me what I can do." I want to hug her, but she's tightened up into a standing ball of nerves, her hands gripping her own biceps as she hugs herself tight. Her eyes blink as her gaze wanders down the hallway, the sound of someone's door opening then falling shut making her blink. Both of us wait quietly as an older man clears his throat and works his falling pants back up over his belly as he meanders toward the elevator. I hold up a hand to wave to him but he just grumbles.

"Vegas, huh?" I turn back to Bailey as her eyes shift to my gaze. She swallows hard.

"My dad's running for mayor. He's the one fighting the Straights. He wants to destroy everything, and he's just this awful, terrible person, and—"

She collapses into me and breaks down completely. My arms wrap around her protectively and I cradle her head to my chest, feeling her wet cheeks stick to my skin. Poor Bailey. My heart hurts for her.

I hold her for a few minutes, waiting out the irrational break that we all need to have sometimes, and then I hold on more as she steadies her breath. I match her inhale, coaxing her to mimic mine, and when she finally breathes out heavily, letting her lips flap, I let a tiny laugh break through.

"Feel better?" I pull back.

Her head wiggles side to side.

"Maybe?" She pauses to glance up then lowers her gaze back to mine. "Not really."

We share a quiet laugh and retreat to opposite sides of the hall, leaning against the walls and looking down at the swirled, colorful carpet.

"They probably pick designs based on what hides vomit," I say, nodding to the design.

"I think it's all meant to confuse and lead you back to the slot machines, actually," she says. I lean my head to the side and let my eyes glaze over enough to let a different picture form on the floor, one that looks like a river leading me down the hallway.

"Huh, I think you're right."

"I am."

I look up to catch her cocky smile and shrug and laugh a little louder this time.

Bailey looks so tired. I doubt she slept, and she was probably in her room waiting for Hannah. I wonder how many texts she's sent. That's why she reached out this morning, I bet. To tell Hannah about her dad, to get it off her chest. I should give them time.

"Hey," I say, leaning my head back toward Hannah's door. "Let me get my things and clear out, and I'll wake her so she texts you back."

Bailey's face goes white, and for a moment, I think she might pass out. I reach toward her and touch her arm, bringing her present. I point to my eyes and she looks into them, matching my steady breath.

"It's going to be fine. She's Hannah. You're you. You guys are necessary to one another, and she'll understand."

Bailey nods but I'm not sure she totally bought into my pep talk.

"And your dad isn't so awful." I lift a shoulder while she

looks on with a more doubtful gaze, her brow drawn in. "I mean, it's not like he buddied up with the cartel and got your mom hooked on dope. He just wants to make his town super safe and keep his daughter wrapped in a bubble and away from harm forever and ever."

She laughs out through a small burst of tears that she quickly dashes away with the back of her hand. Nodding, she steps into me for one more hug.

"You're right, Dustin. Thank you," she says.

I slip away and move toward Hannah's door.

"Don't mention it. Give me five minutes, maybe ten."

She nods and I reach for the key card in my pocket. Before I press it to the door, though, Bailey stops me.

"Hey Dustin?"

"Yeah?" I whisper, prepared to help her through this.

She studies me for a long second, and I start to worry she's going to reveal something else, something that will shatter me. Instead, she gives me a gift.

"You're necessary to her, too. More than any of us."

I flatten my palm over my chest, my fingers covering Hannah's initials, and I pat twice to symbolize my heartbeat. I leave Bailey with a smile and slip quietly back into the room.

"Did you get coffee?" Hannah's gravelly voice calls from the bed. I turn to find her sitting up and waiting amid a pool of soft sheets and pillows that have slipped from her shoulders to reveal her breasts.

I bite my knuckles and she leans back to laugh just before I rush to the bed and pounce on her. She wriggles her body beneath me as I cage her between my arms and legs, giving in to the temptation to bite her pebbled, bright red nipple and saw at it gently with my teeth. I flick my tongue over it before sucking it and then letting go, sitting up on my knees as she lays flat beneath me, her arms splayed out along with her hair.

I want to bury myself inside her again right now, but I made a promise to her best friend, and as needy a fucker as I am, I have to do what's right.

I bend down and press my lips to hers, pulling back as her hands weave into my hair. She whines and I chuckle as our kiss struggles to hold on.

"I have to go. I need to find Alex and make sure things are okay, since we sort of bailed and all. And you got a text or two this morning. I think maybe Bailey's looking for you?"

Hannah blushes and rolls her head to the side, looking toward her phone.

"She's going to scold me," she admits, scrunching her face when she turns back to me.

"Probably. I'll make it worth it," I say, bending down and taking her other nipple into my mouth, sucking it just as raw, then crawling back before she can convince me to stay.

Such a tease, she doesn't bother to wrap her sheet around her body as she moves to the edge of the bed, and when she stands, heading toward the window, I have to physically pry myself from the room.

"You are evil. I have to go. But when I get back, I'll bring breakfast, or . . ." I grab my phone from the small table in the center of the room and check the time. "Lunch. I'll bring lunch. And we'll make the most of the hours left in this room. Or . . . out of it." I nod toward the balcony.

"Promise?" Hannah bites at her thumb and I rush to her to kiss her lips. My hand squeezes her ass as she does the same to me, and my cock stretches, telling my brain to knock it the fuck off.

"Promise," I say against her lips, peeling myself away and gathering my things before dashing from her room.

Bailey is still waiting where I left her, pacing, but when I exit, her eyes flash to mine and I give her a quick nod.

"You got this," I say. "But give her a few minutes. She's—"

"I don't need to know," Bailey says with the wave of her hand, her eyes squeezed shut. We've scarred her for life.

I chuckle my way into my room, and my body is still humming with glee, so much so that I don't notice Alex sitting in the chair in the corner of my room until my second pass through the main area.

"What the fu—"

He stands, laughter spilling from his chest, arrogance oozing from every pore in his skin.

"You have a good night?" He eyes the mutual wall I share with Hannah.

I clear my throat and will my pulse to behave enough for me to play the role of tough guy right back.

"Not any of your business. What are you doing here?" I move around the table, something inside telling me to keep this bulky piece of furniture between us. I'm not sure whether it's to protect me, or him.

"You left last night. We didn't get a chance to talk about the deal and all. And, well . . ."

My stomach twists. I feel sick and I'm sweating so much. I swear he must see it. I keep my steps measured, and breathe through my nose.

"You still want in, right? It's a good deal, Alex. It's going to be a huge success," I say.

"Oh, I believe you. And I know it will. But I was hoping, just to make sure. We'd like to run the labor contracting. We've done a lot of developments is all, and we have standards. It would make me feel better about the millions I'm investing." He moves back to the chair he was sitting in when I arrived and pulls a bundle of papers from the side, carrying them toward me then setting what looks like a new contract on the table.

"We took the liberty of drafting a new agreement with the contracting noted. Not a big change, and you can still have . . . Virgil? Is that his name?"

I nod. He thinks Virgil really is my lawyer. Or he's making fun of me. Probably that latter.

"Have him take a look. I think you'll find it in your favor, though."

I glance down at the first page of words I don't understand. I'll give this to Tommy in the car, but when we get home, I have every intention of letting Mr. Judge look over it with a fine-tooth comb. I have my suspicions, but I don't want to lose what could be a great thing based on the hinky feeling in my stomach. I need actual reasons to blow up a dream.

"Check out isn't until five, by the way. In case . . . you know." He winks then tilts his head toward Hannah's room. My jaw flexes and ire heats my veins, that itch to fight so strong I'm going to have to hit something when he leaves this room.

"Thanks, Alex. I'll get back to you asap." My mouth twitches with all the words I want to tack on like *get your mind off my girl, you fucking fuck!*

"I'll look forward to your call. And hey, good luck at the Series race. I've got a good feeling about you. I may have made a bet or two."

I smile, the fakest damn curve I've ever put on my face, and chuckle with him as he leaves my room. My sound cuts the moment the door closes and I look down at the dirty contract in my hand. So close. I'm so goddamned close. I toss it across the room, papers flying free all over my bed. I don't know what I'm going to do if this turns out to be what I think it is. I'll have to let someone down. I know who I'm not going to disappoint, though. I'm not going to disappoint her ever again, even if it costs me every damn dream I've ever had.

16

I don't answer Bailey's text right away. I want to shower first, pack my things and make my bed without letting housekeeping come in. I want to hide what I did, not that I'm ashamed, but I'm not quite ready for anyone to question it—me—*us*. I don't want my friend to look at me with worried or disappointed eyes. It's different this time. Dustin and I are older, mature. I know what I want out of life, even if I'm too scared to reach for some of my dreams. I'm not afraid to go for this one.

I may not be able to change college majors and ditch a future business degree for one in the arts, but I can be by Dustin's side. And as we grow, I know he'll push me to conquer the remaining mountains I face. I can fight to choose him, to let the world know he's my choice. And I can show my parents that he's worth all our love. I know Bailey loves him too, not the way I do, but in the way a friend loves two souls being together. As cautious as she is with my heart, she also believes in us as a couple. She always has. Even before I did.

My cheeks can't seem to lose the red hue permanently cooked into them. I'm physically glowing, and every time I try to mask the evidence that I've changed overnight, that I've had sex, I feel as though a neon sign lights up above my head with an arrow, flashing the words NOT A VIRGIN.

Again, not that Bailey will care about that. She lost hers our freshman year of college. It was part of her goal to shed her parents' control, and the guy was nice. They met at one of the first parties we went to, and he was a gentleman. I think maybe Bailey surprised him by being so forward. They tried dating a little afterward, but it wasn't that kind of match.

Still, it was nice for her. She came away without regrets, and a piece of me was envious that she had this milestone that carried zero negativity with it. But it also didn't have depth. It lacked love. And I wanted both of those. I wanted to fall into someone completely, to lose myself a little without fear of finding my way out.

I wanted it to be Dustin.

Grin permanently slapped on my face, I open the door to let my friend in after finally texting her to come over. She looks tired, her eyes puffy, and it piques my curiosity about what kind of night *she* had.

"Either Vegas agrees with you, or *disagrees* with you," I joke as she passes through the door. She doesn't laugh. In fact, her body seems stiff, her hands fidgeting as she walks to the bed and sits at the end. Her eyes focus on the carpet as her mouth hangs open with worry lines attacking her forehead.

"Bailey, what's wrong?"

Shit, please don't be one of those Vegas stories!

Her head pops up and our eyes meet. Her mouth snaps shut and she sucks her lips in tight, taking a deep breath through her nose. My mind is running the gamut from she just caught Dustin with a prostitute to she's pregnant—with Tommy's baby! *Oh, God!*

"My dad is running for mayor."

She blurts it out as if it's water she's been holding in her mouth for minutes, and she's dying for air. I blink a few times before breaking into the most relieved belly laugh of my life. I lean back and fold my arms over my midriff, every molecule of my body relaxing after firing up for a full-on panic attack.

"Are you . . . laughing?"

I drop my head back down and meet her stare, her head cocked to one side. The sight of it makes me spit out another laugh, which rolls into that out-of-control kind that makes my voice go hoarse and turns into coughing.

"This is *so* not the reaction I thought you'd have," she says, finally relaxing a little herself and falling back on her hands on the bed.

"Oh, Bails. You have no idea the thoughts I had going. I mean . . . you were pregnant with Tommy's baby—"

"Shut the fuck up!" Her eyes widen and she stands, almost offended at my imagination. We both hold our breath and stare at each other for a beat before breaking into another round of hysteria, this one together.

"Oh, my God. Bless you, Tommy Judge, for making my dad's news seem miniscule!" She sighs as she falls back to the bed, flopping to her back and catching her breath. I fill two glasses with water and bring her one as I sit down next to her.

She props herself up on her elbows and takes a few gulps before giving me a sideways look.

"You aren't mad?"

I puff out a short laugh.

"Bailey, I wouldn't care if *you* wanted to run for mayor against my mother."

"Oh, thank God," she says, falling back down and holding her glass up for me to take. I set both hers and mine on the floor, then flop on the bed next to her.

"He's the one putting up the big stink about the Straights. He pulled all these accident reports and has the highway safety people coming out. Han, he's going to shut it down." She rolls her head to the side and I do the same to meet her gaze.

I shrug as I lay.

"Well, it was a good run. Someone probably should have shut it down a long time ago." It's true. That an entire town has put up with something so reckless for so long, all for the love of speed and octane, is kinda nuts.

"I hope this thing Dustin has planned works out. With the track? That would be . . ." She trails off and returns her focus to the high ceiling dusted with a golden, glittery paint. Everything about Vegas, about this room and this trip, is like some magical fairytale dream.

"He'll get it done," I say, grinning at the thought of Dustin finding success. I start to bite my lip when I feel Bailey's hand slap against my forearm. I giggle and turn to her.

"What?"

"You are blushing, Hannah Judge. Oh-*oh, my God!*" Bailey sits up fast and twists so she's looking down at me. My grin gets stupid big.

"You had sex!"

Unable to bluff through this moment, I slap my hands over my face and peek at my friend through my fingers while my cheeks flame.

"Hannah Banana!" she teases me, poking at my side. I

shift and roll out of her reach before peeling my fingers back slowly to meet her eager expression. She wants details.

"Bails. It was . . . everything. It was literally exactly like I imagined, like I wanted." Memories of last night flood me and my body tingles in response, my legs squeezing together at the thought of Dustin between them, remembering how full I was with him, how empty without him. The ache he left behind is so sweet.

"You aren't disappointed in me?" I mush up my lips and wear a guilty, crooked smile.

My friend blinks at me twice and finally shakes her head while breathing out a laugh.

"I'm honestly shocked it took this long. You know I believe in you two. I just don't like the painful journey. That's all." She lifts a shoulder, and I love how much she cares about me.

"Now, tell me. How big is his—"

"Bailey!" I slap at her. We both fall into laughter, pausing when we hear a knock at my door.

My friend and I both calm ourselves and stand, and while I straighten the comforter on the bed, Bailey goes to the door.

"That's weird," she says, turning to face me after looking through the peep hole. "It's Alex."

As deep as my friend's forehead dents my stomach drops even deeper. There's no reason for him to be at my door, and I'm not stupid enough to fall for him thinking this is Dustin's room instead of mine. This is a calculated visit, and it brings to surface all the things that make me uneasy about Dustin pursuing this deal with Alex.

I'm tempted to simply wait him out and I hold my

breath, making myself as quiet as possible, but it's no use. He knocks again. This time calling me out by name.

"Hey, Hannah. It's Alex. I just wanted to say good-bye and thank you all. Do you have a minute?"

Bailey's brow lowers and mine does the same. I glance to my right, to the balcony, and wonder if Dustin is still in his room. I pick up my phone and shoot him a quick text, letting him know Alex is here before nodding to Bailey to open the door. She won't leave me alone.

Alex flinches a little when he sees her face instead of mine, but he covers it quickly with a slick grin, leaning toward her and kissing her cheek. My friend can't fake a smile worth a damn, so she just steps back after their short embrace and leaves the bewildered slant to her eyes in place.

"I must have missed Dustin. He wasn't in his room, but I'm glad I caught you. I wanted to say good-bye and thank you for making the trip. I hope your stay was . . ."

A disturbing smirk paints his lips as he leaves his thought half-finished. He knows Dustin and I left the club early and he either assumes correctly or has eyes that saw it all. Either way, it makes my stomach sick. I shiver under his glare, acutely aware of my surroundings and all of the ways I can get out of here.

"We had a nice time. Thank you." I force the politeness, but my posture is closed-off. Alex's eyes drop to my crossed arms and he breathes out a small laugh before darting his gaze back up to my face.

"Right, well—" He steps toward me and as much as I want to jerk away, I know that will only make him more persistent. I close my eyes and brace for his fat lips at my cheek. His beard scratches my neck as he breathes against me and I battle my instincts to curl and shudder.

"Until next time." He winks as he steps away, then does the same to Bailey, who opens the door for him to leave and is careful not to slam it behind him even though I can tell she wants to.

"He's bad news," she says the moment she slips back from the peep hole, confirming he's gone.

I swallow.

"Yeah, he is. And it's going to crush Dustin when I tell him, but I don't think this is going to work. I have a bad feeling about it."

And I resent that Alex had the power to completely ruin the blissful daze I was planning on staying in all the way home.

17

I couldn't get back to Camp Verde fast enough. I don't think anyone could, and I'm not sure whether we all have different reasons or my mood is so off that it's infecting the rest of them.

I called Tommy and Virgil down for breakfast so we could pour over the surprise contract. Virgil's natural instinct is to not trust guys like Alex so he didn't even bother to read. Tommy's never liked Alex much either, but he also knows how committed I am to making this work—he's keeping the contract to dig into the meat of it when we get home. The further into this thing I've gotten, the more attached I am to the reality of it. It's no longer a fantasy. I can smell the air out there, feel the track under my feet. I can see future generations of racers, the smiles on parents' faces as their kids realize what they can do on the road. This is probably what Little League parents feel when they buy that first bat. For me, it's a track. It's always been a track. Always the rubber, the oil, the pedal—the machine.

I'm the driver.

We made it back half an hour earlier than anyone expected and it's because I pushed Tom Judge's truck a little more than he probably wanted me to. He'd agree with getting out of Vegas in a hurry, though. I wish I could cut my losses, but Alex really is the only ticket I have to make this work.

Something's on Hannah's mind too. She was quiet the entire way home, and even now as we all unload from the road trip, weary legs stretching in the Judge family driveway, Hannah is distant. After we were so close. There's more to this.

"I see she's in one piece," Tom says, running his hand over the dusty hood of his truck.

"I'll get her a wash for you," I say, glad the only thing left on his truck from our trip is the desert dirt.

"Nah. I'm taking her fishing tomorrow. I'll just get her all muddy again. How'd the foot hold up?"

I roll my ankle a few times and test the tender tip of my toe. I've been too distracted to notice, but it looked as though it healed decently enough when I checked during my shower this morning.

"Feels like I stepped on a fishing hook, but I'll live," I laugh out.

His lip ticks up with a short laugh. He studies me for a few seconds, and I can tell he has more to say. I assume he wants to know how successful the trip was, and I want his input. I'm just not sure I'm ready for him to look over the contract yet and confirm all of the holes and red flags I'm sure Tommy will find. I'd like to live in the dream a little longer, at least while I head down to Phoenix to prep for the race. None of this matters if I can't get my head ready for what comes ten days from now. They don't simply award Gorman's times to me. I have to make my own time trials. And I have to live up to the reputation his team has bought into.

"You know you can call me in whenever you're ready." Tom arches a brow, maybe reading my thoughts.

I offer him a tight-lipped smile and look down as I nod. "Thanks. I appreciate that. I'm trying to do what I can on my own, but I will call on you . . . when I need you. I promise." I look up and am met with a familiar affection in his eyes, an expression I haven't seen in a while. I always loved when he looked at me like a proud dad, and right now? It's one of those times.

"All right, then," he says, placing a heavy hand on my shoulder and squeezing with a little shake as he moves on to carry one of the bags from the back of the pickup.

Everyone's headed inside, but Hannah lingers by the truck, her backpack dangling from her fingers and her feet poking at the ground. I step in close and watch over her head as her family's front door closes, leaving us alone until they can spy at us through the window. I drop my gaze to her and lift her chin with my hand, relieved when her eyes close and her lips part. It's like coming home— kissing her. I was afraid whatever was bothering her on the way home was about us, about regrets. And I don't regret a single damn thing about last night.

Her lips move against mine, stretching into a smile that provokes my own. My tongue slips in her mouth, tasting her, and I bring my other hand up to cup her face, holding her mouth to mine so I can keep this kiss alive a little longer. It breaks finally, but only because she slides her hands along my sides to my back and squeezes me tight, resting her cheek on my chest. I wrap my arms around her and tuck her head under my chin.

"I can't wait to shower the smell of Vegas off of me," she

laughs out. Through all the smoke and dinge Vegas left behind, I still only smell her—her fruity shampoo, her sexy body, her sweetness.

"I have to get to Phoenix tonight. Tommy said he's coming. I mean, Virgil doesn't know shit about cars, and I'd rather know someone in that garage." I'm sure Gorman's guys are tight and know their shit. He's always on the leader board, even if he hasn't won. He's a sloppy driver, so he has to have good mechanics behind him to do what he does. I'm not sure they'll buy into me being their guy right away, though.

"If Virgil doesn't know shit, why you keep him around?" She looks up at me, her chin against my chest, and I slip back enough to look her in the eyes. I let out a guilty laugh.

"I suppose maybe I like the guy." She holds my gaze as her lips stretch into a tight, knowing smirk, but she lets the subject go. She gets that he's a father figure. I surround myself with them when I can.

"Can I come?" She looks up at me with puppy eyes that I wouldn't be able to say no to even if I wanted to. I lift her and spin her around once before setting her back on the ground, her legs so sexy in her cut-off shorts and sockless canvas shoes.

"Of course you can come. I'll even let you drive around the track once if you want."

"Shut up!" She pushes me. I wrap her hands up with mine and hold them to my chest.

"Why are you always hitting me when you're happy?" I laugh.

"Because . . . you like it rough." She wiggles her brows and I laugh harder. I also think that maybe I do, if she's offering.

"We should get inside. Shower and rest a little. I've got to hit the road in a couple of hours to make it there in time for a meeting."

Hannah lifts up on her toes one more time, pressing her lips to mine and leaving them there, her skin tickling mine like a butterfly wing. For a moment, I believe this is heaven.

"Get going then, Eat My Dust," she says, slapping my ass before sprinting out of my reach.

"I'll be right there," I say, mostly so I can watch her go.

I wait outside a little longer after the door closes. I'd like to drive the Supra down to Phoenix, get my mental bearings tooled a bit. I forgot how good it felt to have that car in my hands. I wander across the driveway to where it sits, probably undriven despite how much I'm sure Tom wanted to. He's got too much respect for the thing, though he's probably responsible for half the parts in it.

I do wonder how many times he took the race truck out for a spin. That layer of dirt caked on the wheel wells seems awfully recent. I know *I* didn't put it there. I smile at the thought, but am interrupted when my phone buzzes in my back pocket. I spin to lean against the car while I read the incoming text. I had a feeling it would be Alex, and for a guy who doesn't want me to feel pressured, he's doing all he can to make sure I can't breathe.

ALEX: *Next time you're in town, let's set up a race. For old times. I look forward to hearing from you. Try for Friday. I like Fridays. They're excellent days to ink deals. Good days to celebrate. ;-)*

I black out my screen when I'm done reading and slip my phone back in my pocket. I'm not going to respond. He isn't expecting one. I've seen him operate. He likes deadlines. He's enforced them before. A few fights he's managed have had issues with purses getting paid and the vig getting cashed out. I don't have definitive proof, but I have the sense that Alex's vigs carry a little extra weight, coming with security . . . or a threat.

"Fuck," I mutter to myself, turning back to face my car. I ball my hands together and tap my fist on the roof, my gut twisting in on itself.

I'm about to call Tommy out to have him convince me to walk away from this whole thing when suddenly I'm not alone. It's the last person I'd expect to comfort me out here, even though there was a time when I would expect her first, or at least second, after Hannah.

"You should come in and eat something. Those trips are always hardest on the driver," Mrs. Judge says.

"Oh, yeah. I'm good. Just stretching my legs out." I shake them for affect, but she chuckles, reading right through my lie.

"Dustin, I'm sorry I made you ever feel—"

"It's fine," I interrupt. Like I always do. Before anyone can try to make it right, I stop them and wash away any existence of trauma, or I bury it. That trick doesn't work the same way on Amanda Judge as it does on everyone else.

"You are welcome in this house. And I'm the one who should be out here sulking. I was—" She pauses, drawing in a sharp breath as her eyes gloss over. *Fuck, if she's going to cry.* She fans herself with her hand and I roll my eyes, knowing I can't let her break down. I pull her into a hug and she sniffles against my shirt. "I was so awful to you."

You were. I don't say that.

"It's fine," I say instead.

Lie. Rinse. Repeat.

It feels too good to forgive her, to have her forgive me for loving her daughter. To be accepted. Harboring resentment and distrust is so much work. I'd much rather be hugged as though I belong.

"I did a little work while you were gone. Tom said he didn't know any details, that you were being a little *cagey*." She lifts a brow. I wince because that's the kind of word someone would associate with Colt. I don't want to be cagey. She means well though, so I hold in my defensive instincts.

"I pulled the info on the old Carney place. It's got good bones, but it's in a lot of hurt. You'd get a good price, but you'll need to put a lot of work into it." She shades her eyes with her hand, squinting as she looks toward my truck. "You've made it this far, though, so . . ."

Mrs. Judge turns back to me and her mouth settles into an effortless smile. The worry lines still accent her eyes, but her gut instincts have faith in me. If I pull this off, it's a game changer. I'm just not sure how close to corruption I'll need to get. Alex is my only shot, and I guess I could plead ignorance to anything illegal he does. I have no *actual* proof. I'm starting to rethink letting Hannah's dad take a look at things, though.

"Think the zoning will be an issue?" I'm not totally sure what the various regulations are around here, but that'll need to be ironed out if a project this big is in the works.

"I know a few people who know a few people. I have a feeling you'll get a pretty good hearing. You know, this town's been waiting for someone to be proud of, Dustin. I'm pretty sure you're that guy." She gives me a pat on the chest and walks backward a few steps before returning to the house.

That sounds an awful lot like hero talk, and I'm not sure I'm anyone's hero. I'm merely trying to outperform Colt Bridges' dark shadow. And in the end . . . get the girl.

18

How Phoenix is this much hotter when it's only a hundred miles from home baffles me. It's not just hot out here on the blacktop. It's scorching. My skin burned the first day, and I've been careful to slather on sunscreen and wear Dustin's long-sleeved shirts every time I go out since.

It's been a while since it was only me, Tommy and Dustin out at a track. It's strange to be in a place like this with the two of them. I'm caught between this nostalgic sense that throws me back to my childhood and this feeling that we're where we all were meant to be one day. I'm still an outsider when the two of them get under the hood, but it's different now than it used to be. My brother doesn't beg me to leave them alone, and Dustin—he begs me to stay.

I like having Virgil around, too. It's clear Dustin loves him, and I get why. He's everything Colt never was. I've gotten to know Virgil pretty well these last few days, running errands for Tommy and the rest of the mechanics in the shop. Sometimes we pick up parts but mostly, we're a food delivery service. Virgil doesn't seem to mind. I think he just likes being around Dustin and the other guys. He's widowed and never had kids of his own.

There haven't been many pissing matches over having my brother around. Tommy seems to know he's small-time compared to these guys, but it's fun to watch him work alongside them. He picks up their tricks so fast. My brother would have been an amazing engineer. Unlike me, though, he actually likes business too. He doesn't feel robbed.

"All right, who had the"—I lift the large cup and squint in an effort to decipher the barista's handwriting—Mocha-choca-latte?" A guy named Ernie wheels out from underneath the car and snaps his fingers in the air.

"How the hell you can drink a steaming hot brew in this weather, I have no idea."

I hand him his drink and he winks and says, "Thanks, sweetheart."

Women are rare in this business. I guess it's pretty unique for me to hang around the garage this much. Most of the men who work for Gorman's team are older, in their fifties, and I get the sense that they're used to a *boys' club* of sorts. Misogyny is basically mixed in their blood. I call them out when I have to, but I'm not here to make a statement about how small their worldview is. I'm here to support Dustin and make sure everyone has his best interests at heart. So far, they seem to. In fact, I think the lead mechanic likes Dustin a lot more than Gorman, which might cause a problem if Dustin does well in this race.

"Is that my cold brew? Banana, you're a lifesaver!" Tommy reaches over my shoulder and pulls his drink from the carrier clutched in my hands. Only two drinks remain, both lemonades—mine and Dustin's.

"Where's he at?" I arch a brow to Tommy as he guzzles the first third of his drink.

He pulls his cup from his mouth and practically pants. I can't tell whether he was thirsty or desperate for caffeine. He nods out the garage doors toward the large dirt berm that separates us from the practice track we've been basically living at for four days.

"He's really in his head over this, huh?" I say.

Tommy lifts his shoulders and grimaces, his expression uncertain.

"I don't know. I haven't seen him drive for real in ages. I don't know what his routine is now, but this isn't the Dustin you and I grew up with. Our Dustin would never second-guess himself."

"You think that's what he's out there doing?" I ask.

My insides feel as though I swallowed a dozen butterflies.

"I dunno. Maybe he'll talk to you. We're doing some cool shit in here." My brother's face lights up with an excitement I haven't seen in a long time. He's in his element, no matter what he believes. Even when he doubted going out on the road with Dustin after high school, I knew. His heart belonged in a place like this, with his best friend—with the love of my life.

Dustin is the love of my life.

Tommy heads back to the engine bay and I turn my focus to the wind picking up outside, the orange flags waving with each growing gust. Dust flies from the top of the mound, and Dustin's hat peeks out from the top of the hill. Nothing feels anchored right now—this place, this chance, me and Dustin, Tommy. Everything feels so precarious. I can't help but think Alex and his offer to partner has something to do with it all. He's the one random ingredient that doesn't belong. He's messing with the balance.

I ditch the drink holder and carry the two lemonades up the hill, my calves flexing as my tennis shoes dig into the rough ground. It's a workout to get to the top, but after four days of running up and down this thing, I've gotten acclimated. My glutes are sore as shit, though.

"Hey, stranger. You waiting for a race to start?"

Dustin sits with his knees bent and his arms resting on top. Black jeans, black T-shirt, black hat, black Vans. I'm sure if I touch him, he'll be a thousand degrees out in this sun. He never seems to get hot out here, though. Anywhere. It's like his blood runs cool. He swivels his head and squints to look up at me, the sun shining behind my back.

"I'm always waiting for a race," he says, holding out his hand. I give him his drink and he pats the hard ground next to him. It looks hot, but I can't refuse a chance to be near him. We haven't had much time alone the last four days, and by the time night rolls around, Dustin basically collapses in the RV we're all piled into. Gorman isn't a big name. He's not quite a medium name. It's cool that he's letting Dustin stay in his RV, even though it's a little cramped for the four of us. His sponsor didn't give him much of a choice other than to be grateful, I guess.

I nestle into Dustin's side and loop my arm through his, resting my head on his warm bicep while I sip at my cold lemonade. I try to untangle what's on Dustin's mind by following his line of sight. His eyes seem to be trained on the far curve, which I know from a few test runs is where he loses the most speed.

"You worried about turn three?" I shift my gaze to his face so I can read his reaction, but it remains steadfast. His eyes glued on the road, or whatever he's imagining in its place.

"Not really. I'll get it down. Or I'll crash." He laughs. I play punch his bicep and he catches my fist with his other hand. His head turned toward me, I jump on the opportunity to kiss him, pressing my sticky-sweet lips to his. His tongue passes over my bottom lip before he sucks it between his lips, scraping with his teeth. He backs away to reveal a pleased smile.

"I like it when you taste like summer," he says through a wide smile that dimples his golden cheeks. He lifts his hat and runs a hand through his hair, but it still flies in all directions from the wind.

This track is almost an exact replica of what he's racing on a week from now. It's the reason most of the drivers come here to work out kinks before the big weekend. Who knows, maybe one day they'll be heading to Camp Verde to set up there before the race.

"You know, I still haven't gotten my trip around the loop." I nod down toward the track and Dustin follows my lead, his head falling to one side as he considers my request. I've been dying to drive the car, just once. He took me on a trip in the Supra our first night here, but the stock car only has room for him. And it *barely* has room for him. The steering wheel comes out before he gets in.

"Tommy say how close they are with the car?" He glances back to me and I draw my legs in close, ready to stand and sprint into the garage. He's never been this close to saying yes to letting me drive.

"They looked close to done. Besides, aren't you the boss?"

Dustin's head falls back in laughter and his eyes close.

"Not even close," he coughs out. His head rights and he turns to look me in the eyes, still amused at my suggestion. "Don't let Ernie hear you say that. He's got twenty years or more on me. And Douglas, who is the *actual* boss when it comes to that particular set of wheels, has the power to tell Albert Pierce Financial to pick another driver. He's been Gorman's crew chief since the beginning. He has no loyalties to me. I know the sponsor wanted to get some air time out of this. That's why I'm here."

"You're *here* . . ." I pause to stand, holding out my hand for him to take. He does, glaring at me skeptically as he steps up in front of me. I let go of his hand and fist his T-shirt as I move in close. He smells so good. Even with this unforgiving sun radiating off of his chest. "Because you are the best fucking driver this track—*any* track—has ever seen, and you were born to shatter records and change the game, Dustin Bridges."

His lip curls and his head leans to the side a hint as he brings his mouth close to mine. I look down as our lips draw close, not wanting to shut my eyes and miss the sexy way his jaw flexes when he's just about to kiss me. It does it now.

"Team Eat My Dust, right?" he whispers against me, sucking in my top lip, tugging at my smile. My teeth graze against his mouth as he moves his free hand behind my back and leans into me, arching my back as he deepens our kiss. If it weren't hotter than Hades out here, I'd strip off my clothes and take him right here. Instead, I'll settle for a stint behind the wheel.

"Come on. Let's see about that car."

It's comforting to see that little bit of swagger back in his step as we climb over the hill and back down, into the garage. He lets go of my hand and glances down at me with a smirk before putting his fingers between his teeth and blowing out a loud whistle to announce his presence.

"What?" Tommy yells from somewhere on the other side of the hood.

I smile, loving this return to the familiar. This is how Tommy and Dustin always communicated when we were growing up. They could be blocks apart and all it took was one whistle to find each other. It's their own special brand of Marco Polo. I could never play along because I can't whistle for shit. It was never a problem, though, because one of them always knew where I was. They always had an eye on me, looking out for me. The three of us—invincible.

"I'm feeling like I want to give it another run. How we looking?" Dustin sinks his hands into his back pockets, a nervous habit. He's trying to look casual, and it probably does to the rest of the guys in here. I see the subtleties, though.

The hood drops with a heavy *clunk*, revealing Douglas and Tommy. They're both wiping their hands clean on towels, and I'm relieved to see that they're smiling. I'm sure Dustin is too. I think I understand why he's intimidated by Douglas, as well. I'm sure a little bit of it comes from his loyalties to Gorman and his years on the job, in this world, knowing what it takes, but the bulk of it is likely due to the uncanny similarities between Douglas and Colt. Their voices are close in tone, the same raspy quality from years of smoking. But it's their physical traits too, down to the same thinning hairline, sagging neck fat and oversized Adam's apple. I'd even venture to guess they're the same height.

"I tweaked the throttle a little. If you ease up then punch it through that third turn, I think you'll feel a difference. Might just shave that second off," Douglas says, tossing Dustin his helmet.

Everything about Dustin's body changes the minute that helmet hits his hands. His tight muscles relax, his shoulders drop, his stance widens—I'd bet his dick is hard, too. But before he slips the helmet on, he shoots me a look, then tosses it to me. A foolish grin takes over my face.

"Really?" I'm already slipping it on and reaching for the fire suit before he changes his mind. If I have to, I'll just leap through that window.

"I've never seen a chick so excited to hit two-hunny on a circle before," Ernie pipes in.

"It's Hannah. She's not a chick, she's my sister, and she's come close in the Supra," Tommy says. Clearly, my brother isn't intimidated by the crew.

"Roger that, dude. My bad," Ernie says, saluting my brother then bowing to me.

"But to be clear, Ernie," I shout as I zip up my suit, "Yes, this chick is fucking stoked to hit two-hunny on the circle." I leave him with a coy smile, lift one leg up and thread my body through the window.

Dustin leans in, resting his elbows on the open frame while I buckle in.

"Your sponsor is not going to like this," I say in a low voice to keep it between us. It's not going to stop me. At this point, I'll peel out of here and go rogue if I have to.

"Guess you better not crash, then." He reaches in and tugs my harness tight. "And maybe don't hit two hunny?"

"*Mmm*, can't promise that, babe." I flip the switch and let the car roar to life. If I didn't want to make love to Dustin before this moment, I'm beyond ready now. That's the kind of girl I am; the kind who gets off on the rumble of a Toyota V-8 boasting six-hundred horsepower.

I blow Dustin a kiss as he steps away, a proud smile on his lips, then slip the visor down on my helmet and follow Ernie's guide as I roll backward out of the garage. Douglas is standing at the entrance to the track, and I slow as I get closer to him, a little worried he's going to kill this idea.

He rests his hand on the hood when I stop, and pushes his sunglasses up on his head. He looks over his shoulder at the empty track—nothing to hit, *I promise*—then back to me. "You get one lap. Nobody knows about this. Ever. Got it?"

I flip up my visor as my grin grows, and Douglas rolls his eyes and belly laughs.

"Fucking hell. All right, cut her loose."

He slaps the hood twice and I roar onto the track. The power under my palms ignites my entire body, and I get my feel for it for the first stretch of the track, keeping it around eighty. The wheel is tight, more so than the Supra, and even with my small frame, the space is a tough fit.

"That all you got, Banana?" Tommy's voice pipes into my headset and I laugh right before I floor it and run it up to one-twenty before knocking it down for the first turn.

"You shift like a maniac," he says.

"Yeah, well, who taught me that?" I taunt back.

It's true. I'm sloppy compared to Dustin. I'd get eaten alive out here. But the freedom this single sprint around a misshapen oval has given me a new sense of confidence, an injection of faith. The Straights are nothing compared to this.

The next straightaway open ahead of me, I grind my way back to a top speed near one-fifty. Any higher feels dangerous, so I keep it right there and let the adrenaline course through my veins.

"Woo whoo!" I shout.

"Atta girl," Dustin chimes in.

A rush of shivers travels down my spine hearing his voice, feeling this power in my hands, under my feet, around my body. I smile through the next turn, down-shifting cleaner than before and fire up on the backstretch toward Douglas. I'm half-tempted to take one more turn, but I want the guy to like me. More importantly, to like Dustin, so I slow it down and roll to a stop at his feet.

I kill the switch and climb out, my body vibrating with nervous energy that makes it hard to stand.

"It's a rush, isn't it?" Douglas says.

I hand him the helmet and unzip my fire suit.

"I could get addicted to that." I'm laughing through my words, my fingers fumbling with the zipper. Dustin's calm hands finally cover mine and help me the rest of the way.

"A little jacked, are we?" He's wearing his suit, which means it's his turn to show off. I'm almost more excited to watch this. I've seen it a thousand times, and it never gets old.

"How about this," I begin, stepping free of the pants and lifting myself up on my toes to whisper in his ear. "You beat your time and take that turn like I know you can, and I will let you fuck me in the grandstands tonight when the boys are asleep."

I reach between us and cup his hard-on, giving it a gentle squeeze before slipping away. His wide eyes and lifted brow match the tempted smile tugging at his lips.

"Deal," he says, dropping his helmet on his head and swinging his body into the car in one smooth movement.

The car fires to life and Dustin spins the tires, warming them on his way to the starting line. Douglas snaps his fingers to my brother, and Tommy gives him the headset.

"All right, Dust. You go on my count. You ready?"

I can't hear Dustin on the other end but Douglas begins to count down from five. The trip to one feels like forever, but the moment Douglas's mouth forms the word, Dustin peels off from the start and Tommy, Ernie and Virgil all press their stopwatches to time.

It's laughable how smooth he is on the road compared to me. If I didn't know better, I would swear he's gliding on ice, taking every inch that's his, banking where he needs to and coasting to the middle in the right spot. His first turn is efficient, his time about half a second ahead of where he needs to be, and I squeeze my legs together at the thought of his reward.

"Alright, now ease in. You're going to feel the throttle this next bank, so punch it and don't hold back." I see why Dustin said Douglas is the real master. He looks out on the track like a professor, his eyes dissecting every nuance while his mind calculates every fraction in real time. This man is my brother's king.

Dustin hits the turn and I hold my breath, my stomach riding waves while I mentally will him to beat this imaginary demon that's keeping him from breaking the barrier. He's done this before. He's done it on roads far worse than this, turns much tighter. He's been letting nerves drive the corners rather than his skill, but this time . . . this trip is different.

"Yes," Tommy mumbles just over my shoulder.

I lift up on my toes and my brother says it again.

"Yes."

"Yes!" he shouts a third time, just as Dustin breaks from high to low and comes down the straightaway a full two seconds ahead of his best time.

I bounce on my toes and notice in my periphery that Virgil is doing the same. The three boys are constantly glancing from their timers to the track, their smiles hovering on the cusp of celebration.

"That's it, Dustin. Tear it up, now. Tear. It. Up!" Douglas steps closer to the edge of the track and I join him, my pulse pounding as Dustin gets nearer, suddenly flying by us, the wind in his wake blowing my hair across my face. My insides thunder as he disappears around the final turn, and my brother runs on the track toward the finish line, leaping in the air when he finally stops his timer and spins to compare his clock with Ernie and Virgil.

"Four seconds. Fucker just shaved four seconds," Douglas utters, pulling the headset off and glancing to me.

"How do you know?" He doesn't have a timer in his hand, but before he can answer me, my brother shouts the very same facts before tearing across the infield to jump on Dustin's back.

Douglas stretches at the collar of his T-shirt, his mouth caught in awe, eyes open with surprise.

"I just know," he finally says.

I look out on the field as Tommy and Dustin celebrate, two boys now men seeing their fantasies come true, getting to live them out. We always knew Dustin had what it takes. He's always been special. For the first time ever, though, I get to see that realization dawn on someone else. I do believe Dustin has a new fan.

"Well, goddamn." Douglas laughs, shaking his head as he makes his way toward the rest of the group.

I hang back, knowing my time will come. I've got a debt to pay. And I'm so ready to honor it.

19

Hannah had a little to do with my time around that track. I'll let her take all the credit, despite what I know is the truth—that I ripped through my best time using rage. I let my anger flood my body, and I became a machine, following Douglas's orders and my own instincts. I've always driven like this, determined and fearless. But I've never let myself slip into a place of such anger before. So much hate. I was able to cut off everything that didn't matter to the moment—Hannah included. I lost myself to the goal. One mission.

I wrecked that track out of my hate for Colt, my detestation for my fake mom, resentment for my real one, and for motherfucking Alex Offerman and the line he's making me straddle. And when I realized how good I could be when I tapped into all that darkness, I dove deeper. I reveled in it. And Hannah, she was so damned proud.

It's taken me most of the day to come to terms with the fact I may be two different people. I'm very much the man I try to be. I would put Hannah above anything, even my own life. I'm a survivor and a fighter, and I value the love I've been able to find in the most unlikely of places, love I often don't believe I deserve. I honor the work—mine, Tommy's, the team's. Even Virgil's.

But there is a darkness inside me. I've slipped into it a few times over the last four years. I tell myself it's just addiction in my blood, that my thirst to feel a buzz or black out life's painful parts is simply part of my DNA, something that can't be helped. And I constantly fight against those cravings. I have my whole life.

When I was fourteen, I drank a pack of hard lemonade my fake mom had sitting in the fridge. I got sick fast, and the next day I told Tommy and Hannah it was food poisoning. When I was fifteen, I tried one of the pills Dad had bundled in bags at the kitchen table. I wanted to numb the bruises on my back from where he hit me with a shovel. I slept deep and hard, and the rest was so good I took another pill when I woke up. I spent the two weeks before my sixteenth birthday in a waking slumber, and by the end I was taking two at a time. It happens fast.

My fake mom overdosed for a second time the day after I turned sixteen. I got home from celebrating at the Straights with Tommy and Hannah. I called the paramedics and followed them to the hospital. After I drove her home and tucked her in, I went to my room and pulled the stash I'd stolen from Colt out from my pillowcase and flushed the pills down the toilet. I've kept myself straight ever since. At least, until I left Hannah.

There were a few nights I was blackout drunk. Probably more than a few. Country bars in Oklahoma are a great place to drown sorrows. I always picked myself back up, though. I'd stop cold, for months, and throw myself into racing. I'd replace the high or buzz with my obsession, and when I saw growth, it spurred me on, made me sleep less and work more.

Then Alex would call, offer me a race, a trip to Vegas—a chance to be the *other* me for a little while. A lot of the things I did with him, *for* him, were probably questionable. I didn't care. Alex gave me money I desperately needed, and I threw a race or two. The idea that someone had a pull over me strong enough to make me willingly lose ate at my insides, and so I would visit the darkness again.

The cycle.

Being with Hannah again changes everything.

I haven't felt the pull once since I've been back. Even in Vegas, when I was willingly dancing with the devil, I held on to Hannah's essence—her kiss, her scent, her taste—and I always saw the light. Such a fool to think I could walk the line and not get burned.

Alex called me this morning. He's the reason I was alone, staring at the track. If I don't go in with him on this deal he's going to buy the property out from under me and bring in his own guys. "The opportunity is too good to pass up," he said.

I don't need Tommy's smarts to see what Alex is doing. I knew the minute he gave me those changes to the contract. It was probably his plan all along. He's going to use the track to launder his dirty money. I don't know where that money comes from, but it isn't a righteous place.

I took that rage, the feeling of being trapped, and I turned it into fuel. I've been trapped my entire life. If that's my destiny, I should at least profit from it in some way, shouldn't I?

Two men.

I need the better one to come alive now. I need him

present. Hannah deserves the best of me. I know she dropped that sexy offer as a tease because she wants me as much as I want her. But I don't want this thing between us to burn hot then burn out. She deserves more. She deserves the light.

I haven't worn a suit since the one I scraped together for Hannah's prom. I didn't even need all of the pieces of it when I came home to deal with Colt's affairs. That suit was shit compared to this suit. This suit arrived sheathed in a leather zipped bag, paid for by an allowance I get from the sponsor. The hanger is made of wood. The deep blue color changes color depending on the light, and I swear it feels like silk even though it's not.

I could get used to a life of money.

After my time trials I told Hannah to spend the day getting pampered, to call Bailey and have some fun. I want to take her out, and I wanted time to prepare it all. I also needed to get my head right.

I feel seventeen again, and that feels good. I get ready at the garage, and Tommy helps with the tie. I'm still not sure I'll ever get this thing off my neck, but that knot is solid so I'm rocking it. Hannah's been in our RV with Bailey, doing whatever it is girls do to get ready for a night out. From what I can tell, that consists of mostly giggling.

I tug on the lapel of my jacket, thankful for the night air and a tepid June evening. Clearing my throat, I form a fist and hold it near the door until I finally feel ready. I knock twice and step back, folding my hands behind me and lifting my chin.

"One second!" Hannah calls out.

My palms are sweating, so I do my best to dry them on the back of my jacket before she opens the door. Bailey steps out first, leaving the door cracked behind her as she hovers between the top two steps leading to the RV.

"You better be taking her somewhere expensive because we spent a lot of time on that hair," she says.

A nervous laugh breaks through my even more anxious smile.

"I have something special planned." I hold up my hand to swear it.

Bailey nods then draws the door open, revealing an absolute goddess in a white flowy dress that sweeps against her thighs and cuts down the middle of her chest with this mesmerizing crisscross of golden rope. She's a Roman queen, royal skin bronzed from the sun, smoky eyes that sparkle when she bats her lashes, deep red lips that will be the death of me. Her feet are practically bare, only thin sandals and leather straps that wind up her legs.

"Oh, damn," I breathe out.

"Really?" Hannah sweeps a few of the ringlets that tickle the sides of her face from her eyes as they twirl in the wind. I move in close and offer my hand as she trails down the steps. Her hair is piled up in curls that seem to spill from her head down to her soft, supple skin. I'm going to enjoy unraveling it all later. *Sooner rather than later.*

"I think maybe I'm underdressed," I say, tugging at my tie, which suddenly feels tighter around my neck. It's not the only thing that feels tighter.

Hannah spins so she's standing directly in front of me, our hands tethered at our waists. She glances down and her eyes make the slow journey up the length of my body, her smile owning her face and growing with every new inch of me she sees.

"You look amazing, Dustin. You look like the man I always knew you'd be."

My body visibly quakes at her compliment. She doesn't realize how deep her words cut at the very crisis in my soul. I bring her hand to my mouth and kiss her knuckles as I gaze at her.

"I'm just trying to look like I deserve you," I say. This time, she's the one to tremble in response. I back away and spin, holding out my arm to escort my queen.

"Shall we?"

She loops her arm through mine and Bailey whistles as we walk across the empty lot to the Supra. I let Hannah in, careful to make sure her dress isn't caught in the door, then rush to the other side. I've never been more excited to show someone something. Hannah is going to love this; I know it in my heart.

It took a little smooth talking for me to make it happen, and I may have sold myself to be something a little bigger than I actually am. But I'll tip well. If I have to spend every dime of the money Gorman's team gave me to live on for the next week to make this night extra special, I will. I've eaten ramen and peanut butter sandwiches for days before. I can survive on it again.

"Open the glove box." I nod to the lever in front of Hannah. She eyes me with suspicion but pulls the box open. I didn't anticipate her hair being done up so nice, so she might resist my request, but I really want this to be a surprise.

"Take out the blindfold and put it on before I drive."

Her mouth tightens and curves into this demure smile. She pulls the silk scarf from the box and slides her hands in either direction, gripping the ends and bringing the width of the cloth up to her face. She drapes it over her eyes and ties it loosely behind her head, and I let about a million and one fantasies play out in my head as she does.

"You better not make me car sick," she says as she rests back in her seat and adjusts the seat belt across her chest.

I smirk and bring the car to life.

"I promise, no fast turns until you can see them coming."

Where we're headed is only a twenty-minute drive. It's late enough of a weekday that the traffic in the city won't be heavy, if any at all. I take the interstate for half the distance, then cut through the tall buildings down Central Avenue, stopping at a few lights. The greens and reds reflect off Hannah's skin, and every pause gives me a chance to take in her curves, to remember how they feel under my fingertips.

To adore her.

"Is it pancakes?" She's been throwing out random guesses for the entire trip. I'm glad she's hungry because I do have dinner planned. She hasn't even come close to where I'm taking her, though. I'm not sure if she even realizes we're in the city.

"It's better than pancakes," I say, signaling for the final turn of our journey. I dip into the bottom floor of the garage, wondering if this will give something away.

"Nothing is better than pancakes," Hannah says. She does reach out with her hands to steady herself as the car shifts along the bumps in the garage.

"Reserve your judgement."

I pull into the spot marked with a cone, the way the manager told me it would be. A night guard holds open the back door that employees use to leave at night and I hold up my hand to greet him.

"Good evening, sir," he says as I dash out of the car and offer him a smile.

"Good evening. Thank you for doing this," I say, rushing to Hannah's door and opening it to help her out.

"Can I take it off yet?"

"Not quite yet," I answer, pulling the fabric down a little to prevent her from catching clues on the floor.

"Hey," she says, swatting at my chest. I grab her hand and kiss it, then keep it held in mine.

"You forget I've been through a lot of piñatas with you. I know all of your cheating techniques."

She laughs at my confession but nods with a tight smile.

"I could always see out of the bottom. You and Tommy would swing and swing."

I usher her through the door, my palm on her back as the night guard holds in his laugh at our banter. I'm glad he finds us entertaining. I'm asking a lot for him to be here.

"Yeah, but you broke out all the candy and Tommy and I could see to pick it up. You barely got a thing by the time you were done beating that thing with a bat."

Her honey laugh echoes in the empty hallway, and I note the way she flinches, hoping this is a clue. It's the service entrance; it won't tell her a thing.

"I think I would be really good at telling police where kidnappers are taking me. I'm good at hearing things," she brags. Our guide can't hold in his laugh, and spits out tiny blasts of sound from between his fingers as he cups his mouth.

"Like that! See? Someone else is here. Tommy? Is it Tommy?"

I lean into her and kiss her cheek.

"It isn't Tommy," I say. "And let's not muse about being kidnapped, okay?"

I know she was just being funny, trying to make me break down and let her know where we are, but the mere mention of something like that—of her being a target—sent shivers down my spine. My head immediately went to Alex, to how trapped I am. I can't believe he would do something *that* evil though.

I push those worries to the far depths of my mind and concentrate on the night ahead as I help Hannah into the elevator. I'm like a kid on Christmas morning, only I'm giving a gift instead of receiving. My chest is filled with this warm glow that fires sparks across my nerves all the way from my ears to my toes. I can't wait to see Hannah's face when I pull off her mask. My heart tells me this place will be special for her, will *do* something special for her. It's something I've always known, without even asking.

The elevator softly dings and Hannah holds up her finger, opening her mouth as if that's another clue. She relents quickly.

"Okay, yeah. I've got nothing."

"I know you don't. I'm pretty sure I'm going to completely blow your mind," I brag. Our guide waits in a small chair by the elevator and nods to me that it's okay to continue on my own.

I weave us through a few of the displays to the very center of the most important room in this place. The air is practically sterile, but the place is kept cool and the air conditioning is beading the skin on her arms. I pull my jacket off and drape it over her shoulders. She holds on to it and turns her head, unsure where I've gone. Her lost smile is precious.

"Thank you," she hums. She turns slowly, all of her senses working to figure things out before I reveal it.

"Are you ready?"

She nods, freezing in place. I step up so I'm square with her and take one final breath, exhaling a few of my nerves.

My hands move to the blindfold and I follow the fabric to the back of her head, untying it carefully so not to mess up her hair. She blinks rapidly as I let the material fall away and it takes her a moment to let her eyes adjust. First, she's staring at me, her mouth caught in a wondrous smile that hasn't really resonated with what her eyes are about to see. The moment it does, though . . . I've never been as privileged as I am right now watching Hannah soak in the world in which I've always known she belongs.

"Dustin." Her voice breaks at saying my name, and my chest cracks open. I did right by her.

Rembrandts to the left. Monet to the right. But it's the paintings directly ahead that dazzle her. She had a few Van Gogh prints in her bedroom growing up. I assume they went with her to college. She's always drawn, and I remember seeing her book of sketches and small doodles she brought to the face painting booth when we helped out her mom. She's mentioned studying art over our lives together, and nobody has ever taken her seriously. Art is her passion as much as racing is mine.

She bends down and cups her knees, laughing out once with tears pricking the corners of her eyes. I step to the side and hold my hand to my chin.

"Did I do good?"

She flits her gaze to me, her mouth still caught in intoxicated surprise. I smile behind my palm as I just watch in silence.

"Dustin," she says, making a slow turn where she stands.

The art museum is closed. It closes early during the week in the summer. I'm not sure Hannah's ever even been. Tommy and I came here during a field trip our freshman year and we were too dumb to appreciate it. We liked that we got out of class and sat in the back of the bus with the popular girls for the hour-long road trip. I've always thought seeing this place through Hannah's eyes would be different. I was right. Seeing these works, hundreds of years old yet timeless, reflected in the absolute elation shining in Hannah's eyes is life-altering. I aspire to feel the way I believe she does right now.

"It's our place for the night. There's dinner too. On the patio in the atrium. It's takeout from the Italian place next door, so not quite lobster or steak, but—"

"It's perfect," she says, throwing her arms around me and covering my lips in the cherry red of her lipstick. I'll wear it with pride. I swing her around and keep her in my arms when I set her down, walking her toward the famous piece of the sunflower. I don't know much about art, other than the commercial pieces I've seen in other places. I want her to tell me about everything in this place, as I'm sure she can.

"How did you know?"

I feel her eyes on me before I turn to meet her gaze. I stare at her silently for several seconds, touching her face with the back of my hand and tracing the curve of her jaw as my gaze flits to her red-smudged lips. My lip ticks up on one side as I erase the stray red from her skin with my thumb.

"I just knew," I finally say, shifting my gaze back to meet hers.

In life, people are lucky to experience once that feeling of completely and utterly falling in love. I've had the honor of feeling it three times, each with the same girl. The first when Hannah held me in her arms, away from everyone's prying eyes, behind a trailer at the Tucson track just after Colt ruined my race. The second, the moment she said those words to me, right before I left her sleeping on her parents' couch.

The third? Right this second. And every second that follows. There is something so powerful about seeing the one you love thrive in their environment, grow in the world in which they were meant to be—to see them belong. Hannah belongs in a world like this, and I do everything I can to give it to her.

"I have something for you," I say, bringing her wandering gaze back to me.

I reach into the inside pocket of my jacket for the well-worn yellow shirt that belongs to her. I folded it into a square, so it takes her a moment to unravel it when I hand it to her. Her eyes recognize it quickly.

"I've been searching for this thing," she scolds playfully.

I shrug, guilty as charged.

"I took it with me the night I left. I wanted something to keep you alive in my memory, in case . . ." I look down at the ground between us and sink my hands into my pockets. It's suddenly harder to breathe. I can't say the words out loud, but I took it in case I never saw her again. It lost her scent years ago. I never washed it, and I kept it under my pillow most nights in Oklahoma. I brought it with me when I came home, hoping it would give me strength.

No, that's a lie.

I brought it hoping a time would come, that fate would give me a shot. I wanted to be able to give it back to her. I wanted a moment like this.

"I love it even more now," she says.

"I love you," I blurt out, afraid if I hold back I'll never be able to get the words out at all.

My terrified eyes blink wildly, unable to focus. I've never said those words to anyone, not that I can remember.

I'm sure I probably uttered them to my fake mom as a toddler who didn't know how bad his life really was. Of my own volition, though? Never. Not for anyone to hear. I practiced saying them to Hannah in the open air. I said them in my prayers that I figured nobody heard.

And I said them right now.

"Dustin, you know I love you. Always have," she says, suddenly in front of me, her hands on my face. "You're trembling."

I stutter out a laugh.

"Guess I am."

She has to pry my hands from my pockets, and I let her guide them to her face. The numbness dissipates at one touch of her soft skin. I fall into her eyes, light blue like the brightest day of the year.

"I love you, Hannah Judge. So fucking much," I choke out.

Before I can fall apart more, she lifts up on her toes and kisses me. My lips are caught in this weird state, somewhere between an elated cry and bliss. She holds her kiss to me tight, her lips parting around my bottom one, her tongue brushing against it, awakening my frozen nerves. I come alive at her taste, my hands growing stronger, slipping back into her hair, my thumbs brushing along her cheek while I tilt her head to one side to kiss her the way I want to—the way I need to.

It takes a less than subtle cough to remind me we aren't fully alone, and our lips cling desperately as we part, stopping to breathe with our foreheads together.

"I forgot he was here," I whisper laugh.

"Me, too."

My arms wrap around her and I hold her to me, swallowing her up in my one good suit.

"How about dinner, and then maybe you can give me a tour?" I kiss the top of her head, then spin her to my side, my hand never leaving her body. I won't break this touch until I have to.

"I'd love that."

I love you. I love you. I love you.

We ate dinner on a blanket-covered bench in the middle of the art museum's garden. The perfect square of clear sky above us was speckled with bright stars, the sky clear enough and black without the moon, allowing us to see the universe's crystals despite the city's bright lights that surround us.

I saw Dustin slip the guard a roll of money, at least three hundred dollars. He doesn't have that kind of money to spend on me, but the fact he wanted to, that he did anyway? My heart squeezes with his love and aches that I can't rush this life forward so he can feel the success I know is coming for him.

I don't want to rush, though. I want to slow down. I want to experience every second, every breath, and note it in my heart and mind so I never forget them.

Dustin couldn't possibly have known how deep this gesture would reach. I let our time at the museum be without adding any of my chaos to it. I didn't want to ruin the beauty of him giving me this gift, of sharing the weird things I know about Van Gogh with him while I make him look at paintings for long, silent minutes. He never once rushed. In fact, I had to urge him to leave. I felt bad when I noticed the guard, who we learned was named Marcus, start to yawn.

Dustin let me drive home, which meant I could veer off course if I wanted to, which I did. I followed Central all the way up the mountain to the south of the city. When we were kids, my dad used to take the three of us up here on our way home from races. We liked watching the planes take off from a viewpoint up above. That view is more spectacular at night, and I wasn't done sharing this one with Dustin.

"I bet those curves are wicked fun in this car during the daytime," I say as I roll us into a quiet, secluded pull-off just below the flashing radio towers.

"Daylight being the key word there." He chuckles, unbuckling as I kill the engine. He leaves the car and I join him at the front, and we both slide up to sit on the hood.

I love that neither of us are nervous at the thought of zipping through these jagged rocks at tops speeds. I pushed it as it was in the dark, and Dustin never once gripped the dash. His body remained relaxed, his eyes scanning the road for interesting things to point out in the dark, like the wild donkey grazing in a ravine lit up by our headlights.

"I did a thing that I haven't told anyone about," I confess.

He leans into me, resting his head on my shoulder, lips dusting my skin as he tilts his head enough to look up at me.

"I know you did," he teases.

I lean into him, straightening him up.

"Not that, silly. And sorry to tell you this, but Bailey gets a lot of details."

His eyes widen as he swallows.

"Oh-kayyy." If it weren't so dark, I might catch him blushing.

His feet stretch out and he tugs the tie loose from his shirt. His jacket was long ago discarded to the back seat, the air plenty warm.

"What is this thing you did, Banana?"

I pucker my lips and turn to face him.

"Did I ever tell you how much I love it when you call me that? Just you; not Tommy."

He leans forward and dusts his nose on mine.

"Noted, and very sweet. But quit stalling." He winks and leans his weight on his right palm so he can give me his full attention.

I draw in a heavy breath, then fold my legs up so I can turn to face him.

"There's this apprenticeship at this really amazing studio. It's led by this really amazing teacher, and you learn everything from textiles to interactive digital things, and there's painting, and immersive workshops, and—"

He turns to face me and grabs my shoulders. Our eyes lock, and I'm relieved to see his wide smile.

"Slow down, Captain Excitement. Breathe." We draw in a slow breath together and I let out my nervous energy with a laugh.

"Right. Sorry. Anyhow." I pause, looking down at my hands as I knead them together. "I applied."

I lift my head and tilt it to look at him sideways. I haven't said a word about this to Bailey or my parents or Tommy. I did it as a dare to myself a few months ago. I'd just come back to school after spring break and a series of epic fights with my mother about my future. It was a rebel move, and I never thought in a million years—

"I got in."

I suck in my lips and hold my breath.

Dustin shifts to his knees and braces himself on my shoulders again, shaking me gently, his face marked by his deep dimples and high brow. His perfect hair slicked back with a few loose strands fallen over his forehead so he could match our perfect night.

"Hannah! That's incredible!" He looks up to smile at the sky, and I could cry it feels so relieving to see someone this proud of me.

"Thing is, I can't go," I stammer.

He sinks back down to his haunches and his chin falls to his chest, his mouth open.

"Why?"

I lift a shoulder.

"It's *really* expensive. And it's art, so, you know—"

"Not business." He rolls his eyes. He's seen this debate play out lots of times at my house. Tommy was good, accepting the path printed for him, but I always pushed back against it.

"The art school is actually twice the cost, but with the apprenticeship, my tuition would be cut in half, and I'd work to cover the rest."

"So what's the problem?" His eyes are searching mine, and it cuts me inside just thinking about it.

"It's in Omaha, Dustin. Away from everyone. From you."

Our chests rise and fall as that reality settles into the space and we accept it. After several quiet seconds, Dustin leans forward and cups my cheeks, tipping my head down so he can kiss the top of it.

"So what," he says, falling back.

I laugh out loud.

"So I'll be far away, from everyone. And I can't pay for it anyway, not even the half that will be left, and—"

"So what?" He repeats those two words as if some solution has miraculously unearthed. My chest tightens at all of the unanswered strands that go along with me taking a leap that big. It's one thing to come home for the summers and drive fast out in the desert. It's even not the same kind of risk as leaping from cliffs into icy cold water. This is about my identity, my other true love and going for it.

"What if I fail?"

"You won't." He's so matter of fact. I blink at him slowly.

"I love you." A soft smile plays at my lips and I decide to tuck this conversation back inside, leaving myself with this slice of time where Dustin believes in me so unequivocally that even the most obvious and challenging, real obstacles seem to melt when I look at the world through his eyes.

"I love you," he says, and the words come easier to him than before. They wrap around my heart and pull me close.

I don't tell him that the deadline passed. That they've already given the spot to someone else. That the day I had to decide was the day we sprinkled Colts ashes in the desert and he got the news he'd been dreaming of. The day we kissed in the middle of the road. The day I chose Dustin Bridges over my dreams, not that I was *really* going to take my shot. But that window was open, if only briefly, and I let it close the minute his lips hit mine.

My hand curves behind his neck and I pull him near as I shift to my back and slide down the length of the windshield and hood. I bring him with me, our mouths a fraction apart, our smiles locked in this almost pose, the chemistry palpable.

"You said something about me breaking my best time this morning," he reminds me.

I smile and let my head rest completely against the glass.

"I did," I say, pulling on the end of the loose knot tied between my breasts, unwinding the woven rope from the soft cotton. Once it's completely free from the material, I toss it to the side and turn my attention to Dustin's tie.

"It's not quite the grandstands, but I guess this will do," he jokes. We're under a moonless sky of stars, glitter on the ground far below as the city buzzes with the creatures of the night. Planes float by in the distance and the desert embraces us, not another car in sight.

I slip his tie free from the collar of his white shirt, my fingers working the buttons free one at a time as he drops his head to my chest so his teeth can grip the cotton fold that covers my right breast. He slides it to the side with his mouth, his nose grazing against my hard nipple just as I reach the last of his buttons.

"Ahh," I cry out, arching into him.

He works his shirt from his arms as his mouth searches for my ripe breast. His mouth covers it completely, his tongue swirling around my pink bud before he sucks it raw and turns his attention to the other one. I hold his head to me, wanting him to devour me, and as he trails his kisses lower and lower, I let him.

"My God, Hannah, but you are sweet," he says, lifting the skirt of my dress and pressing his mouth to my inner thigh.

"How sweet?" I bite my knuckle as I look down at him, my knees falling open. He presses his mouth to my center over the cotton strip of my panties and speaks with his mouth against me, sending vibrations through my core.

"So fucking sweet," he says.

My legs start to close around his head, but his hands slide along my inner thighs and keep them open. He kisses me through my panties at first, eventually sliding them to the side and running his tongue along my swollen center. I writhe and moan, thankful we're secluded and alone. I lift my hips so he can slide my panties down my hips and thighs, eventually tossing them to the ground along with the rope from my dress.

"Dustin," I cry out his name.

His tongue enters me and I lean my head so far back I can see the radio towers blinking far above us. His thumb presses where I crave him and his tongue moves in slow, measured swipes along my wet, tender skin, bringing me near climax before stopping.

I'm panting, not able to hide how flushed I am, how out of breath I am, how fucking needy I am. My fingernails rake down his chest as he moves up my body, leaving what I'm sure will be a trail of pink scratches down his skin. When I reach the button his pants, I work it undone quickly, and Dustin holds his weight above me on his forearms as he slides them down his hips along with his boxers.

"I love you, Hannah," he says, his head falling against mine.

I lift my chin until our lips touch.

"I love you," I say just before our kiss prevents words.

My hands grasp his hips as his tip slides against my wet center, my legs widening, begging. He's holding back and I know it's because he wants to get a condom, but I can't wait. I don't care. I'll have his babies. I'll have an entire family with this man. I can't think of a life more complete than that.

"It's okay," I say, my palms on his face as he slips back enough to let me see his strained face. His eyes are squeezed shut so tight, his forehead pained.

"Dustin. I want this, with you. Right now. I don't care. We don't need protection. It's only us. Always," I say.

His eyes open as he pushes into me. My center swells, the ache so sweet, so hungry, and I lift my hips slightly to urge him deeper, and he listens, rocking into me and filling me completely. It knocks my breath from my lungs, and I see the instant concern in his eyes.

"Don't stop" I grab his hips and stretch my mouth into a smile. I pull him into me again, and he groans as I do.

Dustin cages me between his arms, his lips taking tender passes at mine, suckling and nibbling my mouth as his hips rock and he pushes in and out of me. The pace is painfully slow but I wouldn't rush it for the world. He's drawing this out on purpose, taking his time, giving me pleasure before taking what he wants.

He draws my leg up to the side and turns so we're lying side-by-side, his cock never leaving me. Things feel different this way, better, if that's possible. I slip my arms free of my sleeves so my breasts are fully exposed. To be honest, I'm turned on by the way he looks at them. I've never felt my body was anything special, but under Dustin's gaze, I feel sexy and supple.

"Ride me," he asks, and the mere fact he can ask me to turns me on so much that I shift my hips the second he asks and move so I'm straddling him.

My hands find the center of his chest for balance, and he traps my wrists as I sink down on him completely. My head falls back at the feeling of being this full. I sit still as he stretches me wider. When one of his hands leaves my wrists, I dip my chin to see him reach forward and press his palm against me. The sensation rocks me, and a spasm renders my body limp. I fall into him.

"Come for me, Hannah."

I move with him, his hands gripping my ass now, pushing me into him while his hips rock up to meet me thrust for thrust. The feeling builds and my skin gets hotter and hotter, my dress sticking to my thighs, our skin sticking to one another with the light sheen of sweat that builds as we both chase that feeling over the edge.

I tighten around him in complete release as he explodes inside of me, emptying himself with several hard thrusts that threaten to take me away again. I'm dizzy. I'm satiated. I've never felt more a part of a whole, less alone.

I love this man.

"I love you," he says just as I think it.

21

"Gorman Truit is here."

I think this might be the fifth time Tommy has said those words right to my face. I woke up groggy. I woke up late. I barely woke up without Tommy catching his sister's naked body clinging to my side in this sorry-ass excuse for a bed.

"I got it. I hear you." I get up from the bed, my boxers twisted around my body because, well, I just tugged those fuckers on.

"Maybe you want to get some pants on and go out there, make sure you're still in that driver's seat?" Tommy paces while he talks. He does that when he's nervous. And he's nervous.

"Have you seen him yet?" I squint through my headache. I'm sure I look hung over. I'm not; I just didn't sleep. Didn't want to.

"Yeah, I saw him. Shook his hand. He offered to sign a picture for me. What a douchebag!"

I squeeze myself into the tight kitchen space, pull a mug

from the cabinet, and pray the coffeemaker works like it's supposed to.

"You get a picture?" I cock an eyebrow at my friend as I fill my cup.

He parts his lips but doesn't speak, shaking his head in admission of guilt. I laugh.

"Fuck you, all right? I don't meet a lot of famous people."

"Gorman Truit is hardly famous. He's never broken the top ten." I lean into the counter and cross my legs to mask the absolute terror rattling around my chest. Gorman has no reason to be here. He pulled out for personal issues. The rumor on the street is rehab. He's not cleared to drive. It's my car. For this race, it's my car. He can't possibly have the status to ruin that.

I gulp down half the cup, the coffee scorching my throat on its way down. I'm going to either boil this headache away or drown it.

"Good morning," Hannah says, her tired voice floating over my shoulders and wrapping around my bare skin. I smile against my cup and Tommy sees it.

"Oh, fuck. Really?" He waves a hand at us and marches out of the RV.

I set my coffee down and let out a heavy sigh, my back to Hannah. She moves her hands around my waist and rests her head on my spine.

"Were we that obvious?"

"Guess so." I look out at the bright landscape of the dirt lot just outside our door. Tommy swung it closed behind him but it only bounced back open.

"Gorman's here," I tell Hannah.

Her hands slide from my body as she slips away.

"That a good thing? Or—"

"I'm not sure." I shrug as I turn to face her, my hand finding the back of her head and drawing her into me. I kiss her crown and soon her lips, sucking her in for strength to get through this morning. I would give anything to get in the Supra with her and drive back up the mountain.

"Hey, Dust? You in there?" Virgil knows I am. Tommy sent him.

I roll my eyes then close them as I turn to yell over my shoulder.

"Be right out!"

"You should probably put pants on," Hannah teases, tugging at the top of my boxers.

It takes all my willpower to gather her hands together and kiss them before pushing them away. I back out of the kitchen space and offer her the rest of my coffee, which she gladly takes. I throw on a pair of jeans, my Vans and one of Gorman's sponsor T-shirts to show some good faith, and run my fingers through my hair before hopping out of the RV. A small crowd is gathered for Gorman, his guys all pretending they miss him. I've learned a few things over this past week. Gorman isn't beloved. He pays decently, and that's why Douglas has stuck with him for so long. But he's kind of a dick, and he doesn't win.

"There he is!" Gorman saunters toward me as I enter the garage, and I let him pull me in for one of those hugs I really can't stand. He slaps my back hard, and his body smells like gas station cologne. His tan is expensive. I'm guessing it's new, from a salon last night. Have to keep those appearances up and make everyone think you've been on vacation. I'm not even sure his hair is naturally blond. It's very . . . *yellow*.

"Hey, man. Good to see you," I lie. My hands fall to my

back pockets and my eyes scan the room to find Tommy just beyond Ernie's shoulder. His mouth is a hard line, which is a sign that his suspicions are on full alert. *Mine too, buddy. Mine too.*

"What are you doing here? I didn't think we'd get to see you." My voice sounds nervous, like a kid. That's what I am to him. I'm borrowing his grown-up toys.

When I started racing trucks, Gorman was one of the first guys I met on the circuit. He jumps back and forth from stock car to truck, depending on what he thinks he can do better in. His charm works for the brand, I guess. They've been with him for four years. He's thirty-two.

"Oh, just making the sponsor happy and doing a little check in. I wanted to see how the guys were treating you too. They treating you right?" He slings a heavy arm around me and turns to look at his crew.

"Of course," Ernie says.

"Kid rocked the hell out of the time yesterday," Douglas adds.

My chest tightens. I'm not sure it's a good thing to let Gorman know how well I'm doing. He strikes me as a fragile ego. I squint one eye and scratch my forehead, playing humble. Really, though? I didn't just rock the time. I destroyed his. If I can keep that pace up next weekend, I'm placing—something Gorman's never done.

"Really?" His voice feigns interest and pride. I read right through it to its frightened, threatened guts. And that's when I feel the tickle of the dark side. The other Dustin is waking up. The one who got that time in the first place. The one who doesn't lose, who ignores casualties, who acts a lot like Colt.

"I mean, four seconds better than my best time, which is maybe . . . what . . . three better than yours?"

His jaw ticks and his tongue pushes into the inside of his cheek as his teeth come down on it. He laughs through his pissed-off smile. Tommy rubs his palm over his face and turns his back to me, busying himself with anything other than this conversation.

"Wow." Gorman punctuates that single word, the warning clear in the way he says it. His heavy hand slaps my back again. "Good for you . . . *kid.*"

To mask the sudden silence eating all of the oxygen in the garage, Douglas claps a few times and tells the crew to get to work. We make eye contact, and I see his warning. I ignore it. I'm about to walk away when Gorman jerks me back to him, his arm tight around my shoulders, holding me to his side. He gets eerily close to my ear, and I open my stance and crack my knuckles in case I need to take a quick swing.

"You beat my times or place in that race Sunday, and you're fucking done." He steps back and flashes me a toothy smile with a quick raise of his brow.

My only response is to huff a quick laugh through my nostrils, which makes his tough-guy smile calm right the fuck down. He can't intimidate me now. I've turned. This is a different Dustin, and sometimes, I really love being him.

I t absolutely drove Gorman insane that I wouldn't bend to his will. He tried to box me in about a dozen times. At one point, I even thought he was going to suggest we race. He's not allowed to drive, though; I looked that little bit up when he was taking a phone call.

Now that he's gone, I'm left with this pent up energy, and I pour it into prep with Douglas and Tommy in the garage. I think I can handle pushing the throttle a little more. Douglas worries I'll spin out, but everything felt tight out there. My lines were on point, and if I can hold it here, on this road? I can hold it on the series track.

We compromise with a slight angle adjustment on the plate, and I'm gearing up to take it for a spin when Hannah walks into the garage, Alex Offerman's contract in her hands.

"Hey guys, give me a sec." I rush to her, noting the worry lines on her face. I haven't talked to her about the details yet. I'm still not sure how to handle it myself. Tommy said it would worry her, so I've kept it off the table between us.

"What's up?" I urge her into the far corner of the garage as I work on the zipper of the fire suit. She's chewing at her lip.

"You get a chance to look it over?" I nod toward the contract in her hands. It's not that I was hiding it from her. When she glances up at me with deep pools of blue, puppy-sad eyes, I change my mind. I was hiding it. This is why.

"Dustin, you can't do this."

Fuck.

I run my hand through my hair and take the heavy packet from her. I rub the back of my neck and shake the dense contract in my hand.

"I know. There are things I need to work out."

"Dustin, he's laundering money. It's obvious."

My jaw ticks at her tone. I don't think she meant to be condescending about it, but it hits something in my chest and my defenses fire up.

"Yeah, I know. I *said* I'm working on it." I toss it on an empty chair and zip my suit up all the way. I can't bring myself to look her in the eyes. She'll be disappointed and I need *this* Dustin to stick around a little longer to hit the track.

"Just promise me you won't do something without thinking it through. Don't get yourself tangled in something—"

"Something what? That I can't get out of? Promise. Now, can I get back to the car?"

Fuck, that was a dick move.

I give in and glance up. She's working so damn hard to keep her lip from quivering, but I see it. It's too late.

"Gah!" I groan, running both palms over my face. I pinch the bridge of my nose and inhale a deep breath. "I'm sorry. That— I'm on edge. Gorman's visit wasn't great, and I have to do well at time trials. You're right, and I promise, I'm going to deal with it."

My pulse is beating so hard in my chest that it makes my stomach nauseous. Hannah's right that I can't keep putting Alex off. In fact, there's a voicemail from him on my phone that I refuse to listen to. All I want to do is get through this day, and maybe the next. If I can do that, find a balance between my two selves, then the answers to my Alex issues will become clear.

"Okay," she says, her smile fleeting. She grabs my face and presses her lips to mine, holding them there motionless, like a reminder that she is my light and that she believes in me. Thank God she does.

I join the crew again when Hannah leaves, and we take the car for a trial with the new adjustments I talked Douglas into. My lines suffer from the speed, but not by a lot. My time comes out the same, and if I can get used to the feel, I'll be able to gain even more. I convince Douglas to leave things how they are for now under the promise that I'll prove I can handle it. If I have to drive this track through an entire set of treads to be perfect, I will.

Tommy hangs back when everyone breaks for dinner. I'm sure he saw me and Hannah talking. I know he saw the contract. He went over and picked it up and tossed it into my duffle bag as if it's some bit of contraband I should hide. Maybe it is.

"Alex called," I admit to him as I straddle the stool Ernie likes to roll around this place on.

I pull my phone from my pocket and hand it to my friend. Tommy sits on the workbench in the garage and unlocks my screen to see the message.

"What'd he say?"

I shrug.

"You didn't listen?"

I shake my head and bring my gaze up to meet his.

I'm so tired. I feel as though I can't win. Every option leads to ruin. If I go into this business with Alex, I'm in bed with a criminal. I'm Colt. If I don't, he steals my dream and I never get a shot at it. If I don't show well this weekend, I get sent back to the trucks, this time without a sponsor. If I do what I know I can do? Gorman Truit is going to make ruining me his life's mission. Of everything, Gorman worries me the least. I've always been able to handle the road. Driving is where I'm at my best. It's just so damn hard to do with all this weight on my back.

"You want me to listen to it?"

I consider Tommy's offer and decide I've got nothing to lose. I could use his advice, probably. "Put it on speaker."

He does, setting my phone on the bench next to him and turning the volume all the way up.

"Dustin, you were supposed to call me."

Our eyes meet at Alex's ominous greeting.

"I've always hated that guy," Tommy reminds me.

"You sure liked his free beer," I fire back.

He holds a finger to his mouth, hushing me because he knows I'm right.

"I'm afraid I'm going to have to go ahead and close on my own. I do appreciate you bringing me the opportunity. It was a really nice gift. I'll be sure to return the favor one day. Maybe . . . maybe I can host you and that lovely girlfriend of yours for another night in the suite." The only sound left is his arrogant, thick, nicotine-laden laughter before he disconnects.

Tommy and I sit in silence for several seconds as I let his threat soak in. Only, it isn't a threat anymore. It's a big FU and him pissing all over my future.

"Fuck!" I shout, erupting from the stool and kicking it across the garage.

"Maybe he didn't yet. You want me to call him?" He holds my phone up and I chew on that idea for a second. Tommy would love to play gangster and talk tough right back.

"No. That won't do any good."

I walk to the car and wrap my hands around the edge of the engine bay. Why couldn't this problem be something I can solve in here. Tommy and I can fix anything if it's in here. Outside this world, and I'm screwed.

"You could always . . .burn him. I mean, my dad knows a lot of people. The feds worked with your dad."

"The feds *entrapped* my dad."

"Whatever," Tommy says. "All I'm saying is maybe you can beat him to this before he closes on his own."

I let my gaze blur off in the distance and I work through Tommy's scenario. It's not impossible. It's maybe the only way to get what I want. I snap my fingers for my phone and Tommy slides from the bench, slapping it in my palm. I hit RETURN CALL on Alex's message and hold my breath through six rings, preparing myself for his voice-mail. It picks up, his simple message of "It's Alex. Shoot." After the beep, I take a deep breath—and temporarily sell my soul.

"Alex. It's Dustin. I'm in."

My eyes flit up to meet my friends, and I swear I can see the fire burning in my own soul as I look out on the world. I end the call and cradle my phone in both hands, waiting.

A full minute passes, and the rage is building. The walls are closing in.

My phone buzzes, and I hold it up for Tommy to see.

ALEX: *Thumbs up.*

The game is on. I give Tommy a short nod.

"Thumbs fucking up."

22

The closer we get to race day, the lonelier this place becomes. Dustin crawls into my tiny bed, sometimes at two in the morning, his body drained from the day. He still manages to keep himself awake long enough to appreciate me. I'm always kissed. My hair stroked. My skin tickled with the gentle sway of his fingertips along my arm. He puts himself to sleep taking care of me. I lay awake and wait for it.

Sometimes, he's strangely quiet, almost a bit lost. I mentioned the contract two nights ago, thinking maybe he would be open to talking to my dad or having him draft up a counter proposal. He dismissed it quickly, and it seemed to make him angry that I would suggest it. "I have it handled. I'm not stupid," he said. He apologized for snapping. He blamed the stress and said he wants to do this on his own, but I get the sense he's avoiding the red flags because they pick away at the fantasy. I won't push him again until after the race, though. He can't afford to lose focus.

My family is coming in today, though, and we're moving to the raceway. I'll be staying with them in the *much* nicer RV my dad rented for the occasion. Dustin will be pretty much eating, living, and breathing the raceway. His time trial is in the morning, and as expected, he isn't nervous about it all.

"You may be the only person I know who can spend a week with her boyfriend at a dumpy race track and leave with *more* stuff than you came with." Dustin hefts my heavy suitcase down the steps of the RV.

I pat my hand against the side of the rig.

"I'm going to miss this place—*kinda.*"

He laughs out once, and hard.

"Well, I have every intention of using my free pass for a Judge shower whenever I want. I saw that thing your dad rented. Man's travelling in luxury all of a sudden."

Dustin's right. My dad did splurge; I think he's pretty excited. He's been dreaming of this for Dustin almost as long as Dustin has for himself. Those two have shared a lot of fumes and burned through a lot of kart motors to get here. The RV he's bringing to the track is a far cry from the pickup truck shell we camped in for all those trips to Tucson and Nevada.

Nevada.

I can't quit thinking about Alex and that contract. I don't want to bring it up to my dad because it's so impor-tant to Dustin that he sort this out on his own. He feels he has something to prove, even though he doesn't need to prove anything. I have to trust him on his word. He promised. And I need to let go of those last few vestiges of bitterness from him leaving four years ago. I understand why he did. I know what Colt was into, the people who were out to hurt him. Dustin didn't want me to have any part of that.

"I think I see them," Dustin says, drawing my attention back to the present. I twist to face the same direction and shade my eyes from the sun. My dad is maneuvering a tank of an RV down the winding dirt road alongside the track.

"He's never gonna make it out of here," I groan.

Dustin's hand runs along my back and he leans over to kiss the top of my head.

"Nah, your dad's got this. I once saw that man thread a kart on a hitch backward over a bridge made out of particle board to cross a canal."

He leaves me with a grin and wheels my bag toward the oncoming RV. I give him a moment alone with my dad, who hops out of the RV when he decides he's driven it in deep enough. They talk excitedly after they shake hands. Soon, they're hugging. They're finding their way back, and I couldn't be happier. Why my chest hurts so much, I don't know.

"I know that bed is better, but you're going to have to live with Mom in four hundred square feet. You let me know if you want to trade."

I pat my brother's chest and turn to walk backward.

"That's two hundred for her, and two hundred for me. I think I'll manage." Really, I might not.

My mom and I have a lot of shit to overcome. I know the bulk of it is on my plate. I blamed her for a lot of things, for Dustin leaving after her terrible reaction to us. I still blame her for the constant pressure over school, for pushing me to follow her footsteps instead of treading my own. But she loves me fiercely. I see that now. I'm not sure if Dustin made me realize it or if it happened organically. Knowing his life as I do, it's hard to take actual parents—

present and loving parents—for granted, despite how fucking crazy they might make you.

"You ready for this?" my dad says, slinging an arm around my shoulder as he guides me into my new temporary home.

"Sleeping in a bed larger than a shoebox, or race day?" I'm definitely ready for the bed. I step into my parents' RV and instantly feel a million degrees cooler.

"Both, I guess," he laughs out.

"I put your bag in the back," Dustin says, stepping back into the main room.

"Where's Mom?" I mean, this rig is big, but it's not that big. I don't see any sign of her in this thing.

"She's doing some press business or something. She promised to drive up tonight. You know Bailey's dad was planning to run against her?"

I act shocked at my dad's revelation while Dustin walks away so he doesn't have to bluff.

"Wow, really? He would be a terrible mayor." That's not a lie. Mr. Tingle would be about as strict as the mayor-slash-dad in Footloose who banned the town from dancing. In fact, I bet he would try to forbid it in Camp Verde his first day on the job.

"Well, I'm going to shower as soon as we hook up. And if she misses out on the hot water, too bad so sad." My dad laughs at the imaginary gauntlet I throw down.

Dustin takes him out to introduce him to the crew, and before long, everyone is huddled around the number forty-nine car. I take advantage of their distraction and nose around the space, checking out all the bells and whistles this thing has. The kitchen is pretty stacked, which means my mom is probably going to serve up some amazing food. She might know how to push my buttons, but her culinary skills are beyond the imagination. I swear, the woman can throw any random five things into a pot and somehow create something gourmet.

I head back to my room next. This thing has two of them. Mine is the first one, with a shared wall to the bathroom. It's half the size of my parents' but it's all mine. I sit on the velvety bedspread and run my fingers along the soft fur. I woke up an hour ago, but being in here could put me right back to sleep. I'm not sure whether it's the temperature finally being tolerable or the quiet this tiny space somehow provides.

I lean forward to peek out down the hall and out the door, and when no one is in sight, I fall back and put my feet up. As much as I'd love to rest, something is nagging at me.

My mom doing press is weird. We have one paper. Hardly anyone reads it unless it's to see their kid's picture from some sports award in the community section. I can't imagine a Camp Verde mayoral election race about to kick off is news enough for the Valley or bigger outlets. And my dad said that Mr. Tingle backed out, so there isn't even a race to hype.

I turn to social media and run a few searches, but the only big news I seem to come up with is the story about Kyle. He's coming home soon. Maybe that's what my mom is handling. I'm sure there are questions about his accident, people focusing on the Straights. I could see that story getting some legs.

Excited to share the news about Kyle with Dustin, I head back out of the RV and join the male pissing contest underway over the hood of Dustin's car. My dad is quickly winning over Douglas with tales from his drag racing days and all the dangerous illegal shit he used to do to his engine.

"You could have caught fire, man!" Douglas slaps a hand on his forehead and stares in wonder at my dad, who simply nods and agrees.

"I could have. But"—he points to Douglas—"I didn't."

"This all kinda makes those big safety lectures you used to give me and Tommy feel empty," Dustin adds, shifting slightly and catching a glimpse of me. His smile is instant and warms me from the inside.

"Excuse me, boys," he says, leaving the crew and my brother and father as he rushes me, lifting me over his shoulder and carrying me out of the garage. I laugh so loud it echoes against the walls as we leave.

He sets me down just outside, turning my back to the wall in the shade and stepping into me until I'm flat against the brick. His nose runs along my jaw as he grabs my hands and lifts them above my head, cuffing them to the wall in his hold as he kisses me hard and deep. I whimper against his lips and tug his hips toward me so I can feel how hard he is one last time. It's a stolen moment, and it doesn't last long, but it's enough to last me for the day.

When our kiss breaks, he leaves his forehead against mine and drops my hands so he can stroke my cheeks with his fingers.

"Why are you not staying with me again?" he asks.

"Because you won't be around at all, and if you are, you need to rest. And focus. And win."

"Ah, that," he laughs out quietly, dusting his lips against mine one last time before pushing away from the wall and sinking his hands in his pockets.

The wind tousles his hair and his eyes squint in the sun, which has left his cheeks red like his forearms. He needs to hydrate, and he needs rest, but I've lectured him enough about all that. If there is one thing I've learned, it's that Dustin will do what Dustin is going to do.

"Kyle's coming home."

"Oh, yeah?" Dustin's head falls to the side as his smile widens. "When? Today? Is he okay to travel? Should I call them?"

I laugh at how fast his mind works. I love how taken he is with the kid. He's said a few things that make me believe he has a connection to Kyle, a common bond of kids with shitty fathers. I haven't probed. It's not necessary.

"I don't think he's home yet, but he's awake and alert. I read an article that said he's doing well. I don't know that a race track is in his immediate future, but maybe you can give him a call?" Dustin smiles at my suggestion.

"Yeah, I think I will." He pulls his phone from his pocket and holds it in his palm, I think as a reminder.

"You ready, Han?" My dad steps out of the garage and eyes how close Dustin and I are standing to one another. Dustin takes several automatic steps back, but my dad grumbles and looks away.

"This was easier when I could ground you," he jokes. At least, I think that was a joke.

"I'm ready. Co-captain's seat is mine since Mom isn't here!" I skip toward the RV as my dad gives Dustin a final shake of the hand and squeeze of the arm before race day. I blow him a kiss and take off to beat my dad inside. His phone is resting in my seat so I grab it to move it to the captain's chair cup holder, but I notice dozens of messages from my mom noted on the screen.

I lift myself to peer out for my dad and see he's still caught up near the garage, talking to Dustin about something. I open his screen to make sure my mom isn't in an emergency, and the first thing that hits me is a photo of her shaking Alex Offerman's hand in front of the old Carney Raceway. A jolt of panic cascades down my throat, ripping through my chest, and flattening me to my seat.

I flip through photo after photo of what seems to be a press conference announcing Alex's new ownership. He cut Dustin out. Completely. All of the major stations in Arizona are out there. This is the biggest press conference to land in Camp Verde since the mountain to the north caught fire from lightning seven years ago. It's major news happening because of Dustin, and he's nowhere in the middle of it.

I'm sick, and I can't fathom that my mom is aware of how this man stepped in and took over. She's too excited to share the photos and update my dad on the news. They wouldn't be able to look Dustin in the eyes this weekend. They wouldn't be here to support him. My dad isn't that great a liar.

"You ready, Han?" My dad slips into the seat next to me and I twist my palm to show him his screen.

"Oh, hey. She sent photos? Pretty cool, huh?" My dad flips through the same scenario I did, while I look on with my mouth hung open, at a complete loss for words.

"This is going to be a complete game changer. I just hope we can keep that small-town feel. Sometimes things like this have a way of moving in and changing a community for the worse. Dustin swears that won't happen, but I mean, that kid swears a lot of things."

My dad tosses his phone into the cup holder and fishes the key for the RV out of his pocket, pressing a button on the fob that fires up the motor.

"Pretty cool, huh? I can start this thing with a remote. I can even cool it down before we get back in after we're down at the track. I could get used to this. Who knows, maybe your mom and I become those people who wander the country seeing national parks and all that junk."

He looks at me, smile bright, heart full of plans and not a worry in his periphery.

"Yeah, that's pretty cool alright." I swallow my pride and grin right back, choking out my response.

My parents have one half of a story, and I have the other. And if I put them together, I don't know that the tale will be good for any of us. More than anyone, I don't think it will be good for Dustin. *For us.*

I'll bite my tongue for now. I'll keep my ears open and listen for any clue that proves my gut instincts wrong. I won't ruin Dustin's shot. I won't bring this up before the race. Because something tells me even the great Dustin Bridges won't be able to drive his way through this.

23

I t's just the desert.
    Two lanes at dusk.
I'm only racing the car next to me.

I've been mentally preparing myself for the last twenty-four hours. It's not like me to get nervous, but there's more riding this than ever before. It's too late to undo what I've started. If I don't perform today, I'll never be able to keep up my end of the bargain with Alex, and he'll assume full control. I won't have the leverage to hold on to Carney's when Alex goes down. I won't have Hannah. I'll have nothing.

She's not going to be happy that I signed, but I couldn't make that a distraction before the race. She'll understand, especially when she knows that I plan to push Alex out. Sell him out. One wrong move and he's done. If he brings in construction crews and pays them even a ten-spot over what a normal bid is, I'll have him investigated. Our money runs clean. I run clean.

I am not Colt Bridges.

"Ready, killer?" Tommy squeezes my shoulders as he stands behind me and I kick feeling into my legs.

"Always." My real answer is closer to "normally." I'm not ready the way I should be. I feel it. Things are off.

"All you have to do is take top ten," he reminds me over my shoulder.

I nod, scanning pit row. These are the drivers I've grown up idolizing. Most of them have a dozen years on me. Most of them are millionaires. There are definitely at least ten who are better than me—on paper.

I pull my helmet on and fill my chest with air before blowing out hard and turning to look my best friend in the eyes.

"You've got this," he says, placing his hands on my shoulders. I do the same to him and continue to nod as we both look down and feel the moment. It's kind of like our own little prayer. We did this before every kart race when I was a kid. It never failed me. Not once.

I bring my head up and meet Tommy's certain eyes, his smile confident, not a hint of worry in his expression. And with his faith in me, suddenly everything feels right.

"I'm going to win. See you in three hundred laps."

Tommy's lip ticks up at my arrogance and he lightly slaps the side of my helmet.

"There he is," he says.

We pound fists and I turn to climb into the car. Douglas is in my ear first, followed by Ernie at spot. They argue over something I'm not going to pay attention to anyway, so I busy myself with the harness so I can meld my body with the car. That's the only way this works. Me and the car are one.

One focus.

One force.

Other than the constant auditory assault, which now includes Chad, Gorman's team manager, I am completely alone. This is the first time I've been by myself in days, since I walked myself out to the berm on that track, thought long and hard about my flaws and decided to turn them into assets. It's time to block everything out—Alex, my goals, the Judges . . . *Hannah.* She's the last thought I shut out and it's nearly impossible, but if she's anywhere near my thoughts for the next two hours and fifteen minutes, I won't be able to let my other side consume my soul.

I take in my environment and overlay everything I see with the familiar. Those cars in front of me, behind me, and the one next to me are trucks. They're all guys like me trying to prove themselves. They have weaknesses. They can't beat me.

This track is like any other track. The sky is dark, the infield desert, the roadway straight and two lanes. I'm in the Supra. Nobody beats Dustin Bridges.

Nobody.

"You're going to have to break out of that pack early. You're in the middle of the field," Douglas says in my ear.

"No shit," I swipe back.

"Alright, alright," he laughs back.

Douglas and I have found a good groove over the last week. I trust him, more than I trust Chad who is supposed to be calling the shots. Douglas has to listen to him, but I'm only listening to Douglas. Everyone else in my ear is noise. Well, besides Ernie. I guess I'll let the guy who warns me about crashes ahead into my space.

"Pace car is going to get you up to one-ten, maybe a little more. When he peels off and that flag waves—"

"Punch this fucker through the floor," I finish for him.

"Ha ha! Exactly!"

Tommy coined that term for us. It's what he yelled into the headset on my best timed lap. It cracked me up but it did the job. Now, it's my mantra.

I let the voices in my helmet drum on and after a few minutes, I barely hear them. I'll pay attention when I must. For now, I need to find my rage. I brought two things into the car with me, and I unzip my suit enough to pull them out to tuck them under a strap on the chassis. The first thing is Hannah's picture, the same one that got me through four years of hell. I want her with me even if I have to shut her out. She's my anchor, what brings me back after the darkness. But I can't see her until they wave that checkered flag, so her picture is covered by the folded-up paper that has to become my truth for the duration of this race. I slide the birth certificate over Hannah's worn image, the paper folded with the words facing me, a stranger's name staring me in the face. Alysha Solerno, the woman who didn't want me.

My eyes bore into her name as I grip the wheel, my knuckles tightening like a vice as I squeeze. I relax my right hand and slide it along the wheel to the gear shift, feel the rounded top, my hand affectionate in its movements. This is my favorite part of this car. This is where the real power rests. I can punch that fucker through the floor all I want, but if this goes wrong? If I don't shift just right, time is lost.

This is where I win.

Where I am king.

"You ready, kid?" Douglas's voice breaks through and I snap to enough to take in what I need.

"Been ready."

"Drivers . . . start your engines." The command feels the air and excited shivers run down my spine.

I fire up and join the collective thunder that surrounds me. I flip my visor down and inhale the scent trapped inside with me. This is the moment I've been focused on since I was a kid, since that first kart I crashed into a bale of hay trying to corner too fast.

I give forty-nine some gas and let her breathe. She's not mine forever, so I can't really name her. But I can love her. I can treat her right, push her to her max. She'll perform for me because I say so.

We roll with the pace car, and I let the tires feel the slickness of the road. This track is a lot like the one I trained on. Not as polished as it promises, and not as intimidating as everyone says.

We climb as one, my front end inches ahead of seventeen next to me. He isn't a driver. He's just another car. No one here has a name. They're all numbers I need to pass, that I will leave behind. I'll take those numbers down one at a time.

"Feel that curve," Douglas says.

My body sinks into the seat and I take a note of the force, the bank exactly as expected. This is where I will hold the pack. My eyes glaze over as the straightaway comes up and our speed grows. We're hovering at just over one hundred miles per hour, and I feel every engine, every hunk of metal, collectively ebb and flow. It's as if we are one giant beast, heaving our way forward, begging to break free, desperate to climb.

My skin ignites. I'm feeling it now. The other Dustin slips away, and the man who was born to take what's his is in charge.

I downshift through the turn, not even listening to Douglas. My body knows what to do here. This is what we practiced dozens of times. This time, I fly through the corner with restrictions, my speed held back by some red Ford. But not for long. My freedom, it's coming.

I spot the important things—the best place to brake for pit row, the nuances in the roadway where I can distract and pass, the glint of the sun off the walls, the fencing and the fans. The people are merely decoration, just scenery to blur in my periphery. I . . . am alone.

The pace car breaks away and I make my first move, slicing past three cars on the straightaway and slipping in to take the corner tight. I hear the praise in my ears, but I ignore it. Those voices are guides, but I am in this alone. That's how I win. That's how I *always* win.

I explode out of the turn, ditching the attempt to box me in by the pair of cars in front of me, going high to blow by them. I'll burn the fuel and build my position so I can pit in a good position. If I don't take what I want now, it might not be here for me later.

My eyes are glued to the road ahead, the pavement a shimmery mirage of liquid. My tires gripping as I force my way back in. This is the turn where I break into the top fifteen. With the next lap, I will take my spot in the top ten. And then . . . I wait. When the time is right, I'll destroy everyone.

24

It's been years since my dad has seen Dustin drive. The pride in his eyes, the constant grin and zero-doubt in his expression warms my heart. This is how I always pictured it would be, how it was *meant* to be.

Only, my heart is full of worry.

That's not my Dustin down there driving. Something is off.

Yes, he's aggressive. Fearless as always. But at times he's over the edge. His tires have veered too close to danger, his lines on the verge of sliding off-course. I had to close my eyes ten laps ago when he made a move to break into the top three. He was . . . reckless.

I don't want him to die.

With five laps to go, and basically zero fingernails left to gnaw, I'm left to hold my breath several seconds at a time. My body leans with every curve Dustin takes, and my hands squeeze into fists when I think he should brake but doesn't.

I wish Tommy were here. He's in the pit, with Douglas.

Dustin wanted him there, and he needed them, so I'm glad he has him. But right now, my head and my heart are a tangled mess and I'm worried.

No. I'm scared.

My brother has a way of calming me, though. And even though Bailey came and is glued to my back, nervous right along with me, she isn't nervous about the same things. She's on edge because the race is close. It's exciting. My faith in Dustin behind the wheel has always been rock solid. Normally, it's the other drivers I worry about. I don't trust people. He has a target on his back because of his arrogance, because he likes to talk shit before a race, and after. He's the one to beat, and everyone loves to hate that guy.

I'm not worried about the other drivers now. I'm concerned about Dustin, and what he's willing to do. He's already pushed himself beyond danger to get into this position.

Four laps to go.

Four laps, and my mind races forward, predicting his charge, the roll of the car, the crunch of the metal, the wall and the fire. I grip my dad's hand to bring myself back to reality. None of that is happening. It's not going to happen.

"You nervous, Han? He's got this." My dad's confidence is intact. He doesn't know Dustin like I do. He doesn't see what's different. He only sees the boy becoming a man and winning—finally winning for the world to see.

"I know," I lie. I squeeze his hand anyway, but he lets go to look through his binoculars as Dustin makes a move on the straightaway, edging closer and closer to second place, barreling closer to his nemesis—the turn.

I close my eyes and count. In five seconds he'll be jetting toward us. Four seconds until I see the front of his car. Three seconds, he's probably passing him. Two, the crowd is cheering.

One.

My eyes pop open to see Dustin not in second, but in first. He blew by both of them. I'm glad I didn't see how.

"That was unbelievable," my dad shouts.

My smile stretches wide enough to cover my reality and I lift myself up on my toes, perched at the edge, waiting for him to fly by to get a glimpse of his form. Within a heartbeat, he's gone.

"All he has to do is hold."

I swallow the bile threatening to crawl up my throat as I bring my heels down from the high step. We're at the rail, right at the finish line. This is the best seat in the house. My dad spent thousands.

"It's worth it," he said.

My mom is behind us, but other than the few screams early on, she hasn't made much noise. I think she's holding her breath, too. She rarely came with us to the races. She probably hasn't seen anything like this, ever, except back in my dad's time on the Straights. Even that is a fraction of this world and what Dustin is doing.

Three laps to go.

All he has to do is hold his position.

I imagine Tommy's voice, and repeat that line over and over again in my head. I stand motionless, no longer needing to will Dustin to the front. His life is about to change. This track is about to change. Camp Verde, our state, the series and the circuit. Nobody saw him coming.

I did.

At least, I saw *my* Dustin coming. There's a piece of him behind that wheel right now. I see caution fighting to break in, the guarded, defensive nature as he takes the first turn, the speed on the straightaway. But risk is never far away. Winning isn't enough. He wants the time—he wants a record. He blows through the second turn and nearly loses it. The crowd gasps and I almost throw up. My dad holds out his hand though, his fingers spread wide as he looks on through the binoculars. His hand curls into a fist.

"Yes," he hisses, yanking in his elbow.

Dustin made it. He went over the edge and back. His lead is considerable. He took a gamble and won, and that lesson is going to make him do things like this a lot more.

One lap to go.

This is Alex.

The track deal, the line between law and lawless, the lack of worry about what is right and what is in the realm of Colt Bridges—all of it—is Alex Offerman's doing.

I don't know whether he's influencing Dustin or simply allowing everything ruthless and vicious inside a chance to escape. It keeps bringing me back to the most burning question of all—can I still love this man if he isn't the man I love? When he's like this?

If it were just the race, I think I could learn. The race changes a man, just like winning does. There's always been a bond between Dustin and the drive, and separating the two was never easy. Often, when I kissed him, I knew I was kissing the race too. I was kissing the need to be the best, to prove the world wrong—prove Colt wrong.

But I was never kissing questionable morals.

I never kissed someone I thought might not come back to me whole.

He could die out there driving like this.

"Hannah, this is it!" My dad clutches my arm and I step up on the rail and lean forward, my heartbeat slow and steady. Dustin is going to win. Handily. He's going to own the record, by several seconds. Gorman is going to hate him and Dustin won't care. The money is coming. The sponsors are coming. The dream has arrived.

He could die out there driving like this.

My ears fill with the whirl of engines as Dustin blurs by us first, the seventeen car next. The rest pile through, racking up points and dollars and their next big sponsorship. Smoke billows from Dustin's back tires as he burns out on the track, eventually stopping and lifting his body halfway out of the car. Tommy rushes toward him followed by a throng of reporters and cameras. He's swallowed up by a crowd in seconds, water tossed from bottles in the air as his body is hoisted from the car and carried on shoulders by people I don't recognize. My parents are hugging and my mom cries happy tears.

I'm crying too. Faking the smile.

The love of my life just disappeared completely, and it happened right in front of my eyes.

Ernesto's is Dustin's favorite restaurant. My parents took him, me, and Tommy there for his fourteenth birthday. It isn't the most expensive place in Phoenix, but it costs a lot more than the diners and burger joints we're used to.

It was the first time Dustin had shrimp. That dish is literally all he can seem to talk about as we pile into the restaurant to celebrate. My dad reserved the back room, planning to celebrate Dustin's finish no matter what place it was. Nobody imagined it would be first. Nobody but Dustin.

He's kept me close to his side since I met him out on the

track. My legs carried me down there as my heart beat for his, searching for my love. Even our kiss felt different. I wrote it off to the attention, to the moment. Strange things make things seem strange.

Dustin pulls a chair out for me and I slide in, smiling as I glance up at him. He's trying to come back to me. His hand lifts my chin and he bends to kiss me while my brother eggs him on, calling us "gross." That attempt only makes Dustin guide our kiss deeper. It isn't tender, and it isn't for me. He's showing off. I feel the difference.

Once everyone gets seated and the waiter takes our drink orders, my dad dives right into reliving the race. It's been hours, and they've done this several times already, but no one at the table seems tired of hearing it. Douglas looks more relaxed than I've ever seen him. Even Chad, who isn't anyone's favorite on the team, seems bought into the hype. Gorman hasn't called, or if he has, no one has acknowledged it. I know he isn't happy. That's the one thing Dustin said to me during the chaos.

I swung my arms around him on the track, kissed him, and he shouted in my ear that "Gorman is done and I was his ruin."

Conner Maydrip, driver of the seventeen car, kissed his wife's belly a hundred feet away from us then slid up to cradle her face and mouth "I love you." That was what my Dustin would do. That's not what this one did.

"You look gorgeous," he says, leaning into me from the side. He plants a kiss on my cheek and I smile as I spread my napkin over my lap. I wore the white dress. I'd always planned on it for this moment. He must know, recognize it. I turn to him to bring it up, to ask what he thinks of my dress, but his focus is already to the other end of the table.

I sit back in my chair and listen. It's just the rush from

winning. Later on, when we're alone, he'll open up and say all the things he's supposed to. He'll tell me about the track deal, about the details and how it happened. I got the talking points from my mom, which were the same ones I got from my dad. The backstory doesn't seem to be in their knowledge base.

The waiter shows up with a round of shots. There are ten of us at this table, including most of the members of the team. My dad got one for everyone, but I pass on mine. Dustin doesn't.

"There he is!" my brother celebrates, holding his shot out to toast and clink his tiny glass against Dustin's.

"To speed, and the goddamn king of it all," my dad says, a little dramatic but heartfelt and well-meaning.

Dustin lifts his glass and drains it into his mouth, sucking in his lips to get every last taste of it. He glances my way when he slams the shot glass down and does a bit of a double take, no doubt catching the frown lines on my forehead.

"Oh, hey, it's just one. That's it, I promise," he says, leaning in and pressing his tequila-ruined lips to mine.

"I know," I lie, smiling and nodding as he returns his attention to the rest of the room.

I look to my brother, but he's loving this side of Dustin. Tommy doesn't even acknowledge me, rehashing some conversation he heard the crew having next to them. When everyone laughs, I realize I drifted away and wasn't listening. I laugh for no reason at all. I laugh because everyone else did.

I wish Bailey was here. She made it to the race but left after congratulating Dustin. She's trying to secure one of three internships with our governor's office for next semester, and while I spend the night with a bunch of guys covered in grease and smelling of gasoline, she's wearing a business suit at a dinner for twelve candidates. It sounds like a stressful nightmare, but right now I might trade places with her. I feel horribly out of place.

The rest of the dinner progresses the same. One drink becomes three for Dustin, and my mom racks up a bottle of wine all on her own. She's getting loud, and a few times she's mentioned the track deal and celebrating. This will be "her legacy as mayor," she says. Dustin gets quiet when the talk of that comes up. He quits looking my direction.

The longer the night drags on, the harder it becomes to keep my mouth shut. Questions pile up, and the growing feeling that I was left out of this on purpose presses on my chest so hard I can barely breathe. Dustin refuses one last shot when Douglas offers to buy a final round, and I'm relieved. He's buzzed, and judging by the way his hand keeps flirting with the edge of my skirt and my upper thigh, I'd say he's quite amorous too. But he isn't drunk. His heart is in there, as is his mind. We are going to have a conversation tonight, the very minute we're alone.

"Hannah, honey. Help me to the bathroom," my mom blubbers. She reaches toward me across the table, over half-filled drinks and cleaned plates. I get up and excuse myself before she knocks something over.

"Come on, drunk lady," I tease. She giggles and my dad mouths "thank you" to me from behind her back.

My mom doesn't do this often. A politician is always on.

I hold her steady as she points out every woman's hairdo on the way to the bathroom. She claims to love them all, to want to try that for her next cut. I don't dare mention that she won't be able to do most of them since she shaved the back of her neck and chopped off most of her hair to her ears. Somehow this half-bob, half-pixie cut works on her, but I don't think it would ever suit my face. I get my shape from my dad..

"I'll wait right here," I say, letting go of my mom's arm when she clutches the stall door. She waggles her finger at me.

"All right," she mumbles. It takes her a few tries to get the lock in right, but when she does, I turn my attention to the mirror to mess with my hair and run my fingers under my eyes where the liner has smudged.

"You know, I'm really glad everything worked out," my mom rambles.

"Uh huh," I respond, only half listening.

"It was all my idea, you know."

I drop my hand and flit my eyes to the reflection of her stall door.

"What was?" I'm a little more interested now. Maybe she's going to put everything to bed over this Alex deal. Maybe she has some key piece of information that'll make it all make sense.

"The money."

I blink a few times. She's not making sense. I smile and hold in my laugh.

"Oh?" I spin to rest my ass against the counter. I fold my arms across my chest, the chill from the restaurant making me regret wearing this dress.

"I didn't think your dad would do it, though. And when Dustin left, I was afraid he threatened him or something, you know?"

"Uh huh," I prod. My chest tightens. This is not in my mom's head. This happened. This is real.

"I said, 'Tom, that poor boy left without a penny to his name,' but your dad told me the story. I thought we'd give him more than ten thousand dollars but your dad said it would be enough. He had talked to his uncle and he was expecting him. He just left sooner than we thought."

"Right," I hum. My mouth hangs open and my eyes can no longer blink.

My parents . . . paid Dustin to leave? And he accepted it?

"Anyway, I'm glad it all worked out."

My mom says something else that I don't hear because the bathroom door closes behind me. My ears are closing up, the whoosh of blood rushing over my ear drums at a steady pace to match my stride.

"Excuse me," I mutter, sliding behind the chairs to get to my seat to grab my purse. I look down at Dustin, the king sitting in his throne, and wait for the look on my face to resonate with him.

"We're leaving. Now." I hold his gaze for a breath, then slip behind him before he has a chance to question my reasoning.

"Dad, I have to run. Thank you for dinner. I'll see you later. Tommy, we'll talk." My brother and father hold up a hand and nod as I leave. They're too involved in having a good time. My mom is probably still fumbling her way out of the bathroom. I don't slow to see whether Dustin is following me or not. I'm not sure I want him to. What comes next? It's going to hurt. There is no way for it not to.

I press the fob and unlock the Supra, getting in the driver's seat and cranking the engine. I check the mirror and see Dustin scanning the parking lot several yards behind me. His gaze lands on the car and he skips from the curb and slowly jogs my way in his slick pants and slick jacket, ready with his slick lies.

The door opens and the air that rushes in bursts my protective bubble. I clamp my teeth down.

"Are you okay? Are you sick?"

He shuts his door.

"Yep," I respond. I give the lot a quick glance in the rearview then pop the gear into reverse, peeling out backward and hammering into drive. We dip through the curve and I fishtail a little when I enter the street.

"Slow down there, speed racer," he jokes, steadying himself by pressing his fingertips to his window.

I don't have words for him, and the longer we drive in silence, the more rigid his body becomes in the seat next to me. It takes him five miles to speak.

"This is about Alex," he says.

My eyes flutter closed and a short laugh blows from my nose.

"Sure. It's about Alex," I say.

I'm that girl he left behind. I'm an idiot for ever letting her go. She never would have let this happen. She would have seen it coming.

"Han, I can explain."

"Can you?" My tone is clipped, and he sighs in response.

That sound, his breath exhaling, his exasperation—it grasps hold of my body, and my only response is to pull to the side of the road and get out of the car.

"Hannah! What the fuck!"

I march down the middle of the street in the center of East Phoenix, Mercedes and BMWs honking as rich couples swerve to miss me. I don't even know where I'm walking to, I only know that I need to walk.

After several seconds, the Supra rumbles up next to me.

Dustin reaches out the window and brushes my arm with his hand.

"Let's talk. Let me explain, Hannah. Come on!"

I stop hard and place my palms on my hips as I look up at the hazy sky. The city is too tainted with light to see any stars. That's all right, they don't belong in this moment anyway.

I lick my lips then bite my bottom lip as I nod. My thoughts are darting and weaving, but my conclusions consistently come out the same. I have to hear him say it, though. I need resolution—conclusion.

I turn to face him, his expression full of panic, and for a beat, my heart aches with the natural instinct to take care of him. I bury that feeling fast and march to the passenger side of the car.

"Pull into that lot or something. You've been drinking," I say as I get inside. I slam the door shut and close my posture off to him.

Dustin nods and drifts to the right side of the road, signaling and pulling up to a closed record shop.

I don't expect him to start the conversation, so when he does it takes me by surprise and forces me to turn in my seat to look at him.

"Alex was going to buy it out from under me, Han. He was going to move. He texted me that he already had."

"And so you what? You called him and said 'Wait for me'?"

His brow pulls in tight, and even though those probably weren't his words, I can tell I came close to hitting the nail on the head.

"No, I mean, it wasn't like that." He's stammering, and it's not like him to not know exactly what to say. Dustin isn't good at lying to me. He doesn't want to, but he feels he needs to. That's how I know it's going to hurt.

"What was it like?"

He takes a deep breath and leans back into the driver's seat, his hand pinching the bridge of his nose. That tequila doesn't seem such a great idea now, I bet.

"Me and Tommy talked about it, and we're going to catch him in the act. Tommy's already figured out who we need to call when we have proof, and he made sure the contract didn't have a stipulation that would prevent me from buying Alex out."

"So you and my brother set up a sting. And you just figured you'd win today and have a flood of money that would get you out of trouble when this deal goes south?" It's not the first time he's taken risks with money, actually. Before, his lifestyle dealt with hundreds and thousands. This game plays in the millions.

"But I knew I would win," he says, almost laughing through the words. He leans his arm on the steering wheel and lets his head fall to the side so his perfect hazel gaze can hit me.

I huff out a laugh.

I have always loved his confidence, but I have never questioned his loyalties before. I knew, no matter what the risk, that Dustin's heart was in the right. I'm not so sure anymore.

"Han, you have to believe me."

And here it is, the reason why. Do I? Should I? Believing him was a lot easier before my drunk-ass mom blabbed all her secrets in the ladies' room. It's always easier to believe someone when you don't know the lies they're capable of.

"Tell me, Dustin. What are you going to do if you find

out how much money you can make laundering with Alex? What if it's thousands?"

He spits out a laugh.

"First, it won't be. And second, fuck that. I'm not about that."

I swallow hard, my pride.

"So, it would take millions, then?"

His eyes flinch and his lips part, almost as if he's considering it, but he shakes his head.

"No, not even millions. Hannah, you're being nuts. If he goes that direction, he's out. If not, then nothing to worry about."

"So, you wouldn't sell your soul for a few thousand dollars?"

He crosses his heart.

He actually crosses his fucking heart.

Tears prick the corners of my eyes and my breath quakes with a sharpness as I ready myself for the hardest question of all.

"Would you sell me? For say . . . ten thousand?"

The answer is obvious and fast. His jaw drops a tick, flexing at the sides as his lips part and his pupils dilate, his eyes taking in all of me.

"Would you, Dusty? Would you leave me forever if someone gave you ten thousand dollars?"

His body shrinks, his weight sinking lower, his head falling into his shoulders. The truth cuts me right down the center and I choke out a single cry.

"Hannah—"

"Don't!" I hold up my hand, swearing him away from me. "Don't touch me, Dustin. Don't . . . don't lie to me. Don't give me excuses or tell me this is different. I don't want to know that Alex is different, that he's worth more. I don't want to be worth less. I don't want any of it."

I'm no longer able to contain my tears, but I let them cut down my cheeks in silence. Dustin kills the engine and hammers his fist against the steering wheel. I'd give in if the voice in my head wasn't screaming at me not to. This is all for show. He's mad he got caught.

"My dad paid you to leave me."

"I didn't want the money," he insists.

"Then, why did you take it? Why did you go?"

Red eyes meet mine and his mouth opens without words. He shakes his head as his own tears run down his cheeks.

"I had no choice, Hannah. It was dangerous."

"Bullshit," I fire back. "You always have a choice."

He nods, then turns his focus to the front of the car, leaning forward with both fists resting on the wheel.

"I choose you," he says.

"But you didn't." The truth never lines up with his logic. What really happened diverges from what he says, from what he thinks he wants. From what he *says* he wants.

"If Alex makes you thousands of dollars, Dustin, you're going to take it." I feel sick leveling him with such an allegation. I'm attacking his character. It's hard not to.

"I won't," he says, shaking his head, his gaze lost to the dark storefront and the neon sign that reads CLOSED.

"I don't believe you. I can't."

He punches the steering wheel again, twice, then flings open the door to pace along the sidewalk behind me. I sit in the car and let myself cry. I wring out my tears so when he comes back, they'll be done. I find the girl he left, and I put that shell on as armor.

He tugs open my door and kneels on the ground, his hands fisted together in prayer as he falls into my lap.

"Please, Hannah. I was going to pay your dad back with my winnings. I only wanted to keep you safe."

As if owing my dad is the problem here.

"So you went into bed with a gangster," I croak.

He looks up at me, his weight heavy against my thighs. His eyes are so lost, his heart clearly shattered. It's nothing compared to the thousands of pieces I'll have to pick up when I leave this place.

"I want to go home, Dustin. All the way home." I turn my gaze away from him. I can't look at him anymore. I'll get soft and give in.

"Okay," he whispers. He stands slowly, dusting the debris from his pant legs as I hold out my hand for the keys. He drops them in my palm and I get out of the seat. He waits outside the car as I move to the driver's side, and I pause to look him in the eyes above the car.

"Then what?"

He knows.

I know.

"I'm not like you, Dustin. I won't leave without telling you. So . . . then, I'm packing my things and I'm leaving. I'm not sure where I'll go. I don't want anything to do with my parents. I don't want anything to do with you. My company? My presence and my love? They aren't for sale. You got a bill of goods. A real lemon of a deal. But hey, you've got your track, and Alex. So enjoy."

I manage a tight smile, a smug one that hides the kicking and screaming happening inside.

"So this is good-bye?" The new Dustin is rearing his head, a look of incredulousness tempting his face. His eyes squint; his lips pucker. I get it. It's easier to be mad. I was. I still am. But soon? I won't be. I won't be anything but whatever I decide. And as painful as this is, that future feels hopeful. There's light there, at the end.

It's just lonely, but I've had practice at that.

"Unless you want to drive a hundred miles to Camp Verde to say it again, yes . . . it is."

He blinks at me, his face stoic, eyes suddenly stone cold. His lip sneers and he breathes in through his nostrils as his hands fall to his sides and he looks out at the traffic rushing by.

"Nah, I'm good. You go on."

I nod, my heart breaking but my head telling it to hold on a little while longer.

"Maybe you can call Alex to come pick you up," I say, my last words to him—ever. I get in the car and roar the engine to life, wasting no time before backing out and pulling into traffic. I don't bother looking at him in the mirrors. I don't want to remember him any way but the awful, cruel way he chose. He did that for a reason, to make this easier for both of us. I have to believe that because the only other option is that his heart is completely black, and I'm not ready yet to write off his soul entirely. I want to wish it well. I want to root for it. I just can't be there to hold it tight.

So this is what it feels like to lose.

Hannah drove off and I sat on the curb in the heat of the Arizona night and fucking cried. I called her. She didn't pick up. I texted her—too many times. I got angry at her, angry at me, at her father and mother. I thought about killing Alex.

What was left by the time Hannah's dad came to pick me up three hours later was a ghost of a man. Unlike me, Hannah has no problem letting people know she's leaving and not coming back. When she left the record shop parking lot, she called her brother, who was drunk off his ass. He's lucky because he probably won't remember the things she said. Neither will her mom.

Tom, however? He remembers everything.

"She'll come around," he says.

My forehead hasn't moved from its resting place on the window. I've counted the light poles as we passed each one. One hundred forty-seven.

One hundred forty-eight.

"You hear me?" He leans forward toward the steering wheel while stopped at a light. I shrug, my fist in my teeth. It's the only thing that keeps me from crying.

"Your wife's car smells like roses." It's making me sick. I guess he couldn't really drive the whole damn RV here to pick me up.

Tom sniffs the air and glances around the dash, finding the culprit—a fragrance clip on the air vent. He plucks it off, rolls down the window, and tosses it out.

"Better?"

I give him a crooked smile that lasts about half a second.

"This isn't about you," he says. He's tried to sell me on that line a few times, but I kinda think it is about me. I'm pretty sure it's *only* about me.

"Hannah and her mom have been at each other's throats for months. It's been building. She wants to go to some art school. As if that will pay the bills, ya know?"

I let his critique linger in the cab for too long. My inner voice fights against him, wanting to tell him that she should get to do what she wants, that race car driving is as much a pipe dream yet he seems okay with that. Too much time passes, though, so instead I settle on, "She's really talented."

It takes him a few seconds to respond.

"She is."

At least we agree about that.

We finally reach the RVs, and despite his efforts to get me to join him in his nicer motorhome, I opt to suffer in the one that brought me here. I'm not much in the mood to talk about anything, especially Alex and the ten grand I still have to pay back to the Judges. It's the first thing I'm doing when my money comes in.

"Dustin, listen," Tom says, stopping me before we part. My defeated body turns slowly to face him, arms sagging at my sides. The back of my shirt is glued to my skin from sweat, my jacket draped at my side, hooked on my finger. I'm just some poor kid playing dress up.

"You should be celebrating," he says. "I'm sorry you're not. You've done nothing wrong. This is my mess, and I'll fix it. Try and focus on that incredible race you won. I've never seen anyone drive like that. You, son? You're the one who's talented."

I raise my lip to try for a smile. Whatever expression I make passes well enough and Tom bids me good night, climbing into his trailer while I head toward mine.

Tommy's sleeping in the bed I normally crash in, and Douglas and Ernie are already snoring in theirs. The only thing left is one Hannah slept in, with me most nights. It's the only place I want to be and the last place I want to be at the same time. I crawl onto the small mattress, ducking my head for the overhead bin that still houses some of her things. The yellow shirt is tucked under the pillow. She'd been sleeping in it. I lay flat and bring it to my nose, inhaling . . . *remembering.*

Tom can say I did nothing wrong all he wants, but didn't I? I keep replaying Hannah's questions in my head, her anger and accusations. She was so certain with her words. She believed them to her core. If Alex breaks the law but makes me thousands while he's at it, will I still have the stomach to turn the money down?

Hannah was right. I've thought about it, even if I don't want to admit it out loud. I've even fantasized about letting it ride a while and raking in money. That's how it is when you've never had anything; once you get a taste, it's hard to go back to hard work that might not pay off.

Especially when breaking the rules pays so well and so easily.

Maybe she's better off without me.

Maybe I'm a lot more like Colt than I ever cared to admit.

The last thing I remember is staring at the stain above my head and practicing all the ways I planned to apologize this morning. I'd get someone to drive me to her house or I'd rent another car. I've got a credit from the last one since I turned it in early.

As the sun flickers against my face through the makeshift curtains Hannah strung up in the side window, I work to open my eyes. My body feels heavy, like a brick. I didn't drink very much at all, so I know it's not a hangover. It's my heart, my fucking broken heart.

I rub my face and pull my shirt the rest of the way from the waistband of my pants. I can't believe I slept in this shit. My yawn stretches my mouth wide, the inside cottony. Desperate for water, I roll from the bed and crouch until I'm clear of the low-hanging ceiling. Tommy is sitting on one of the plastic chairs in the kitchen, staring at his coffee.

"Works better when you drink it," I say.

"Uh," he grunts.

I pour the rest of the pot into a mug and drag another chair in the space to face him. Unlike my friend, I take a big drink before staring at the steaming surface.

"Hannah called," Tommy says.

"Figured," I say.

I take another drink, but he keeps staring at his liquid. We let the silence settle, as uncomfortable as it is.

"I guess I talked to her last night, too."

"You did."

He nods, rubbing his head before bringing his gaze up to meet mine.

"Dust, she sold you out."

I chew at my lips for a minute, trying to sort out the hidden meaning or make sense of what he said. Hannah left me and ran my heart through the fire and back again, and she had a right to do those things. Not sure how any of it is selling me out.

"She called Alex."

I blink at my friend, my mind working its ass off to catch up to his news. Why would she call Alex? What's to gain there? Unless—

"Fuck."

"Yeah, fuck," Tommy says.

I bolt from the chair, knocking it over in my haste, and set my mug down by the sink so I can pace.

"Everyone knows. I mean, not *everyone*, but my parents and Virgil. I think Douglas maybe figured things out too. But it's cool. You look like the good guy."

"How do I look like a good guy?" I hold my arms out, wanting to rid myself of this smothering wrinkled shirt.

"She told Alex you were working with the feds—"

"Which I'm not!" *Yet.* I blink rapidly, both versions of me battling. I planned to, yes, but then Hannah left, and then I started thinking about simply playing it by ear. And maybe I never was going to go through with it at all. The Judges were so excited. Her mom was excited. The town.

"Fuck!" I swing my arm across the counter, sending my

mug flying through the room, coffee splattering in all directions and porcelain cracking into bits.

I rush back to the small bed and riffle through the sheets for my phone, checking the time. It's past noon. Gah! So much time for things to get really bad. This isn't how any of this was supposed to go.

I check my messages, but still nothing from Hannah. Not a word. I hover over the text string I sent her last night, all of my begs and pleas. I want to ask her why. I want to explain. I want her back.

Alex is going to kill me. Probably literally.

I sit down and swallow bile.

"I feel sick," I shout to my friend. He squeezes into the space and sits on the floor in front of me while I hyperventilate.

"The deal is dead. Kiss the Carney track good-bye."

I squeeze my eyes shut hearing his words. It can't be dead. I'm *this close!*

"You wanna tell me about the ten grand now?"

His voice is different for this question. That's the tone of a brother offended on his sister's behalf, and maybe a little on his own. I rub my temples and stare at the floor.

"No, I don't," I admit.

He waits me out, probably hoping I'll break. It's no use, though. I've got too many things to sort through. I've got my own ass to save somehow, my life to protect. That little part of me that thinks maybe it's for the best if Alex puts me out of my misery scares the shit out of me. That voice is there, though. I can't deny it isn't an option that I give the smallest weight to. Weight is weight.

It takes me an hour to process what I know, and I almost call Alex a dozen times before finally deciding what a bad idea that is. I change into jeans and a clean shirt and jog over to the Judges' trailer where Tommy sits around the table with his parents. I'm hoping his dad explained the ten grand thing, but even if he did, I can't say he'll see it any differently than Hannah did. The circumstances were different, though. I wasn't being bought off. I was given the means to survive so I could keep her safe.

That's all meaningless when you take it into consideration in the shadow of my dealings with Alex. And that's where I went wrong. I aimed too high. I wanted too much.

I got greedy.

"Dustin, how could you be so stupid." Tom lays into me. I never let him see the contract. His son did, and that should count for something, but I'm not going to sell Tommy out. I need all the friends I can keep.

"I really thought I could handle it. I wanted to make something happen. I wanted it for you," I say, looking to Hannah's mom. Her eyes sag, her expression full of pity.

I pull out the last open chair and flop into it. It feels as though I spent the past four years being pummeled by life only to get this little glimpse of what it could be like if I had it all. It's all so cruel. All of it.

I swivel in the chair until my gaze meets Tommy's, his stare leveling me with heated judgement.

"Will you tell Tommy that I didn't take a bribe to leave four years ago? Please?"

"You didn't?" Tommy questions.

Tom slaps his hand on the table and stares at the wood grain.

"No, he did not." Tom turns to meet his son's stare, holding it so long I start to sweat. Tommy does his best to brush him off, but his dad doesn't let him, slapping his hand down again. We all flinch.

He turns and points at Tommy. His finger always looks so long when he does that.

"I made that choice. Not him. You understand? I made him leave. I told him to go for your sister's sake, because of Colt. I didn't want any of those bad things Colt was tangled up in to find their way here, to this home. To Hannah. To you!"

Tommy nods, understanding seeping in. Tom turns to me, sliding his palm across the table, leaning in.

"And then you go and tangle yourself in that same damn shit your dad did. And you brought it here. Because *you thought you could handle it.*"

I suck in my lips and take the brunt of his anger. I own it and accept it. Because he's right.

"I did."

I did.

"Development agreements fall apart all the time," Hannah's mom says. "It's fine. It's going to be fine."

Her panicked repetition of that word gives me the sense that she doesn't quite believe it yet. I let her ramble on for the next half hour. We all do. We do it because it seems to make her feel better. I sit and listen because I have nowhere else to go, no one else to be with. The only solace I have is that none of this will hit the press. Alex won't let that happen. My record stands. My life in this world is solidified. I won't be going back to trucks any time soon. I only hope I don't end up in a ditch.

"I have to get some air," Tom finally says as his wife repeats herself for a third time. I have more sympathy for her than I used to. Being mayor is her life. I think if I wasn't able to rationalize that I wouldn't lose driving over this, I'd need to replay the possibilities over and over again too.

"I'll come with you," I say, leaving Tommy with his mom. He eyes me as I leave, and there's still a tinge of anger in his stare. I'll let him hit me if that's what he needs. Punch me square in the jaw. But his dad is right. I didn't leave because they paid me. I took the money because they insisted. I took it to survive. Because even if I *had* to leave, I still needed to live.

I follow behind Tom toward the hauler. Virgil stands from the roof, whistling to get our attention. He waves us over and I jog to catch up to Tom. He's still steaming, but he isn't yelling at me so forgiveness is in my future. At least, I hope it is.

I try to slow him down when we step into the back of the hauler. I want him to enjoy this. It's a pretty cool space, the bottom floor an entire garage and parts storage along with a small kitchen and sleeping quarters. It's not quite the luxury bus he picked up, but this one also hauls around a hundred-thousand-dollar race car on the second floor, so that kinda means it wins.

He isn't interested in a tour, though. His stride is long and consistent, taking the steps two at a time until we're on the rooftop. The boys have a table set up and a game of poker going. The mood out here is a lot better than the one in the Judge's RV, so I'm glad for that.

"You guys want in? We're playing with coupons because nobody has actual cash. You can Venmo your buy-in." Douglas shakes his phone, ready to take payment.

"Yeah, sure. What's buy-in?" Tom takes a seat and nods to the empty one. I do as I'm told, happy he wants me around.

"Fifty," Douglas says.

"Cool. Sending a hundred. Deal us both in."

"I can pay my way—"

He waves a hand and leans to the side, squinting his eyes as he looks up at me.

"This isn't a bribe. And neither was that other thing." He pulls his phone out and sends Douglas our buy-in. "You're family."

I have to stare at him for a second after that. I haven't heard him say those words in a while, and even now, I don't quite believe them. But I need them.

"Now, if I take your money in poker the mob isn't going to show up to shake me down, are they?" Douglas doesn't break his eyes from his cards as he makes the joke. It takes a second, but eventually everyone laughs but me. Even Tom.

"I had it handled."

"*I had it handled.*" Tom mocks me the same way his son would.

"Hey!" I protest. I throw in two coupons for my first bet. Everyone matches. That sucks because I'm bluffing.

"Why didn't you just ask your uncle?" Virgil throws in. His question makes zero sense.

"Ask him what?" I throw in three and take three new ones, which aren't any better than the last. I'm even bluffing about having a pair.

"To partner with you on that track thing. I always wondered that. You seemed so bent on this Vegas guy."

I throw in my entire hand, folding before the round of betting gets going again. It wouldn't matter if I had four of a kind right now, because what the hell is Virgil talking about?

"Virg, I love you man, but Uncle Jeff wouldn't be able to sponsor a lemonade stand with me, let alone a full raceway. He's not even really my uncle, it turns out." That last bit hurts. One more reminder of the shit cards life dealt me.

"I don't know anything about that not being your relative part, but I do know the man has millions."

Tom throws his cards in, and we both gawk at Virgil, who seems oblivious to our shock as he reorders the cards in his hands. He finally glances up to meet our stares.

"Oh. You . . . didn't know that?" He practically laughs with surprise.

"The man lives in a shithole. He lives alone. He drives those crappy trucks around and picks up help, paying guys a day rate to move people's shit for them." I reach back in my mental files in search of context clues, but absolutely nothing stands out.

"He doesn't really need anything. And I think the man simply likes being alone." Virgil shrugs as if his answer clears everything up.

"He always was a bit of a loner," Tom adds.

"He dated Ava Cruz, queen of the Straights!" I add, nothing making sense. It didn't make sense when she told me that, but now it really doesn't fit.

"That's right!" Tom leans back in his chair, his thoughts on old times.

"No! That's *not* right! None of this is right. Jeff is a millionaire?" I'm standing now. Douglas and Ernie throw in their bets to call Virgil, who sinks everyone with a straight.

"Nice hand, boys. Nice hand." He sweeps the coupons into his pile, acting as if our conversation is done.

"Virgil!" I hold my hands out as he looks up.

"You never heard of Miller Trucking?" He's shuffling the cards while talking. It's this whole mysterious side of the man. He's part card shark, part secret keeper.

"He does the moving for free. He likes to pay guys who

need a job, and he usually helps out seniors who can't afford to hire help."

I shake my head and widen my palms.

"What?"

Virgil chuckles as he deals.

"I thought you knew."

I look to Tom, who shrugs.

"Man wasn't very cool in high school. Beats me." He takes his cards and winces, and I can tell it's an act. The man's probably holding aces.

I sit back down and play my cards about as well as I did the first time. In fact, I fold six hands in a row. I'm merely going through the motions, busying my hands while my head tries to make sense of everything Virgil said.

Why wouldn't I ask Uncle Jeff to partner? Why wouldn't he say yes? We didn't spend a lot of time alone together, but the man was kind. He was busy, but he was kind. He seemed supportive of what I was trying to do. And despite his penchant for living in no-man's land in complete squalor, he seemed to have a pretty good head for business.

For the first time since my world came crumbling down, I breathe. I almost smile. I don't know that I'll be able to do that for real for a while, but I can feel my heart regulate. That vision I had for my future, it feels less fuzzy all of a sudden. It's only missing one key part, and that's because she thinks I traded her for cash. Turns out, she sold me for something way worse. She did it for vengeance.

THREE WEEKS LATER

B ailey isn't taking my calls anymore. I don't think she'll hold this grudge forever. She understood my pain. She was the only one who did. She's angry that I left before our final year of college, though. I couldn't do it anymore.

She'll make new friends. I'm sure there are a ton of girls who will want to be her roommate. She'll probably have an easier time studying. I won't be there to distract her and drag her to parties and cry over my broken heart. I'm a lot of friend to handle. Bailey deserves better.

I have more faith in her than I do myself right now. Omaha is in the middle of America, but it feels like a different planet. I think it has more to do with my complete change of major than the actual city I'm in.

I took Dustin's advice the minute I got to Camp Verde and I called the instructor with the art program. He wasn't able to give me the apprenticeship. That spot was taken, as

I feared, and the student had no intention of dropping out. But he did offer me a work-study opportunity. It's going to mean a lot of long nights and I'll have to be okay with scrubbing toilets. If it means I get to do what I love? I think I might be.

The answer to my next worry fell into place too. I needed a place to stay, and it turns out the founder of the art institute is an older woman in need of a tenant in the apartment above her garage. All I have to do is convince my parents to pay the rent. I had enough for the first month, and it seems the least my parents can do, given that they ponied up ten grand four years ago just to make me miserable.

Still, it's the ask that seems impossible. I've been sitting on this bed, staring at my phone, dreading this call, for an hour. My mom doesn't even know it's coming. I leveled them with the news that I was dropping out of Northern and moving to the Midwest to study art. They barely contained their laughter so I told them to fuck themselves. I tossed around the idea of calling my dad instead. He's always softer with me. I think maybe he broke my heart a little more, though. It isn't fair, and the broken pieces aren't even, but it's true.

"Are you all right, honey?" Sheila, the founder who owns the house, isn't so good about knocking before entering. She's bringing me more quilts. It's ninety degrees outside, but she swears it gets cold sometimes. I think I have plenty of time before November.

"I'm fine. Thank you." I give her a proper smile. I don't want her knowing all the baggage I bring. "Probably home-sick," I add.

Sick of home, is more like it.

Sick. I'm actually really sick. My stomach has turned

over about a dozen times today, and I keep breaking into major sweats.

"You don't look so good," Sheila says, setting the blankets on the end of my bed and holding the back of her hand to my forehead. "You don't feel hot. Maybe . . . clammy?"

It's like that word, the root of it—*clam*—is some sort of trigger. I hate seafood, and the thought of it sends everything in my stomach hurling up my esophagus.

"Excuse me!" I hold my arm over my mouth and sprint to the bathroom where I hurl everything I've ingested today into the toilet. I don't feel better now, but I don't feel worse. That's something, I suppose. I slide down so I'm sitting on the floor and tug the flusher, getting rid of that awful smell.

"Oh, wow, you eat something bad? That cafeteria at the school isn't very good. You're better off packing something from here."

"I'm fine," I say. I don't feel fine at all.

"I mean, it's either that, or you're pregnant." She laughs at her own suggestion, leaving me in the bathroom alone.

Holy. Fucking. Shit.

It's only been a few weeks, maybe five? But it's possible. It is definitely possible. I crawl back out to the room, grabbing my phone and Googling every pregnancy symptom I can find. Everything I read seems to match up to how I feel. I'm probably projecting. I should get a test.

I get to my feet and collect my things, but before I reach the door, my stomach lurches again and I have to drop it all and rush back to the bathroom for another round.

The sweat comes and goes as fast as the wave of nausea. I've never rooted for food poisoning or the flu more in my life. This cannot be possible. This isn't happening.

I wait long enough to feel certain that I'm stomach-stable enough to get in the car and go two miles down the street. I buy two tests, and hit the restroom at a burger place next door so I don't have to wait. It takes me almost a full minute to pee, and I'm not sure whether I'm dehydrated or nervous. The test, however, doesn't take nearly that long to deliver my fate.

Two lines.

Two *definite* lines.

Two very obvious, very pregnant lines.

The second test comes back exactly the same. I set them both on my knees as I sit in a fast food restaurant bathroom stall, my underwear around my ankles. I blink, staring at the two tests so hard that my eyes blur them into one single stick.

I'm having a baby.

I'm pregnant with Dustin Bridges' baby.

A man I love and hate at the same time, if that's possible. A man I've saved from himself so many times, the last one only a week ago when I stopped him from getting in bed with a very dangerous character. A man I watched lose himself to temptation. A man whose real mother lost him to a father who wasn't fit.

I'm terrified that Dustin has too much Colt in his blood. But this is his baby. He has to know. I have to tell him.

I have to.

Just . . . not now.

EPILOGUE

THREE YEARS LATER

I didn't sign up for this part of our friendship. I've been hiding in this closet for an hour watching Tommy and Bailey watch a movie. Every now and then, they start to make out. At this point, I'm not a great friend for capturing their special moment. I'm a creep.

I sink into the coats, glad at least that the Judge family closet is well-stocked. He could have popped the question at our place, where there are a lot of uncomfortable places to hide. He wants this moment to be special, though. His parents are waiting upstairs and the Tingles are in the garage, probably freezing their asses off. Mr. Tingle keeps texting me, asking if it's time yet.

It's way past time. *Come on, Tommy. Man up.*

Bailey leaves the couch with the empty popcorn bowl, and I get ready when Tommy steps away from the sofa and gets on one knee. He turns around to give me a thumbs up and I start recording on my phone.

It's two days until Thanksgiving, and the Judge kitchen is packed with more food than I knew existed. Hannah is coming home, the first time she's been here since she left. She's bringing her daughter. Leaving *the guy* in Omaha. I'll be heading to Vegas, paying my debt.

It's fine.

It's not.

Bailey is telling Tommy something about the movie they're watching, something about the couple being a couple in real life, and my friend is having a hard time balancing on his knee. I chuckle at his nerves and decide to narrate this for them.

"Oh, Bailey. You have no idea how shitty that man's balance is. He must really love you. I kinda hope you start doing all of the dishes by hand so I can watch him suffer."

I zoom in and catch Tommy's face as he turns and grits a smile at me. He's laughing too, but he's hurting plenty.

Finally, Bailey shuts off the faucet and leaves the metal bowl upside down to dry on a towel. It takes her a few seconds to realize what's happening when she sees Tommy on the floor, but the moment it hits her, her hands cup her mouth and she freezes in place.

"Bailey Tingle, you put up with my shit something fierce. It would be my honor if—"

"Fuck, it's cold. It's colder here than it is in Omaha, I swear!" Like a hurricane, Hannah blows through the front door, crashing into the middle of her brother's proposal, her best friend's big moment—*my life.*

A man walks in behind her, holding a sleeping toddler over his shoulder.

My blood boils.

"Where should I—" He stops when he realizes Hannah's

frozen inside the door, her eyes on everyone in the room. Thank God I'm in the closet.

"Were you—? Is this—? I thought you're just dating! Bailey?" She pivots, taking turns pointing her finger at her friend and then her brother. "Oh, my God!"

"And right on cue, Hannah enters the house and fucks everything up," Tommy moans.

He gets to his feet, but before he can settle in to be angry, Bailey leaps at him and wraps her arms and legs around his body.

"I do, Tommy Judge! I do! I do!" She practically pries the ring from his hand and shoves it on her finger before kissing the man senseless. I feel my mouth start to smile and I almost open the closet door. Then I remember.

Hannah.

I text Mr. Tingle and a few seconds pass before they enter the room. Tommy's parents rush down the stairs. Everyone is celebrating, almost ignoring that Hannah is in our presence. The occasion is too happy to ruin. I stop recording when the scene basically devolves into one big group hug.

I'm going to have to leave this space eventually, so I decide now is as good a time as any.

"Congratulations, man," I announce as I step from the closet. I hand Tommy his phone and do my best not to look to my right. I can feel her eyes on me. I bet they're bluer, wider, more dangerous.

I hug my friend, and then Bailey. They thank me and Bailey gushes about the ring, showing it to me as if I haven't seen that fucker every day for the last six weeks.

"I'm so happy for you," I say, the conversation feeling forced because of the *other* thing happening in the room.

"You made it. I didn't think you were getting in until

tomorrow," Tommy says through an awkward grin. I lift my brows to him as he moves past me to hug his sister.

"We wanted to beat the snow. It's supposed to nail Flagstaff by morning."

It physically hurts to hear her voice.

"I'm sorry," Bailey mouths.

I shake off her apology. It doesn't matter. This moment had to happen sometime.

It's been three years since my uncle gave me the seed money to buy the track, and in that time, with Tommy's management, we've turned it into not only the Miller Racing headquarters, but a premier training facility for young racers.

That track? It's the love of my life. I'm never leaving it. And as long as Hannah has roots here, the grandparents of her child here, then there's a link forever tethering us to one another.

"I should probably hit the road," I say, deciding maybe leaving for Vegas a day early isn't the worst idea.

"Mommy?"

I nearly made it out without breaking, but in all the revelry, a two-year-old girl woke up confused and wanting her mom. So fragile, so small; her voice sounds like her mother's. My chest hurts.

"Baby, come here. I got you."

I turn to see Hannah take the girl from *that man*. He was just some artist. A special one, but her teacher and nothing more. Sure, he's "the best in the world," but so am I. Hannah's parents have only seen their grandchild a few times. Their relationship with their daughter is still a bit rocky; however, it's smooth as silk compared to mine.

Awkward glances dart around the room, all of them

starting toward me then sliding away in quick apology. I have to get out of here.

"Who's that man?' Her question is quiet, and I think I might be the only one to hear it. I know I'm the only one to hear Hannah's answer.

"He's no one, baby. Go back to sleep."

And that's my signal.

"Alright, well. Congrats you two! Tom . . . Amanda. Mr. and Mrs. Tingle? Have a wonderful Thanksgiving." It takes every ounce of strength in my body to make this final turn. "Hannah. George."

"It's *Jorge*," he corrects.

"Yeah. Whatever." My meter for being polite has run out.

"You're not staying for Thanksgiving? I thought you all were tight here."

"Hannah," Tommy chastises. I can't believe she's starting already. We really do bring out the best in each other.

"I have a date in Vegas. Busy busy," I say, dropping that locale on purpose. Tommy's told her about the mess she left for me. He hasn't shared exact details about my arrangement, but she's not stupid.

"You do love Vegas. Almost more than—"

"Don't," I cut her off, stepping in close. I don't need us putting on a show. Neither does her brother and Bailey.

Her mouth hangs open, and for one split second, her bottom lip quivers as her gaze moves to my mouth. The thought of kissing that surprised look off her face crosses my mind. I quickly dismiss it.

"Let's be better than that," I say, and she snaps her mouth shut. The smug look disappears with it and she simply nods.

"I have to put her to bed." She moves past me, but as she does, her daughter grabs the collar of my shirt, bunching the corner in her tiny fist for a brief second. It slips away as Hannah moves toward the stairs. She smells like an angel, and her eyes are blue, like her mom's. Her hair is a sleepy mess, which I can relate to. I wave as she disappears up the steps, and she bunches her fist a few times in response.

My mouth waters with the desire to forget. Before temptation ruins me, I get myself out of the house.

"Alright, then, I'm off. Tommy? I'll see you Monday. Bailey? You're an idiot for loving him."

"I know, but I do," she says, slinging her arms around him and kissing his cheek.

Nobody saw those two coming. Yet now that they are, I can't fathom them any other way.

Unfortunately, I can't see Hannah and me any other way than what we are, either. That's probably for the best, too, because what I have to do to make Alex Offerman leave me alone isn't something she'd like. Not one bit but I have to do it. The funny thing is, though?

It's her fault.

THE FUEL SERIES CONCLUDES WITH
BURN - OUT JULY 30, 2021

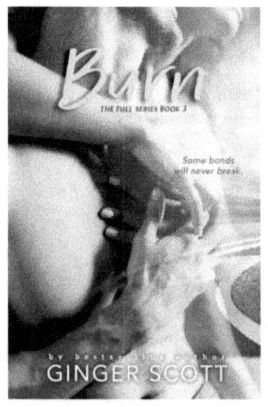

ACKNOWLEDGMENTS

Hannah and Dustin have grown up! My thanks are the same as with Shift, but I wanted to add a special note of appreciation up front for my readers. Thank you for taking this leap with me and trusting me to put your heart back together. I promise, this heartbreak will be worth it! I got you.

This series has been such a rush to write. I cannot wait for my readers to experience every moment of it. I wanted you to have something special this summer. Of all summers, this one called for something big. I hope this book hits the spot for you.

I have a lot of people to thank for helping me get this baby over the finish line. (Get it?) As always, Autumn, you steer me in the right direction. I am forever grateful for your expertise, but even more for your friendship. Aly Stiles - you are more than a critique partner, you are literally a life coach. I'm not sure I know how to write without Rebecca Shea sitting across from me at a Panera. My betas for this baby, Jen and Shelley, you were patient and guided me so much. And Brenda Letendre, YOU were my Rusty

Wallace. You kept me going when I was running on empty, and this book shines because of your editing. I'm so deeply proud of it, and I have you—all of you—to thank for that.

Mom, boys, and my gear-headed brother—you are the soft and chewy center of this book. But my sweet Lesley, you are the heart. It beats with your spirit. This series—it's for you. Even if you're too shy to read the saucy parts lol!

Thank you for taking this journey with me. If you enjoyed this book, please consider leaving a review, talking about it with a friend, forcing it in someone's hands, shouting about it out the car window—pretty much anything. (Only kidding a little.) My readers are the only reason I get to do something with these stories in my head, and I am profoundly grateful. Now, back to the race. ;-)

ABOUT THE AUTHOR

Ginger Scott is a *USA Today, Wall Street Journal* and Amazon-bestselling author from Peoria, Arizona. She has also been nominated for the Goodreads Choice and RWA Rita Awards. She is the author of several young and new adult romances, including bestsellers Cry Baby, The Hard Count, A Boy Like You, This Is Falling and Wild Reckless.

A sucker for a good romance, Ginger's other passion is sports, and she often blends the two in her stories. When she's not writing, the odds are high that she's somewhere near a baseball diamond, either watching her son swing for the fences or cheering on her favorite baseball team, the Arizona Diamondbacks. Ginger lives in Arizona and is married to her college sweetheart whom she met at ASU (fork 'em, Devils).

FIND GINGER ONLINE: www.littlemisswrite.com

f facebook.com/GingerScottAuthor
🐦 twitter.com/TheGingerScott
📷 instagram.com/authorgingerscott

The Harper Boys

Wild Reckless

Wicked Restless

Standalone Reads

Candy Colored Sky

Cowboy Villain Damsel Duel

Drummer Girl

BRED

Cry Baby

The Hard Count

Memphis

Hold My Breath

Blindness

How We Deal With Gravity

www.ingramcontent.com/pod-product-compliance
Lightning Source LLC
Chambersburg PA
CBHW070634260626
47161CB00007B/2700